Any Other Night

by

Anne Pfeffer

To my parents,
who read every version of this book
and cheered for me every step of the way.
Love you, Mom and Dad

Acknowledgments

I couldn't have written and published this book without the following people:

My fabulous writing teacher, Linzi Glass, whose ideas and advice improved every page of this book, and my talented fellow students: Adele Plotkin, Traude Gomez Rhine, Shelli Lether, Leba Haber, Sylva Kelegian, Jean Monte, and Linda Williamson.

My writing buddy, Cortney Pearson, who's been so generous with moral support and manuscript reads.

Meredith Efken, who helped me give shape and structure to my book.

Deborah Brodie and Eric Elfman, who gave encouragement and editorial help.

My teen consultants: Brandon Touloujian, Leonardo Lawrence, and Carlos Villegas.

The special fans on Inkpop.com, who stayed in touch and supported me all the way: Jake Smith, Andy Dennis Doiron, Dana Jacobs, Jesse de Angelo, Diane Stiffler, Lia Sunny, Maddy 11, Raven Paramour, and Peyton (Retroplaid). Also the many, many other Inkpoppers who read this book and gave such great and supportive comments.

Christian LeGraand, who supplied spot-on tennis knowledge

My brother, Robert Tolone, who advised patiently and whenever I called on artistic matters.

Dalya Moon, the talented author and designer who created my cover.

Chapter One

Any other night, I'd be down for driving my best friend Michael to the party, but tonight is different. Tonight is the Sweet Sixteen birthday party for Emily Wintraub.

Who I think I'm in love with.

Not that I actually know her, by the way—I've never actually spoken to her. But all of that's about to change.

I send Michael a text. *i want to get there early.*

Michael never gets to parties early. His answer comes back to me. *why?*

But then he remembers. *u gonna talk to her tonite?*

yeah

awesum—go for it dude. I'll meet u there

So I shower and wrestle with my hair to make it lie smooth, but it goes all wavy on me anyway, and put on a nice shirt and sports jacket and splash on some manly cologne. I take off in my prize possession—the hot, red BMW 3 series convertible that my folks gave me for my sixteenth birthday. I pull into the Malibu Breakers Club parking lot at exactly 8:05, thinking Sweet! I'm the first one here. I'll have her all to myself.

Cool and self-confident, I saunter down the steps to an area of beach where they've put up this canopy over a dance floor and tables set for dinner. The sight of Emily nearly knocks me over. She looks amazing, with this flower or something in her hair and this little dress that goes in and out in all the right places and stops mid-thigh, so I can scope out her legs.

I can't believe this. Even this early, she's surrounded. She's standing with Derek Masters, the six-foot-two-inch captain of the school basketball team. He wears his hair gelled and spiked, but it actually looks decent on him. I've heard he can sink a basketball from mid-court blindfolded.

Derek's got his hand on her back like he owns her or something. Not only that, but there's a freaking mob of kids hanging around them, all wanting to talk to her.

This was not part of my plan.

I force myself to chill and wait for my chance to get her alone, spending the next forty-five minutes hanging with these guys I know while Masters and some other clowns monopolize her on the dance floor.

This party blows. If it weren't for Emily, and the promise I'd made myself to talk to her, I'd get out of here and take a walk down by the water.

Now, Michael's making his entrance, slouching his way toward me through the crowd. There are a lot of people here by now, since the Wintraubs invited our whole junior class from Pacific Prep Academy.

He's still got his tan and sun-streaked hair, left over from the summer, and he's wearing faded jeans and his favorite leather bomber jacket.

"Hi Michael!" A posse of girls in tight partywear waves to him, but he just lays one of his super-charming smiles on them and keeps moving.

He reaches me, slapping me on the back. "Yo, Ryan! Lead me to the drinks!"

We wade through the sand to the drink table and inspect the offerings.

"A piss poor selection!" Michael declares, viewing the sodas and other non-alcoholic choices. "You want a Coke?" He pours one for each of us. "For the real refreshments, we'll have to wait until Chase gets here."

"Chase? He's coming tonight?"

Chase Cavanaugh moved here to LA with his family about three months ago, in June, and started at Pacific Prep this fall.

"Yeah. He's on his way. When he gets here, you wanna come with us to the parking lot? Do some serious partying?"

"Gee, lemme think a minute—no thanks." I do a quick scan for

Emily, checking out the dance floor and dining area, where guests are now chowing down fajitas and enchiladas.

"Aw, c'mon!"

I don't see her anywhere. "Michael, that guy's bad news."

"No worries, dude," he says, taking a drink from his cup and studying the ice sculpture on the drink table. He tilts his head sideways, squinting at it. It's a man wearing a sombrero.

"Does this thing have tequila running through it?" Michael sounds hopeful.

"No." Since he took up with Chase, it seems like all Michael thinks about is getting loaded. I look around again for Emily, but she's nowhere in sight.

His eyes begin to sparkle. "Let's take it."

Maybe she's off hooking up with one of those dudes from the dance floor. Someone who got to her before I did. My stomach does a few flip flops at the thought.

"What? The sculpture?" Already, I see the possibilities for humor. But not at Emily's party. "No way."

Maybe she's hooking up with Masters. More flip flops—a lot of them now.

"Come on," he says, "this thing's a prank waiting to happen!"

"Forget it!" But the idea would be so excellent, under other circumstances, that I have to ask, "What do you mean, take it?"

"I dunno. Move it to a more appropriate location. Like maybe, the men's locker room?"

Just then a girl walks up to Michael, Maura somebody. She's skinny, with a pale, rabbity face and this habit of clearing her throat every ten seconds. She kind of sighs as she looks up at him.

Still no sign of Emily.

"Hi, Michael!"

This girl has no chance with him. None. A billy goat would have a better chance of winning the Kentucky Derby.

"Hey, Maura," Michael says. "You keeping track of those polygons for me in Geometry?"

Maura nods. "If you want to come over and study some time…"

"You know me. I never study more than one day before a test. But can I ask you questions sometimes during class?"

"Sure!" Maura looks thrilled to be getting even that much attention from him.

Michael jokes around with her for a few minutes, then looking off into the distance, says "Jeez, Maura, I promised someone I'd meet him, and he's here now." He manages to sound genuinely sorry. "I'll see you around school, okay?"

She leaves, glowing like she just won a cruise trip, while the two of us stare after her.

"I think you've found your woman," I say. Speaking of which, by now I'm ready to lead a search party for Emily.

"*Right.*" He laughs a little, then shrugs. "She's not so bad. She's nice."

That's the thing about Michael. For all his craziness, I've never heard him say a mean word about anyone.

A stocky guy in a rumpled shirt wanders up and punches Michael in the arm.

"Hi, Chase," I say, without enthusiasm.

His eyes are red-rimmed, and he hasn't shaved in probably a week. From his dressing and grooming habits, you'd never know this guy's dad is almost a billionaire. "You ready, dude?" he says.

"Ready!" Michael sways as he steps forward, and for the first time I realize he's on something, or maybe he's drunk. He had it under control, so I didn't notice it until now. *Crap.* And he's planning a visit to Chase's car trunk.

"I'd better go with you," I say. Or start to say, because a vision appears before me. She's coming down the steps from the club with a couple of other girls, her dark hair swinging, her body curving in ways that I find endlessly fascinating. It's Emily, and she's headed my way.

Chapter Two

The first time I noticed her was at afternoon car pool. It was last year, before I turned sixteen and got my Beemer.

In fact, it was not Emily that I saw first, but her dog, a golden lab who looked a whole lot like my own dog, Jasper, who had died. I was waiting on the curb in front of school for Rosario, our housekeeper, to come, when a white sedan showed up. A dog's head rammed through the open back window, joyously spraying saliva. His whole body wiggled with dog love at the sight of a girl with skin like the pinky-white interior of a rose and shiny dark hair swinging past her shoulders.

I would trust a dog's judgment. This girl had to be excellent.

"Hey, Toby!" She didn't seem to mind when he lunged halfway out the window and planted his slobbery lips on her face. I was impressed. Not all girls could handle that. I didn't know who I was more jealous of: the girl, for having the dog, or the dog, for getting to kiss her.

After that I started seeing her around campus all the time, walking with her friends or studying in the library. She had this smooth dark hair that I wanted to touch and this light in her eyes that just wouldn't go out, as if she was never bored or mad or in doubt about anything. Me, I lived in a world of doubt. I wanted to meet her.

And now she's walking in my direction.

"Go without me," I tell Michael.

"You sure?" Then he catches sight of Emily and, raising an eyebrow at me, heads off with Chase for the parking lot.

Emily arrives at the drink table, and for the first time this evening, she's alone. I move in on her.

"Happy birthday, Emily. I'm Ryan Mills."

She gives me one of her fantastic smiles. "I know who you are. I've seen you at school."

My heart does a kickflip, but I keep it together. She and I had exchanged a few accidental glances last year that jolted me down to the soles of my Converse high tops. I wonder if she remembers them, too.

I wish I were more of a chick magnet, like Michael. He has always been taller, tanner, blonder, and more buff than me. I'm stuck with medium brown hair and an average build, so I try to make up for it by projecting coolness whenever possible.

"I think you're in my history class." The school year has just started, and it's the first thought that enters my mind. It's a completely random thing for me to say. No way is she in my history class.

A cute crinkle appears between her eyebrows. "You're not in Hellman's European History, are you?" Hellman's is the AP class for brains. Me, I'm in the regular class with all the boneheads.

"European History's my favorite," she says. "Especially English history."

"Oh yeah?" I trot out the miniscule amount of knowledge in my possession. "Like Henry the Eighth, right? And all those wives?"

"Six wives," she says. "The way you remember what happened is: divorced, beheaded, died; divorced, beheaded, survived."

Someone bumps into me from behind, saying, "Sorry, dude." I don't even turn my head. Emily has these incredible black eyelashes. Her eyes aren't exactly gray or exactly blue, but more like gray-blue, the most amazing eye color I've ever seen.

"He sounds like quite a guy," I say. "You would think the word would have gotten around he was a bad bet."

"It did, but when you're king, you have a lot of options."

"I guess so."

Not only is Emily hot, but she's smart. She's wearing something loose on top that slips down a little to one side. My eyes follow the curve of her neck and shoulder.

"Have you been to England?" I ask.

"No, but there's this program where you spend the summer studying at Oxford." She sighs a little. "I would die to go."

And I would die to kiss the side of her neck where it meets her shoulder. I look into her eyes, and it feels like we are the only two people on the beach. Surprisingly, the band is playing a sort of good song, kind of an uptempo thing. Emily glances in the direction of the dance floor.

"You wanna dance?" I figure I can get by with my one-step-to-the-right-one-step-to-the-left all-purpose dance move. We dance our way through a few songs, smiling whenever our eyes meet, but finding it too hard to talk over the music.

Then, the band transitions to a slow song. Not sure what to do, I hold out my arms in dance position and say "Shall we?" in what I hope is a suave manner. A second later, one of my hands is holding hers and the other is on her waist, and we're rocking back and forth to the music. There's probably six inches of space between us, but that's okay.

I can hardly believe I'm doing a slow dance with Emily. "Great party," I say.

Emily looks doubtful. "You think? It really isn't me."

Okay, so it *is* pretty cheesy, but on the other hand, I can't complain when I'm here with Emily in my arms. "Why are you doing it?"

"To make my Great-Aunt Lydia happy. She's a member here and paid for the whole thing."

The fact that Emily's not into this party makes me like her even more. Now there's only about three inches of space between us.

"That's pretty cool of her," I say.

"She's sweet." Emily's hair brushes my shoulder. "She always tries to give us things that my dad hates to accept."

"But he said 'yes' to the party?"

She gives a sad nod. "Kind of a waste, don't you think?"

"At least we're out on the beach." My arm somehow finds its way around her, and she moves closer to me.

"I know!" She looks up at me through her black eyelashes. "That's what I was telling myself: at least we're not in some horrible banquet room."

"I was gonna go take a walk by the ocean. It's a beautiful night."

"If it weren't my own party, I'd go with you."

We're dancing really close to each other now. Her hair is right there, so near my face that I could brush my lips against it. Her eyes are these gray-blue pools, and I'm swimming in them—no, I'm drowning in them.

A loud thud, followed by the sounds of people yelling and swearing, plates and glasses breaking, and a couple of screams. The band's singer stops in mid-lyric.

A voice says, "Get up, dickhead."

Unfortunately, I know the voice.

It's Michael.

I've seen him high at a party before, but never like this. He must have been worse than I thought earlier, or done some heavy consuming in the parking lot, or both, because he can barely stay on his feet now.

He's laughing at Chase, who is sprawled out on the sand. A folding chair is lying on its side. Not only did Chase take down the chair when he fell, he managed to pull a tablecloth half off one of the dining tables, sending plates of food into people's laps and on the ground. The kids who'd been sitting at that table are wiping salsa and guacamole off their two hundred dollar jeans.

"Dude!" Michael is shaking his head at Chase. "You're such an asshole!" They are both laughing hysterically. For a moment, anyway, until Michael gets this weird expression on his face and projectile vomits into the sand.

"Gross!" "Ew!" A big space clears out around Michael. He glances up, catches sight of me standing next to Emily, and starts to wave. You would think he'd look embarrassed, but no.

"Ryan! Get over here, man."

"He's a friend of yours?" I can tell from Emily's voice that this is not earning me any points.

"Uh, yeah." This would not be the time to tell her he's been my friend since kindergarten—my best friend, in fact.

"Ryan!" Michael is waving to me to come.

"I guess I better help him out," I mutter and slink over in their direction, trying to ignore the puzzled look she gives me. As I walk up to them, Michael crooks an elbow around my neck, leaning on me. He reeks of Jack Daniels and vomit.

14

"Jeez, Michael!" I try to unhook him from my neck, without success. "Get off me!"

I've never seen him this crazy and out of control. How could he do this to me at Emily's party? "Dude," I say in his ear, "get it together!"

I put out my hand to Chase, who ignores it. Like the genius he is, he attempts to pull himself up using the tablecloth on top of him, thereby sending the other half of it sliding off the table and onto him, along with a load of plates and half eaten burritos.

Emily rushes forward, sending out a dirty look that includes me. Or maybe it doesn't. Maybe that's just my paranoid imagination.

"Get up," she says.

Chase rolls on the sand, his shirt riding up so that we are treated to the sight of his beefy belly. I would bet the two of them are on a lot more than just Jack Daniels. Michael's pupils are the size of poker chips.

"I said get up." Emily's tone of voice says *Don't mess with me.*

I finally peel Michael off my neck, but he wobbles and almost falls. I grab his arm, holding him up and trying to think how to show Emily I'm nothing like these two.

Meanwhile, Chase looks up at her from the sand. "Nice ass." He goes into more fits of laughter, and even Michael laughs a little.

A thundercloud passes over Emily's face. She grabs a pitcher of virgin margaritas from a nearby table and, with all the speed and fierceness of a good tennis serve, upends it over Chase's head. People start to point and laugh as more and more sand sticks to the wet parts of him—which is most of him.

This girl's going higher and higher in my opinion, while I'm sure I'm falling like a rock in hers.

"Hey!" Chase makes a weak grab for her legs, but he's just trying to save face.

She sidesteps him and picks up a bowl of salsa. "Leave. *Now.*"

Two security guards suddenly appear and pull Chase to his feet. A man who I guess is Emily's dad looms up beside her, then moves in on Chase and the two guys. He has this uptight, clenched-jaw look to him that makes me think I wouldn't ever want to piss him off.

Chase tries to take a step and falls down again, causing

everyone to spin in his direction. I'm still holding Michael's arm, but now I notice how green he is. "Emily!"

She turns back to me.

"I'm gonna get him out of here, okay? Before he hurls again."

"Thanks." She gives me an uncertain smile and looks me up and down, like she's trying to figure me out.

Why did Michael have to be such an idiot tonight? I help him up the steps, get him inside the club, and look around for someplace private. Seeing a door marked "Stairs," I pull him through it into a service stairwell.

I half-carry him up a flight of stairs, then stand there with him, catching my breath. When he tilts sideways, I ease him onto the stairwell floor, then sit next to him. We are silent for a few minutes. Michael leans back against a wall, his eyes closed, while I think about Emily.

If it weren't my own party, I'd go with you. I can almost hear her voice.

"Ryan?" Just saying my name seems like it's hard work for him.

"Yeah?" Memories of what happened three years ago come back to me: Michael lying cold and pale on the ground, my terror that he was going to die.

"You know Chrissie? From the club?" He means the tennis club, where we play together twice a week. Michael gets out the words slowly.

"What about her?" I ask. She's maybe twenty. She cashiers at the Pro Shop and teaches lessons to the kids. Chrissie's really hot, but kind of a ditz, I always thought.

"I had sex with her."

Random thoughts roam my brain. Chrissie's a grown-up. A drop-dead beautiful grown-up.

"Once. In the Pro Shop. At the club."

Michael having sex is nothing new. He's way ahead of me on that score. The word "sex" brings me right back to thoughts of Emily, to me with my arms around her, her gray-blue eyes looking up at me. Before I have time to say anything, Michael doubles over.

"I'm gonna be sick."

Grabbing a metal trash can, I shove it at him just in time. Maybe I can go talk to her for a minute before we leave. Just to check in and make sure she's not mad at me.

When he's done, I set the can in a nearby corner. It stinks, but we may need it again.

"You're not driving home," I say. "I'll take you."

But he's got something more on his mind. "Hey, Ryan?" He's still struggling to get the words out. "I gotta tell you …something … kinda bad." He looks around, as if he thinks he'll find someone in the stairwell with us, listening in. "Don't tell… anyone else, okay?"

He has *more* bad news for me after ruining Emily's party? "*What?*" I only halfway hide my impatience.

He groans, bending over, holding his stomach. "Man, I feel like crap."

"I'm taking you home," I say, but then I look at my watch. The party's almost over. For all I know, Emily thinks that I'm shooting up with Michael in the stairwell, or off trashing a bathroom with Chase. If I want to talk to her, it has to be now.

"Listen, Michael, I need to go for a few minutes."

"Why?" He slurs out the word, looking confused.

"Lemme go out and see what's happening," I tell him. I look at my watch again. "I'll be back soon." Michael can wait a couple of minutes. It's the least he can do, after the way he screwed things up for me out there.

"Nah, dude, I don't … feel so great." Michael does look pretty bad. "Can we just go?"

"I wanna say good-bye to Emily."

"Stay here, man. Please. I'm not doing so hot." He reaches out, and for a moment his grip tightens hard on my arm.

I shake him off and start down the stairwell. "I'll come back for you."

"Hey, *Ryan!*"

"*What?*" One last time, I turn back.

Using all his energy, Michael lifts his arm and gives me a salute. His eyes burn a hole in me. They are an intense green.

"Soldier Rock!" he says.

Instant flashback. I'm eleven years old again, standing on the top of Soldier Rock with Michael, looking down. *You can do it, Ryan. You're a beast.*

17

Fast forward to the present. I'm back in the stairwell with Michael, thinking of Emily. Whatever's bothering him can wait.

"Hang in there, man. I'll be back soon."

He's safe here. I'll just be a few minutes.

I run down the stairs and outside to the party area, where servers are carrying off tables and chairs, and the band packs its equipment. I finally find Emily in the middle of a knot of kids. It seems like every single member of the junior class has to discuss the Chase-Michael mess with her and say goodbye and thank her—all in slow motion, no less.

"Ryan!" It's my surfing buddy, Jonathan Takahara. Jonathan is this interesting combination of hard-core surfer dude and major Science Geek. He's looking pretty rad in a white shirt, dark gray jacket, and thin red tie. "Man, what was up with Michael tonight? Who was that dude he was with?"

I guess Jonathan hasn't met Chase yet, since school only started two weeks ago.

"It's a new guy who got Michael back into drugs over the summer. He's an asshole, if you ask me." I glance Emily's way. There are only about three kids left talking to her.

"How did Michael meet him?"

"Their dads know each other. Chase's dad called Nat about investing in a film."

"How come he didn't call *your* dad?" My father's higher on the Hollywood food chain than Nat is.

"I don't know, but I wish he had." Then Chase would have called me, and I would have kept Michael away from him.

Finally, there's an opening in the crowd around Emily. "Gotta go," I say.

"Later, man."

I beeline my way over there.

"Ryan! Are you leaving?" Emily asks.

"Soon. Hey, I'm really sorry about what happened. Those guys totally messed up."

"Yeah, they did," she says in a level voice. She gives me that searching look again.

"Michael's not usually like that," I tell her. "He was into drugs really bad when we were in middle school, but then he cleaned up his act for, like three years. It's just that—this summer—well, he kind of fell apart again."

She listens to me, her face serious. "He needs help. A *lot* of help."

"I guess he does. He's waiting for me now. I'm gonna drive him home."

Now she almost looks admiring. Maybe it's the light. "Smart. You're a good friend to him—I can tell."

"Oh, I don't know..." My face goes hot from the compliment.

"My friend Chloe was telling me Michael's usually really nice. She likes him."

"A lot of girls like him," I say, then wish I hadn't. "I mean, he's pretty hot, and all." *Shut up Ryan.*

Emily shrugs. "He's not my type." Her eyes drop down, then up to meet mine, and her cheeks turn this watermelon pink. It looks good on her.

"*Really?* So, who *is* your type?" I lean in toward her, while she blushes some more.

She laughs and shakes her head. "I'll tell you some other time." The eyelashes flutter down and up again, making my breathing stop. "If you're nice to me."

I want to ask, *so is there going to be another time?* But her father is waving to her to come. "Emily, step on it!"

She looks over in his direction, then back at me. "I'd better go."

Not yet! "So I guess I'll see you at school?"

She nods. We make toe-curling eye contact for a second before I head off, my mind going over every word we said.

I'll tell you some other time. Does she mean she'd like there to be another time? *If you're nice to me.* Should I call her?

I return to the stairs and run up, stopping when I see the stairwell is empty. I check my watch, and my stomach drops into my ankles. I was gone *half an hour.*

I am a total, gaping asshole.

"Michael?" I call out, fear pumping through my belly. No sign of him. I start to run, grabbing in my pocket for my cell.

I race down the stairs and through the entry area out the main doors to the valet station. Panting, I arrive and begin to punch in Michael's number. "Did a guy come here – tall, blond – to pick up a black Mustang?" I ask one of the guys in a Breakers Club jacket. He wears a name tag that says "Jed," and I've seen him around the club before. I hear Michael's recorded voice, telling me to leave a message.

"Yeah. Maybe ten minutes ago."

"How could you give him his car? He was wasted!"

"Don't look at *me*. I didn't help him." Jed turns away from me.

I can't believe I left Michael alone for all that time. I can't believe they gave Michael his car.

I hand in my valet ticket and wait until my car is brought around. I cringe as I drive down Pacific Coast Highway, expecting at any moment to see police lights and Michael's Mustang crumpled in the road. But everything's normal. I even take the most likely route to Michael's house, to be sure he's really okay. The house is dark and his car nowhere to be seen. He probably put it in the garage and went to bed.

I'm practically weak with relief. Michael just dodged a bullet.

I drive home thinking about Emily again. I wonder if I should call her tomorrow.

Chapter Three

The next morning, I wake up in a tangle of sheets. My mouth tastes like the floor of a city bus. *Where's Michael?* Panic rises in my throat.

Chill. You know he got home fine.

I pull myself out of bed and walk to my bathroom, peeling off my underwear as I go. I fall into my glass enclosed shower and turn on the hot steam. Twenty minutes later, wet hair combed but already curling in weird directions, I'm dressed in my tennis whites. No matter what else is happening, Michael and I play tennis every Sunday at eleven.

Should I call Emily? I think back to the awesomeness of talking to her last night. *If it weren't my own party, I'd go with you. I'll tell you some other time. If you're nice to me.*

I drag myself down to the kitchen to see my mother facing an army of caterers, all glitzy young Hollywood types in black jeans and white t-shirts. Every single one, I would bet, is an actor looking for his big break. I wonder if they realize whose house they are in.

Mom sees me and sways over to me in her suspension-bridge shoes.

"Honey, did you have a good time last night?" She tries to run a hand through my hair, but I dodge backwards, acting as if I'm really trying to let a mob of caterers pass by.

"It was okay. What's the party for?"

"You remember," Mom says. "It's the mother-daughter tea party for Elsie Williams."

Yeah, I do remember now. It's a fundraiser for The Elsie Williams School, where my sisters go. Molly and Madison are in the second grade there.

"What time did you get in?" Mom asks. Then, without missing a beat: "Hello? Yes, this is Nadine Mills." She's talking into her headset. She taps her foot while she listens and mouths the word "Sorry" to me.

"It's okay," I mouth back.

"But I specifically ordered the linens in Fuchsia," Mom is saying, squinting as if somehow that will help her hear. "No, I can't hold. I need to speak to a supervisor."

A caterer is stirring the contents of a round copper pot on the stove. I hear the sizzle of butter and smell something incredible, something sweet and spicy. My stomach growls.

"Morning," I say to Ro.

Rosario is standing at the gigantic center island, cutting strawberries. Our kitchen is so high-tech, I think you could use some of our appliances to orbit the globe. My mother sure doesn't use them for cooking, although Ro does.

"Good morning, Ryanito." She's wearing one of her long swirly skirts with lots of fabric. I used to hide in her skirts when I was little, while she pretended to look behind doors and in cabinets, saying "Where can Ryan be?" She has lived with our family since I was one month old.

"Thank you for your help. It just takes talking to the right person, doesn't it?" Mom ends her phone conversation and begins checking a clip board and firing off instructions, while her assistant, the hyper-efficient Brittany, scribbles notes. "The photographer and Cupcake Table begin at 11 sharp, the magician at 11:30. Lunch is at twelve fifteen, no make that twelve thirty."

My mother's so thin a Chihuahua could pull her over. She's worked hard to look that way. She's in this pair of stiletto heels a lot like the ones she broke her ankle in two years ago.

"I think heaven must be a place where you can wear flat shoes," I heard her tell Dad one time when I was about ten. "My feet are killing me!"

"Why can't you wear flat shoes now?" I asked.

"I just can't."

Dad winked at me. "According to her, it's not in her job description."

"But Mom doesn't have a job."

"She's married to me. That's a job!" Dad said, laughing.

Though Dad gets along great with Mom, I stopped talking to her years ago. Her body is here on earth, but her mind and soul live in a distant universe. Why should I tell her anything, I think, when a day later, it'll be forgotten? She doesn't listen, or maybe she doesn't care.

Hearing a buzz, Ro looks into a security monitor and punches a button, rolling open the wrought iron security gates at the bottom of the hill.

A giant Rent-a-Party van grinds up the driveway. Mom teeters out to meet it, with me following behind. While I stand at the top of the front steps, she talks to these two bruisers in Rent-a-Party overalls, rapping out instructions, as the huge guys bob their heads up and down.

I see my father in the driveway, preparing to flee. He's pulled his Mercedes out of our five car garage and is loading his golf clubs into the trunk.

"Hey, Dad." I look down at him from the steps. "Who're you playing with?" I played golf once or twice with my father back in the days when I spent time with him.

Mom is making the Rent-a-Party guys move their van closer to a service path that runs along the side of the house. No way will she let them carry folding chairs through the living room.

"There you are," Dad says. "I thought you'd be sleeping in." He slams his trunk shut and steps around toward me as he answers my question. "I'm playing with Jared Abernathy. I want him for the lead in *Mystery Moon*."

Dad's directing the film, which Michael's dad, Nat Weston, is producing. They've worked together on a bunch of films. Dad used to talk to me a lot about the films he made, but not since the time of Michael's overdose, three years ago, when I put both my parents and Michael's in the Ryan Mills Parenting Hall of Shame.

"How about you and I plan a game for next weekend?" Dad says.

I shrug. "Yeah, sure, why not?" I say, but I don't mean it.

Dad gets in his car and rolls off down our long driveway for his morning of deal-making.

Grabbing my cell, I head up to my bedroom. I punch in Michael's home phone number and hang up when their voice mail kicks in. I try Michael's cell. Same thing.

Again, I think about calling Emily. I force myself to pull out the Pacific Prep student directory, which lists her home number. I punch in the first half of the number, then hit "off," then doodle on a piece of paper and spend a few minutes throwing darts at my dartboard.

C'mon, you wuss. This time I punch in her entire number and let it just start to ring before I hang up. I can't do it. I never even talked to her before last night. I'll look for her at school and casually go over... I hear the theme song from *The Godfather.* My ring tone.

"Hello?" I say.

It sounds like a kid, a boy maybe nine or ten. "Did you just call us?"

Crap.

Chapter Four

"Is Emily there?" I immediately kick myself. Why didn't I just say it was a wrong number?"

"Yeah. Who's this?"

"Ryan Mills, but I can…"

"Emilyy! It's Ryan Miills!"

Well, there's no backing out now, I think, since this kid has just notified all hearing creatures within our galaxy that I'm looking for his big sister. There's a moment of jumbled up breathing and jostling noises, after which I hear her voice.

"Give me the phone."

"How much you gonna pay me?" He is cracking up.

Scuffling sounds and then, "Ryan?" It is Emily. "Don't mind him," she says. "He never fully recovered from his lobotomy."

"I'm sorry to hear that." There's one of those silences where I can tell we are both smiling into our phones. But then it ends, and it seems as if someone should say something. *Something clever.* I clear my throat.

"So what are you doing right now?" *That wasn't it.*

"I'm supposed to be working on a paper, but instead I'm looking at last spring's yearbook."

My eyes go straight to my bookshelves across the room. Sure enough, there's my copy of the yearbook, which up until now I've seen no reason to open.

"Is your picture in there?" I'm already crossing my room, reaching for the book. It is thick and glossy-paged. On the front cover are a photo collage of Pacific Prep students, all at least a 7 on the Attractiveness Scale, and the embossed title, *A Myriad of*

Memories.

"No," she says quickly. "My picture was left out by accident. A *huge* mistake. Most unfortunate."

"Ha ha, nice try." I've got the book in front of me and am sprawled on my bed, leafing through the sophomores. I reach the "W's." There's Michael and, one photo over from him is Emily's class picture. She looks young and cute, with her hair pulled back in a headband.

"Good picture," I say.

"Not really, but now I get to look at *yours*."

"Aw, I wanted to see your other photos first." I leaf back to the index. "You have… wow, *six photos* in the yearbook."

I gulp a little. I'm willing to bet that the only shot of me in there is my stupid class picture, which every kid gets to have, even if he's a brain-dead serial killer.

I start looking up Emily's photos while she tells me about them. She's in the Honor Society, the Songbirds a cappella singing group, and the Young Historians Club. It turns out she's also in three Advanced Placement classes, although at least there are no photos for that.

"You're awesome," I tell her.

"Thanks. But I'm not."

Some of the photos are group shots, so we compare notes on the people who we like and don't like, and then go on to things that annoy us.

"You know what bugs me?" Emily says. "People who say 'no offense' right before they're about to offend you. They go 'No offense, but …' and then they say something heinous."

"I know what you mean. Like 'No offense, but your face looks like road pizza.'"

"Exactly. It's so passive aggressive." She adds teasingly, "By the way, I just calculated that there's an 87% overlap on the people we like."

"I guess that proves we have the same taste."

"Yes."

A woman's voice surfaces in the background, talking to Emily.

"Now?" Emily says. "Ryan, my mom says we have to go. But I'm really glad you called."

"Yeah, same here." *Glad* is not the word. *Ecstatic,* maybe. *Delirious.*

"So, I guess I'll see you at school?" she says.

"Yeah, uh …. Maybe we could have lunch together one day. "

"I'd like that."

After we hang up, I bound to the mirror and do a few muscleman poses. I examine my biceps. I have game. I am a beast. Wait until Michael hears I practically have a date with an Incredible Woman.

Michael. I stop flexing my muscles. What time is it anyway?

I look at my watch, and with a strange, twisting feeling in my stomach see that it's eleven fifteen. I've done it again—forgotten Michael because I was talking to Emily.

I was supposed to meet him at eleven. Why hasn't he called me?

Feeling strangely off balance, I go downstairs again. The party has started. Mountains of pink and white flowers decorate our entryway. A magician in a tuxedo and top hat waits to begin his show, while Brittany helps the little girls sitting at a low table with colored frostings and sprinkles. Each is decorating her own cupcake.

I end up going through the kitchen and butler's pantry, past the laundry room, and into Rosario's quarters. She never locks her door, and I know I'm welcome to hide out there. I practically lived in Rosario's room back when I was five and six. Nowadays, I only visit when things get really bad. Today, I don't know exactly why I'm here.

Ro's living quarters are just a small bedroom and larger sitting room. The sitting room has a sliding door to an outside bricked patio. Ro has a hammock in one corner of the patio, plants, and a couple of shade umbrellas. There are wind chimes and bells that I used to like to listen to when I was little.

I flop into the hammock and call both of Michael's numbers again and get the voice mail. Michael usually answers his phone, but maybe he lost or forgot it somewhere. I swing back and forth in the hammock, thinking about Emily and how easy she is to talk to and what a stud I am for getting a lunch date with her.

I doze off for a while in the hammock, then check the clock. It's 12:30. I get Michael's voice mail again. I'm sure there's a good explanation, but I'm antsy enough now that I'm even considering calling his parents. Scrolling through the listings in my cell phone, I come across Michael's mom's cell number. I haven't used this number since the Big Rift of three years ago. I call it now.

"Hello?" she answers.

"Yancy?" Yancy Weston designs shoes and handbags and she's huge, according to the girls at school. Now that she's making perfume and stuff, she's home even less than usual. "It's Ryan. Hey... I'm trying to reach Michael. Have you talked to him since last night?"

I wait, as the silence between us gets weird and uncomfortable, until I have to fill it with something, anything. "We were at a party, and, well, it's a long story, but he took off before I could drive him home. And now I can't reach him."

Yancy's voice sounds cracked, old. "I'm at the hospital," she says. "Michael's gone."

Chapter Five

Michael's gone? Where did he go?

"He was in an accident on PCH. Nat was with him."

"At the accident?" Yancy's speaking something that sounds like English but can't be, because nothing she says makes sense to me.

"No. At the hospital." She chokes back a sob. "Nat was with Michael when he died."

I swing my legs out of the hammock and jump to my feet, then grab a lamp stand as I feel myself get dizzy. I wait for the patio floor—and my stomach—to settle.

"*What!*" My head's still spinning a little. "When did this happen?"

I hear Yancy's story in small, disconnected pieces. *Lost control of his Mustang on Pacific Coast Highway. Hit a road divider.*

Thrown from the car. Massive head injuries.

Never woke up.

He died around four in the morning, she says, with his dad beside him. Yancy had been in San Francisco, but flew back and only got to the hospital a few hours ago.

Each word from Yancy's mouth is like a drop of water on my forehead, a kind of Chinese water torture. The words are dripping, dripping out the rhythm of *Michael is dead, Michael is dead.*

But wait a minute. Yancy doesn't know what she's talking about. "I *drove down* PCH all the way and even went to your house, looking for him. There was no accident!"

"Ryan, Michael went *north* on PCH." There are tears in Yancy's voice.

Michael had driven in the wrong direction. He was too wasted to even find his way home. And I deserted him.

"You saw him last night, Ryan?" Coming at this moment, Yancy's question feels like an accusation.

"Yeah, I saw that he wasn't … in the best shape, so I told him I'd take him home. But then I had to leave for a few minutes. And he didn't wait for me. And the Breakers Club valets let him go."

I left Michael alone when he needed me. All I could think of was myself and chasing this pretty girl around, and now, because of me, Michael is dead. I feel sick as I think back over our last conversation. He asked me to stay with him. And I blew him off.

I killed Michael.

With the hand that isn't holding the phone, I've twisted one of my fingers painfully in the rope of the hammock. I twist it even more, until it hurts like hell, then loosen it as I talk. I do it over and over. Twist it, loosen it. Twist it, loosen it.

"Did you say you offered him a ride?" Yancy asks me.

"Yeah. But I had to leave. I was only gone a few minutes. I told him to wait, but he left on his own." I should be saying, "I made him drive there in his car, then left him alone for half an hour when he asked me to stay. This is all my fault."

Her voice gets hard. "Nat's calling the Breakers Club about this. We're furious. They should *never* have given him his car!"

I am still twisting the rope around my finger. I notice that, the longer and harder I do it, the more purple the tip of my finger becomes. I wonder if I can make gangrene set in. Maybe if I hurt my finger badly enough, I'll stop feeling the intense, burning pain that's in my throat and chest.

Yancy says she'll call us about the funeral, and we hang up. I suddenly think of the expression *My heart is heavy*. My heart feels heavy. My chest feels so full of pain that I think it will explode, and my heart will roll out onto the ground and lie there, beating by itself.

I tell myself that I did my best. Anger hits me hard and unexpectedly. This isn't all my fault. My mind reaches out for anyone I can blame.

First of all, Chase, who poured drugs and liquor into Michael, when he was already drunk. And the Club. That valet handed Michael a death sentence when he gave him his car.

And then there's Yancy. She was a crappy mother, clueless,

always gone. No wonder he ended up the way he did.

My cell phone rings, and it's Jonathan. "Ryan, man, forty foot waves at Surfrider today. You up for it?"

Pacing back and forth on Rosario's little patio, I dodge a long string of wind chimes and stare out across a lawn that slopes down toward our swimming pools.

Michael is dead, I tell Jonathan. "He had an accident last night after the party."

There's a long silence.

"Michael *died?*" Jonathan's voice trembles.

"Yeah. His mom just told me."

Jonathan does a giant exhale on his side of the phone. "No way, man."

I feel like a hand is gripping my chest, making it hard to breathe. "I gotta go," I say. "Will you tell people? I don't think I can do it."

"Sure."

"Thanks," I say.

• • •

I lie in the hammock, waiting for Ro. Sunday's her day off, but Mom must have asked for a trade, to have Ro during the party. I fight off a wave of panic and focus on trying to breathe. Finally, I hear her footsteps.

"There you are," Ro says.

I stand up. "Michael died last night. In a car accident."

Rosario steps backward, her hand flying up to her mouth as it opens in shock. She has watched Michael and me grow up together. Seeing her eyes fill with tears, mine do, too. She puts her arms around me, like when I was small and would still let her hug me. We are both crying now. We sit together on her old sofa, while I tell her the story.

Then I trudge past the laundry room and through the kitchen, looking for Mom. I need to tell her about Michael. In addition to our dads' working together, my mom does charity stuff with Yancy, and our two families take vacations together every year.

The tea party's still going, with all the mothers and daughters

31

eating lunch outside. I find Mom sitting between my twin sisters. Molly has put bows in her hair and is looking around, all excited and drinking tea from this little cup. Maddy, slumped over, gives me a gloomy look and pulls at the neck of her dress. I speak into Mom's ear in a low voice. "I gotta talk to you."

"Now, Ryan? I'm busy!" But, seeing my face, she gets up and lets me lead her to a quiet patio, feeling the worst I've ever felt in my life. As I tell her about Michael, she sags a little, going pale under all that stuff she wears on her face. I put an arm around her shoulder to steady her, and she leans against me. She's so small and thin, it's like holding a baby bird.

"We have to call Doug," she says. She pulls out her cell phone, reaches him on the seventeenth hole with Jared Abernathy, and gives him the news. The connection's bad, so Dad keeps breaking up. In between the static, words and phrases come from the receiver—*call Nat, tragic, coming home now*—until right at the end, before he and Mom hang up, I finally hear one entire sentence.

"Thank God Ryan wasn't in that car with him."

Chapter Six

That night, I lie in bed and think of Camp Evergreen, where Michael and I went for five summers, starting when we were eight.

Every summer started the same way. The first free moment we had on the first day, Michael and I would run down to the lake to fish for crawdads. On this one side of the dock near the shore, where the lake was only two feet deep, you could see crawdads crawling over the stones. They were the same dull brown as the rocky lake bottom and looked like lobsters, only a lot smaller.

All we did was tie a string around a chunk of bacon or baloney from the camp kitchen and lower it in front of a crawdad. Once it had sunk its claws into your bacon chunk, it was not letting go, even if we hauled it up into the air. We kept our prisoners in a pail of water and eventually slipped them back into the lake.

Some crawdads were easier to tell apart from the others. That was how we knew we were catching some of the same ones over and over. We even gave names to our favorites.

"Okay, Captain Hook's going for another ride," I would say, hauling up for the fourth time a big one with a missing left claw.

"Come to Poppa, Elvira." That was Michael, as he repeatedly pulled up an unusual all-black one with a thing for baloney.

"Face it, these things are stupid," I told Michael. "They just get caught over and over."

"We're the stupid ones," Michael said. "They've gotten dinner, and meanwhile, all we've got's an empty bucket." We cracked up, picturing the crawdads with their full bellies down on the lake bottom, laughing at us poor, pathetic humans.

I hadn't thought about the crawdads for a long time, until this last summer, in fact. It was about two months before Michael died. He and I were at one of the Lobster Barrel restaurants with some friends. I remember Jonathan was there, and they were giving out these red plastic lobster key chains for an anniversary celebration. One of them arrived with our check.

"Ryan, look, it's a crawdad!" Michael had said.

"It's a lobster, man," I said.

"For us, it's a crawdad. We used to catch crawdads," he told the rest of the guys. "At camp."

"They look like lobsters," he went on, "only bigger."

"Bigger?" Jonathan said. "I thought crawdads were small."

"No, they're huge," Michael said, straight-faced. "How big was that one crawdad you caught, Ryan? Ten, twelve pounds?"

"At least," I said.

"Not only are they huge, but they're *mean*," Michael said. "This big one chased Ryan around the dock and then clamped his claw on his big toe and wouldn't let go."

"You're so full of it, Weston," one of the guys said.

"No, it's true," I said. "Except Michael got his facts mixed up. It wasn't me who got chased around—it was Michael. And it wasn't his toe the crawdad bit—it was his dick."

The guys started laughing. Kyle, down at the end, threw a bread roll at Michael, who caught it and lobbed it back to Kyle.

"Ryan, my dick's way too big for a twelve pound crawdad to get his claw around. It must have been *your* dick you're thinking of."

Jonathan jumped in. "Michael, you're *doubly* full of it. Although the part about Ryan's dick, I'd believe."

After we'd pooled our money to pay the bill, Michael got up from the table.

"I'm gonna find you one, too," he said to me. He asked a waiter, then walked around past a few empty tables until he found an abandoned key chain and handed it to me.

"Now we each have one," Michael had said. "To remember the crawdads by."

I get out of bed, go to my desk, and open the drawer. There it is, sitting in the paper clip cup. My crawdad. I wonder if Michael had kept his.

I'll never see him again. I climb back into bed with the crawdad in my hand and lie there for a long time, barely moving, barely even breathing, it seems like. I lie there for hours, staring at the ceiling, until I finally fall asleep.

Chapter Seven

Jonathan must have done his job telling people, because I'm accosted in the school parking lot on Monday morning as soon as I get out of my car. First, it's by some girls from the varsity soccer team – Mamie, Jessica, Lauren, and... the last one is Katie, I think. Their faces are red and soggy from crying.

Maybe I should have stayed home from school after all, the way my parents suggested. But I'd wanted to keep busy, to stop myself from thinking.

"Ryan, what happened on Saturday?" It's Mamie talking.

"Michael had kind of a lot to drink that night," I begin.

"He wasn't just drinking!" Lauren says. "I saw him snorting coke in the parking lot. That new guy was daring him to do a second line."

Heat fills my chest and throat. "Did Michael do it?" I ask.

Lauren nods.

A crowd is gathering around us: three guys from the old gang at the Westside Academy for Boys, where Michael and I went to elementary school; Brent and Oliver, who Michael and I know from freshman English; and a couple of other kids who I don't know that well.

"Where did you go with him, Ryan?"

"Into a stairwell. I stayed with him up until the very end. But I had to leave him for a minute, and that's when he gave me the slip."

Emily floats through my mind, small and out of focus, then drifts away. Anger pulses through me, anger at Chase and at myself.

The bell rings for class. Our group migrates indoors, with me still trapped in the center like the yolk of an egg. As we enter the building, the cluster of people around me finally breaks up, but I'm still not free.

In front of me is Ballbuster Anderson, our headmistress. She's really small, but she's tough as beef jerky. As usual she looks like this butch military official, standing there in one of her weird man suits. It's navy with brass buttons, but pint-sized. She wears it with a white button down shirt, and something hanging around her neck. A scarf, maybe.

"Hey, Miss Anderson." I keep replaying that evening in my mind, like a video, except I keep changing the parts I don't like. So many small mistakes. If I'd done even one thing differently, he'd be alive. If I'd driven him to the party, the way we planned, he'd be alive. If I'd stayed with him in the stairwell, he'd be alive.

"Mr. Mills," she says. "I'll give you a late pass to class. Tell me what happened."

So I do. She listens with this terrible expression of pain on her face. Michael practically had a chair with his name on it in Anderson's office, getting hauled in regularly for things like cutting class, pranks, or not turning in homework. He used to joke that Anderson was secretly hot for him and looked for excuses to call him in.

When I finish, she clears her throat, but her voice comes out sounding high and strangled. "Thank you. We're having an assembly at eleven thirty. You may go to class."

As I travel through the now empty halls, I have this weird feeling that I've forgotten something that I decided wasn't important, when in fact, it really was. It's a strange feeling, and it bugs me. I push the thought away and slide into my seat in English.

• • •

After each of my morning classes, I am surrounded. I tell my story over and over. I don't see Chase at all, but wouldn't blame him if he kept a low profile. Just thinking of him, I feel the metallic taste of anger in my mouth. Michael was fine before Chase came along.

At eleven twenty, the loudspeakers announce an all-school assembly in the gym. Unlike most of our assemblies, where the kids are talking and horsing around, we file quietly up into the bleachers and sit down immediately, waiting for Miss Anderson to speak.

I can't help scanning the bleachers for Emily, wondering how she's doing. As if Michael and Chase's little stunt wasn't bad enough, to have a kid die on the way home from her party — sixteen has been a real downer for her so far.

They've brought out a podium, which sits reflected in the shiny gymnasium floor. Ballbuster walks in, looking shrunken and tired. From where I'm sitting, I can just see her forehead and some puffs of reddish-blond hair above the microphone. She taps the microphone, testing it, then steps up onto something, because now her face bobs into view.

"I think you've all heard that we have lost a member of our school, Michael Weston." Miss Anderson stops for a minute to collect herself.

I wonder what she's going to say about him.

"Many here know that Michael was full of high spirits and had his own special way of enjoying life." A few kids laugh, hearing her say that. "I think a lot of people will miss him, and I know I will."

"Dr. Winters and a team of others will be available to meet with students who have questions or concerns. A memorial service is scheduled for Friday. My door is open, and there will be a box by my office for your suggestions on how we might best commemorate Michael's life."

She stands there for a second, then says, "Perhaps a moment of silence would be appropriate."

We sit there, motionless, the entire student body and faculty of Pacific Prep. The only sounds are sniffling and blowing of noses.

"Soldier Rock," Michael had said to me. Only he and I knew what that meant. If I'd been paying attention that night—really listening to him—I would have realized he needed my help. And he'd be alive right now.

I look at my hands, wondering if Michael's here in the gym, watching us. Knowing him, he'd probably be up to no good.

A strange thought passes through my head. I could just see Michael's ghost pranking his own moment of silence. I almost tense up, expecting explosives to go off at any minute.

Wall Art. That was one of Michael's ideas. We would take firecrackers, insert them into Hostess Twinkies, and explode them against a wall, creating amazing spatter patterns of cake and marshmallow cream.

But Michael's ghost isn't here, or isn't in the mood to prank.

Miss Anderson looks up, says, "Thank you," and dismisses us.

Chapter Eight

Classes are over, and I've somehow survived my first day back at school since Michael died. Now I just have to figure out how to get through the rest of my life. Turning a corner, I walk along a bank of lockers. The place is emptying out as kids go home for the day.

Ahead of me, I see Emily at her open locker door. Catching sight of me, she straightens up a little and stands, waiting, as I walk up to her.

"Ryan, I'm so sorry about Michael." Her voice is as soft as a featherbed.

I stare at her, like a wounded animal, unable to speak. If I talk, I might start blubbering and disgrace myself.

"How are you feeling?" she asks. "Are you all right?"

Everyone else has just wanted the grisly details of Michael's last moments. She's the only person today who has cared how I'm doing, not that I deserve any sympathy.

"I'm okay," I say. Then, "Well, not really."

And just then, Chase wanders by, wearing his usual "nobody's home upstairs" expression. It's the first time I've seen him today. The sight of him in a t-shirt that says "Party On!" has me clenching and unclenching my fists.

When he notices us, I almost think for a moment he's going to turn and run. But he comes up to us.

"Hey, you guys. How's it going?" he asks.

"How do you think?" I say stiffly. Red is running along the edges of my vision.

"Yeah. Tough break about Michael." He sniffles, as if he's congested, and starts with this hacking cough.

"More like a tough break *for* Michael. Seeing as how he's dead and all." I'm viewing Chase through a haze of red, as my anger builds.

"Yeah, it sucks that he's gone." Chase shifts from foot to foot and moves his shoulders around. "Okay, see ya." He turns to leave.

"*Excuse me?*" It is Emily. "That's *it?* After everything that happened this weekend, that's all you have to say?"

Chase's cough is a deep rumble in his chest. He gives us a wary look. "Hey, I didn't mean to mess up your party. I was just having fun."

"At everyone else's expense!" Emily looks at him like he just crawled up out of a sewer.

"Well, you don't have to be a bitch about it," he says.

The next thing I hear is a grunt of pain and surprise, along with the sound of bodies hitting metal locker doors. My hand hurts like hell. I'm watching it all from a great distance, a tiny moving picture tinged in red. I've somehow pushed Chase against a locker door. I crack my fist into his ribs for what I realize is the second time, and then the third time.

I want to hurt him—as badly as I can. I pull away from him, then lunge forward trying to body-slam him into the locker again. Chase is a lot heavier than me and is really strong for a guy who looks so out of shape. He pulls back his right fist and clocks me.

As I reel away from him, hands fall on my shoulders and arms, pulling me backward. I'm ready to attack Chase all over again, but a couple of guys hold me down. I am panting as the red waves in front of my eyes begin to dissolve. I catch glimpses of people around me: Chase, nursing the hand that hit me; Emily, so intense she barely seems to breathe; and Ballbuster Anderson, arriving on the scene.

"He just went crazy!" Chase says to Anderson. "For no reason."

I can still feel my body smashing into Chase's, hear him hitting the locker with a satisfying groan. "He called Emily a bitch."

Anderson's eyebrows shoot up into her hairline. Then she is marching us down to her office. It doesn't matter that she's a pygmy—four foot eleven, or something like that. Miss Anderson walks large. I've never been to her office before for a discipline problem. I've never acted this way in my life.

"I will deal with you one at a time," she says. "Mr. Mills, please wait outside until I have finished with Mr. Cavanaugh."

It's almost four o'clock by now. The hallway's empty, except for Emily, who has followed us and sits waiting for me on the long bench across from the Admin Office door. She wears one of those short, tight skirts that all the girls have and is sitting the way all the girls do, with her knees pressed close together. Her hair's pushed off her face, which is pale and serious.

Even in my state of total misery, I think she's beautiful. I'm afraid she thinks I'm an ass, but then she pats the place next to her on the bench. Like a dog, I scramble over to sit beside her.

She puts her hand on my arm. "That was .... eventful."

"Yeah." I touch my temple, where Chase hit me and wince. "I don't usually go around jumping people."

"Just people who deserve it, right?" She leans toward me a little, and I catch the scent of lavender. Her eyes sweep my face, taking in my injuries. "You might have a black eye tomorrow."

"I feel like an idiot."

"Don't. You were *amazing!*"

"Really?"

Her lips are the perfect shape and color. I can't stop looking at them.

My head begins to pound, and suddenly, all I can think of is Michael, taking off on his cosmic rocket ride into death. Inside me, I feel a tearing, as if something huge and made of steel—a battleship or a skyscraper— is being pulled apart.

And Emily sees the expression on my face and doesn't ask a bunch of dumb questions about how I feel, but just looks at me, and I say "It's Michael," as the pain rips into me.

She puts her arm around me and squeezes—hard. Her hand, which grips my right shoulder, is surprisingly strong. I can almost feel strength flowing out of her fingers and into my shoulder, straightening my back. I feel myself relax.

"I miss him," I say.

The sympathy in her eyes is like a warm bath.

If girls were flames, most girls would be a single match, a mere Bic lighter. Emily, on the other hand, would be an inferno—a raging, thousand-acre forest fire.

Chapter Nine

Chase is completely uninjured by my brutal attack. Miss Anderson gives him a detention period and makes him write Emily a note of apology. As for me, she tells me to sleep a lot this weekend and gives me the phone number for Dr. Winters, the school psychologist.

"For grief counseling," she says. "In case you want to talk about it." I crumple the phone number and toss it in the trash on the way to my car.

By five thirty, I'm pulling up our driveway. The two polar opposite feelings of pounding Chase's flesh and Emily's arm around me have left me in a strangely good mood, but tired. I think I could sleep for a week.

As I leave our garage, Alberto, one of the gardeners, is finishing up for the day. His kid, Hector, is with him. Every once in a while, when his daycare falls through, Alberto brings Hector to work with him. He knows my parents don't mind.

Hector is four. He has a toy shovel and rake, with which he is scooping a hole in the dirt by some bushes.

"Hi, Alberto," I say, then drop down to squat on my heels as Hector comes running. He has a round baby belly and these perfect, tiny baby teeth that look like the mini-Chiclets we used to get in our Halloween bags.

"Dude," he says in his husky four-year old voice. His eyes take in the cut lip and rapidly swelling bump on my temple.

"Little accident playing soccer," I tell him. "So, you remember the secret handshake?" I look very serious as I say this, and he does, too. Hector can never remember the secret handshake, probably because it changes every time we do it.

"No, Hector," I say, "it's right fists together, then left fists together."

"No, man," he argues. "First you gotta slap it like you mean it."

I hit my forehead, avoiding the rapidly swelling part of it. "How could I have forgotten?" Then I pick him up and swing him around a few times, while Hector yells in delight and Alberto watches, smiling.

"Later, buddy," I say and go into the house, where Molly and Maddy are sitting on bar stools at the kitchen island with a plate of cut up apples. They're wearing the same sad expressions they've had since they first heard about Michael, but when they see me, they leap off their stools.

"Did you have a fight? Did you win?" Maddy is bouncing up and down beside me. She has blonde hair and freckles, while Molly's dark, like my dad. I was eight when they were born. For a long time, I ignored them, but ever since they saw Michael overdose and almost die, I've kind of looked out for them.

"You poor thing! Does it hurt much?" Molly's eyebrows come together, and her mouth puckers into a little "O."

"I'm fine. I crashed into a guy playing soccer in P.E."

"Put this on your head, Ryanito. Then sit down, and the girls will set the table." Ro brings me a towel with an ice pack in it, and I take a chair.

"Any chance the rents will put in an appearance?" I ask her.

"They will come to say goodbye, before they go to dinner."

Rosario is taking a roast chicken, surrounded by potatoes and carrots, out of the oven. Molly and Maddy have already laid down just four placemats, for the three of us and Ro.

They don't even bother to ask anymore.

"Ryan," Maddy complains. "My backhand sucks. Will you help me with it?" She's into tennis in a big way.

"I've noticed you tilt your head as the ball comes to you," I tell her. "To judge the shot right, you need to look at it straight on, with both eyes. I'll show you this weekend."

"Well then, you have to do spelling words with me, too!" Molly says. "So I can win the school spelling bee."

"You got it." I touch the ice pack gingerly to my swollen temple

Rosario serves our chicken and vegetables. We sit at a table in a bay window off the kitchen. Since it's mid-September and still light out, we can see the garden, the fountains and off in the distance, our tennis court and pools.

We've just started to eat when my parents roll through the kitchen on the way to their real lives. Mom's got this dress on that's embarrassingly short, and Dad has these sunglasses that I guess he thinks make him look cool.

"Mom! Dad! What a nice surprise!" I say in the fake, bright voice that I use for needling my parents. Anger slithers out of my mouth and crawls around the kitchen, like a cockroach.

"We're going to a screening," Dad says. "Then a late dinner." He takes a closer look at me. "What did you do to yourself?"

I repeat my soccer story.

"Thank goodness you don't play football," Mom says, making one of her invaluable contributions to the conversation. "Don't wait up for us."

"We wouldn't think of it!" I use the same bright tone as before.

Both Dad and Ro have that *Not again* expression on their faces that they reserve for my sarcastic moments.

"Ryan, you must *respect* your parents," Rosario says after they're gone.

"They should stay home once in a while!"

I'm sure Ro agrees with me, but she keeps it to herself. "Have some juice." She fills our glasses.

"You guys doing okay?" I ask the girls. "Have you been thinking about Michael?"

They nod. "Miss Ellen says he's gone to a better place," Maddy reports. "Is that true?"

"I don't know," I say. "I hope so."

They tell me and Rosario about their day. Second grade is hard, because Maddy, who is in a different class from Molly, got the cool teacher, while Molly got Miss Cruella. Her real name's Miss Priscilla. Molly, at age eight, is bitter.

"So, today," Molly complains, "Miss Cruella's yelling at Cameron Fiske, yelling *maniacally*, but then the door opens and Mr. Palmer walks in, and just like *that*"—she snaps her fingers—"Miss Cruella starts talking in this fakey, sweet voice, pretending like she was being nice all along." She sniffs in disgust.

We talk about ways that Molly can deal with Miss Cruella.

"Why don't you just be so bad," Madison suggests, "that they move you to my class?" She's struggling to cut her chicken, having a hard time, but refusing our help.

"Why would they do that?" I ask.

"Well, I mean, if Miss Cruella doesn't want to have her anymore."

"Mmm, I don't think it works that way. She'll just get into trouble." I hand Molly the juice pitcher, and she fills her glass.

"Many times," Ro observes in her accented English, "there are difficult people. With the teachers, you must be polite. You must obey! But, *inside,*" she points to her chest, "you are *yourself!* You still have your own mind, your own heart."

Molly thinks about it. "But then I'm just *copping out,*" she says, using an expression she heard in one of Dad's movies.

"It's called *playing the game,* Moll," I say to her. "Ro's right. If you know how to play the game, it means you're smart."

We finish dinner and help Ro clear the table. Ro insists on it, not because she's trying to get out of work, but because she feels it's her job to raise us right.

"I made dessert," Ro says. "Ryan's favorite."

She sets in front of me a piece of warm apple pie with vanilla ice cream. It's her homemade pie, the best in the world.

"Thanks, Ro." When I take a bite, the flavors of apple, butter, and cinnamon hit me like a surprise. This is the first food that hasn't tasted like cardboard to me since Michael died. I see him, sitting with me at this table only a month ago. "Do you remember, Ro?" I say.

She nods, her eyes filling with tears. The thing we're remembering is, this pie wasn't just my favorite. It was Michael's, too.

Chapter Ten

"I keep wondering if Michael's spirit is here," I say to Jonathan. "You know, like maybe Michael's here watching us?"

"He might be," Jonathan says. He's sitting across from me in the school cafeteria, with his black-framed glasses and a t-shirt that says "Tokyo." Although Jonathan's an LA kid, like me, his parents came here from Japan.

"You know those people who have near-death experiences?" he continues. "They actually die, and they go down a tunnel toward a light and float around in the air looking down on people. But then something calls them back to the living."

"Maybe that's what happened to Michael," I say. "Except no one called him back."

We're in my usual corner of the cafeteria, the gathering place for guys who went to the Westside Academy for Boys before coming to Pacific Prep. On a normal day, there might be half a dozen guys sitting there.

This week, in honor of Michael, the Westside group fills three long tables. Other kids pass by the tables or stand around in groups—talking and trying to take in the news that one of us has died.

Then, I remember something. "Jonathan! Michael said he had something to tell me the night he died. He said it was bad, and I had to promise to keep it quiet. But then he didn't get the chance to tell me." Guilt stabs me again. I wouldn't even listen to him.

"Do you think it was for real?" Jonathan and I both know that Michael had a flair for drama. He liked a good story.

"I don't know. Maybe he was in trouble for drugs."

"Do you know anyone else he might have told?" Jonathan asks.

"Not really." Lots of people liked Michael, but I was the person he spent most of his time with.

I push away a bowl of glue-like vanilla pudding in front of me. Just the sight of it makes my throat close up. "I'll take it," says a sophomore at the end of the table. I'm glad I don't have to look at it anymore.

"Remember Michael's phone call?" somebody says. "Back in kindergarten?" We all know what he's talking about.

Michael had made his mark early at the Westside Academy for Boys. In fact, it was the day I met him, the third day of school. I was learning my way around the place. In the Admin Building they had an old-fashioned pay phone on a wall, and as I passed by, I saw a blond boy on the phone, laughing to himself. He saw me and waved me over, pointing excitedly to the receiver. I could hear a woman's voice saying "Hello? May I assist you?"

Michael slammed the receiver back in its cradle and said, "Run!" And we both did, me clueless as to what was going on. Near the little-kid playground, we stopped. Michael was doubled over laughing.

"Who did you call?" I said.

I had my answer within a few minutes, when the distant sound of police sirens wafted across the campus. A couple of police cars turned into the school gates and pulled up in front of the Admin Building. It was lunch hour, so kids and teachers started running in that direction.

Michael's eyes were round as silver dollars. "Shit!" he exclaimed.

I was blown away. At age five, I couldn't believe I knew someone cool enough to say *shit*.

"I hung up!" he said. "What are they doing here?"

We stared at each other. "Don't tell anyone," he said.

Silently, I shook my head.

It took a few hours to straighten everything out. Our headmaster, Mr. Stamford, sent the cops away with apologies and did an investigation into who had called 911. I never said a word. But Michael did. Too excited to keep his mouth shut, he also told Jake and Sam, saying "Don't tell anyone!" Of course, they did, and Michael was busted by the end of the day, making his first of many visits to Mr. Stamford's office.

After that, for me, no one was ever as much fun to hang out with as Michael. And people told him that Jake and Sam had talked. I was the only kid who had kept his secret. Within days of his famous 911 call, Michael and I were best friends.

It's time for class. As I head for the cafeteria door, forks and knives clatter, plates clink together, and trays slam. I escape before I lose my hearing.

When I think about it later, I realize I am the only one who always eats lunch at the Westside table. The other guys often sit with new friends they made at Pacific Prep. Even Michael did, sometimes, when he was alive. It's weird, I think, that I'm the only one who still hangs exclusively with the old crowd from grade school.

Chapter Eleven

On Wednesday, instead of school, I go with my folks and Rosario to the cemetery for Michael's funeral. We've left Maddy and Molly at home with Yolanda, Ro's niece, who fills in for her on days when Ro isn't working.

"We don't *want* to see Michael get put in the ground," they said. They'd already suffered through Michael's near-death by overdose at our house, so it was hard on them to learn that Michael had died for real this time.

Dad's hands tighten on the steering wheel as he drives. "I can't imagine what Nat and Yancy are going through."

"Ryan, I sent them a lovely arrangement of orchids," my mom says.

That should make up for the unexpected death of their son. I almost say it, but decide it would be tacky to get nasty on the day we come together to remember Michael. So I just think it, instead.

Rosario gives me a side-long glance, as if she's wondering if I'm going to mouth off again.

"Ryan?" she says. "Did you have classes this year—with Michael?"

"Physics," I tell her. I suddenly think of something. "He would have been my partner. You know, for labs and this big project second semester. Now, I'm going to have to find someone else."

Rosario has witnessed me and Michael in action on other school projects, pulling stunts like starting a six week project four days before it's due. I can see her mind working.

"In this class," she asks. "There are serious boys?"

"Yes, Ro." I give her a face like I'm mad at her, even though she knows I'm not. "There are serious boys." Like any serious boy would want me for a lab partner.

Ro pats my hand. "Michael had a good heart," she says. "He always made me laugh."

Me, too.

After we park at the Rolling Meadows cemetery, we walk to the funeral site. The Weston family plot's a really nice grassy area under some shade trees. From here, you see rolling green canyons and the spiky outline of downtown LA off in the distance.

Nat and Yancy wanted to keep this service small. They've agreed with Miss Anderson to an all-school memorial service tomorrow in our gymnasium. But today, there are only about thirty people, those closest to Michael and his parents.

The ceremony's short and simple. Memories of Michael roll through my head. The tennis games. The summers on the beach—boogey boarding, surfing and throwing Frisbees.

I stare at the ground until the ceremony finally ends. My dad motions to me to leave, but I mouth, "Just a minute." I go stand by Michael's open grave.

I told you I'd drive you home.

I'd meant to come and say a private good-bye, but all I can think is: he's down there. Michael's in that little box, soon to be buried under six feet of dirt. I am trying to take long slow deep breaths to get rid of the panic I'm feeling.

Why didn't you wait for me?

A girl walks up and stands next to me. It's Chrissie, from the tennis club, who, on the night of his death, Michael told me he had slept with. I'm too unnerved to be polite.

"What are you doing here?" I ask. No way did Nat and Yancy invite her. They don't even know she exists.

"I heard Bobby Baker was invited, so I just tagged along," she says in her accent that's pure Southern fried chicken. Bobby's the club pro that Michael took lessons with, and he's an old friend of the Westons.

Chrissie's dress, and even her shoes, are purple. I notice, because it's a funeral, and everyone else is wearing black or dark gray. She has daisies stuck in her hair.

"Michael had a beautiful spirit," she says. She pulls a daisy from one of her curls and gently drops it into his grave.

Chapter Twelve

It's noon on Thursday, and Michael's not here to have lunch with me. Just like we always played tennis on Sundays at eleven, we always ate together at school on Thursdays. I think we both liked the routine in our lives. We knew what to expect.

I'm heading toward the cafeteria when, all of a sudden, Emily's walking toward me."Hi, Ryan!"

"Hi." We both stop.

A memory is coming to me from my other life, the one I had before Michael died. She and I were going to have lunch together. I remember in a vague, distant sort of way that I was excited about it.

"Are you going to eat now?" I ask.

"Yes. I brought something from home," she says. A beat, then, "What about you?"

"Same."

I guess I should ask her to have lunch with me.

But I always sit with Michael on Thursdays.

I don't say anything.

"Would you like to eat lunch together?" she asks a second later. "Or maybe it's not a good time ..." Her voice trails off.

I'm hearing her as if through ear plugs. She's far away and out of focus. I want to answer her, but my throat clenches shut like a fist. It takes me a minute to get it operating again.

"Okay," I say. "Do you want to sit outside? In the Quad, maybe?"

I find a spot in the shade under some trees, and we pull out our lunches. I have a plastic container that Rosario packed with leftover beef stew, but I don't bother to open it. I haven't been hungry all week. Emily has a sack lunch with a sandwich, peach, cookie, and thermos.

I wonder if Michael's watching us and what he thinks of me for having lunch with a cute girl the very first Thursday after his death.

"Chase wrote me that apology," Emily says. "You want to see it?"

"Yeah." I take the piece of paper she hands to me from her backpack and read:

Dear Emily,
I'm sorry I called you a bitch. That was innapropriate. Also, I'm sorry I was rude at your party.
Sincerly,
Chase Cavanaugh

"Hmmpf," I say. "He didn't exactly strain himself."

"No, but he did apologize about my party when he didn't have to. Miss Anderson didn't know about that."

To Emily, Chase is just a party wrecker, and I'm the warrior who defended her honor. She doesn't know that Chase and I are both killers, Angels of Death. We have that in common.

My tongue feels thick and my brain foggy. "I was supposed to play tennis with Michael. That morning after the party."

"Did you play with him a lot?"

"Every Sunday, at least, and during the week, too, sometimes."

She touches my hand. "You must miss him."

"Yeah."

Her eyes, her calmness, her hand on mine—it's like being wrapped up in a soft blanket. The tension's draining from my shoulders, and I can breathe again without that tight pain in my chest.

She takes a small bite from her sandwich.

Once again, I'm staring at her perfect lips. What would it be like to kiss her?

Am I allowed to be thinking this way so soon after Michael's death? No one's told me the rules.

"Do you ever play in tennis tournaments?" she asks.

"No. I used to, when I was a kid. But when I was about twelve I quit. My coach was all on my case about it."

"Why?"

"He thought I could do well if I tried harder. But I didn't want to spend four or five hours a day on tennis."

I'm acting normal and answering questions, when what I really want to do is put my head on her shoulder and go to sleep for a long time.

"Now that ... well ... I'm going to have to find a new partner." I stare down into my untouched beef stew.

We are quiet for a minute.

It feels safe, sitting here with her.

I want to say to her, do you know that you smell like lavender? Do you know what it does to me when you smile, when your hair moves across your cheek like that?

"Hey," she says, "Would you give me a lesson some time? I'd be terrible, though. I've never played."

"I'm not sure I'd be a good teacher," I say slowly, although I probably would. I'm really good at tennis and teach Maddy stuff all the time.

Emily's eyes open wide. "Okay, sure, it's no big deal." Her shoulders slump, and she looks down, her cheeks pink.

I'm a jerk to make her feel bad, and after she's made me feel so much better.

I tell her the truth. "It's not that I don't want to. It's just that I'm in a weird place right now."

"I understand. You don't have to."

"No, I want to. I'll give you a lesson. Maybe in a few weeks, okay?"

"Okay." Another silence, then Emily says "I guess the school's having a memorial service for Michael? Tomorrow?"

"Yeah." The pain and the tearing sensation are starting again. I know it's only been a couple of days, but will it always be like this? I look down at the grass.

The bell for class rings, interrupting my thoughts. I leap to my feet, then reach down to help her up. My hand closes on hers, setting off a storm of electrical activity in my body.

As Emily comes up beside me, my brain signals my hand to let go of hers, but it won't. For a few long seconds, it just keeps hanging onto her hand as if it's suddenly very important—a lifeline.

And Emily doesn't seem to mind; at least, she doesn't pull away.

Finally, my fingers move enough to drop Emily's hand. But I can still feel it in my own, warm and alive, even after we've said goodbye and I've gone off to my endless afternoon classes.

Chapter Thirteen

I'm in the kitchen with Ro, Maddy, and Molly. Ro's making lunches, while I go through the motions of quizzing the girls for their spelling tests. "Maddy— 'chuckle'," I say. She begins to spell it out.

"Rosario!" Mom walks in. She's got about a pound of make-up on and this clingy T-shirt and pants, along with her usual pair of gravity-defying shoes.

She interrupts Maddy in mid-spell. "I need my cashmere sweater—the moss green. Do you know where it is?" She directs a little smile at us, her three offspring, acknowledging our existence.

"Miss Nadine, I took it to the dry cleaners yesterday. Remember, you gave it to me?"

"I did?" Mom stops short, considering her options. "Well, can we get it today? I need it for the Teen League luncheon."

"Hey, Mom," I say. "Did you know that, in some countries, entire families live in spaces the size of your closet?"

"Ryan." Rosario shakes her head at me, but I ignore her.

"It's true. I saw this thing on the Internet about comparative home sizes around the world."

Mom turns her back on me. "Well, Rosario?"

"I will call the cleaners." Ro dials, while Maddy and Molly finish their milk and start to put on their shoes. We need to leave for school in a few minutes.

As always, my mom's wearing a ton of expensive jewelry, including a chunky gold necklace with these red stones called garnets. I recognize the necklace, because I helped Dad choose it for her at Tiffany's when I was twelve.

Dad had picked me up from the tennis club one Saturday and

said he had an errand to run on the way home.

"I'm getting something for your mom," he told me. "Some jewelry."

"You already got her jewelry," I said. "For her birthday." We were in my dad's Mercedes, as he turned onto Rodeo Drive in Beverly Hills.

"Yeah, but now our wedding anniversary's coming up."

"So you have to buy her more jewelry?"

"Well, it's good to do *something*."

Dad parked the car and led me into Tiffany's. He had obviously called ahead, because waiting for us was this amazingly tall woman with silver hair piled high on her head.

"Mr. Mills, what a pleasure to have you back!"

"Hi, Rhoda! What do you have to show me today?"

Rhoda whipped us past glass cases and people in black clothes into a private room, where she had laid out all these trays of necklaces and bracelets. The garnet necklace was the best one, even though Rhoda called it a "choker," which didn't sound very romantic to me.

Leaving Tiffany's, I remember Dad saying, "The thing with women is, you gotta sweep 'em off their feet. Make 'em feel special. You know why?"

I shook my head.

He leaned down toward my ear, as if he were telling me a secret. "There's an old saying. 'If momma ain't happy, ain't nobody happy!'" And he laughed at his own joke.

"Would something bad happen if you didn't do it?"

"No," he said. "But I *like* doing it."

I look at my mom, standing there in the kitchen. Judging by the gold hanging off her arms and neck, she ought to be pretty darn happy.

Right now, though, she wants that sweater. Rosario's on the phone, turning to Mom. "He can rush it through, but it will be very expensive."

Mom frowns at this annoyance. "Well, I just have to have it. Be a love, Rosario, and pick it up by eleven?" Mom blows kisses to the three of us and a second later is out the kitchen door, walking down the hall to her office.

Maddy, Molly, and I say good-bye to Ro, and I drive the girls to their school, then head off for mine.

Chapter Fourteen

Jonathan falls into step next to me on my way to class. He's one of the few people at school I can stand to be around since Michael died.

"So you and Emily, huh?" he asks. He must have noticed us having one of our lunches or sitting together in the Quad, talking. It is Emily, mainly, who has gotten me through the last couple of weeks, pulling me out of my black moods with her steady friendship.

"What? No, we're just friends," I say.

"*Right.*"

"No, really." She and I are just friends, and I have a bad feeling it'll have to stay that way.

"She's in a bunch of my classes." He doesn't say it, but he means the AP classes. "She's very cool. She's *hachimenreirou.*"

Jonathan breaks into Japanese every once in a while. He speaks it at home with his family.

"What's that?"

"It means *perfect serenity—beautiful from all sides.*"

Wow. Jonathan nailed it with that one. "I can't believe you have a word in Japanese for that."

"We do." He gets an evil look on his face. "We also have *bakku-shan.* That's a girl who's pretty from the back, but from the front, it's like *no way.*"

I try to look disgusted at him, but I can't help smiling. I've known Jonathan since the second grade, although not as well as Michael. "What's your point, Takahara?"

"Just that an asshole like you could do a lot worse than Emily."

"Thanks for the tip, asshole."

There's something I've been wanting to ask him. He's into all this weird spiritual stuff, and sometimes we talk about it.

"Jonathan, do you believe in karma?"

Because I do. I believe that everything you do somehow comes back around to you eventually. The night that Michael died, I made enough bad karma to fill an ocean.

"Yep." Jonathan answers instantly.

I reach up and shift the strap of the loaded backpack that's biting into my shoulder. Not sure I really want to know the answer to my next question, I ask it anyway.

"What happens if you've got a lot of bad karma? Do you go to karma hell?" We turn a corner and pass some guys we know, raising our hands briefly to them as we go by.

"Kinda, yeah. If your karma's bad enough when you die, you get reincarnated as some lower form of life."

Great. I'm probably scheduled to come back as a sea slug.

"On the other hand, you can work off bad karma and create good in its place."

I get this image of a giant worksheet in the sky, where the karma gods keep track of how everyone's doing. Right now, I've got a whopping balance of negative karma.

"How do you know all this?" I ask.

"I have two uncles and three cousins in Japan who are Buddhist monks."

"You're kidding!"

"Nope. My father's the black sheep of the family, because he went into the import/export business."

So Jonathan knows what he's talking about. I can redeem myself, if I do good deeds. But what about Emily? Since I lost any right to be happy when I left Michael in the stairwell that night, the karma gods would probably count being in love with her as a bad deed on the worksheet.

Jonathan brings my thoughts back to the hallway. "Ryan, did you ever figure out anything about Michael's secret—the thing that was bothering him?"

I shake my head. "I have no clue."

There's no one else he would have told. Letting it go doesn't feel good, but I don't know what else to do.

"Okay, well, see you later," Jonathan says, and we go to class.

Chapter Fifteen

Emily has put on white gym shorts, a white polo shirt, and a pair of white Keds, the color scheme being a requirement of my tennis club. She looks cute, with her hair up in a ponytail. She's going to have her first tennis lesson.

It has taken me a while to get up the nerve to go back to the club. I park my car and get out, setting my feet carefully on the asphalt of the parking lot, as if I'm not sure it will hold me. I would go around to open Emily's door for her, but she's already out and pulling the tennis rackets from the back seat.

"The last time I came here, I was with Michael," I say. "In fact, probably the last *fifty* times I came here, I was with Michael."

Her forehead wrinkles. "Do you want to do this? We could go somewhere else."

"No." I grab a couple of cans of balls. "I promised you a tennis lesson."

I'm wearing my best, most professional looking whites. In addition to giving her a few pointers, I wouldn't mind showing off to Emily the true God of Tennis that I am.

As we walk through the club gates and onto a court, I follow close behind her, grateful I'm not here alone.

"You won't laugh at me, will you?" she asks.

I bounce a tennis ball. "Only if you're really bad."

"Don't!" She wags a stern finger at me as the corners of her mouth turn up in a smile.

Once again, I'm drowning in those gray-blue eyes. I have to force myself to say, "Okay, well, I guess we should get started."

I demonstrate a basic forehand and backhand, and we practice for a while. I hit gentle shots straight to her, while she tries to get anything at all back to me. I shouldn't be, but I'm appreciating the sounds and feelings of tennis again: the grip of my feet on the court, the thwack of the racket strings against the ball. My mind stops churning, and my senses take over. It's sweet relief, like when a good, strong pain pill kicks in.

Emily's hitting balls out of bounds, into the net, and even backwards, gritting her teeth and saying, "I'll get it! You'll see!" And after a while, she does get it, hitting three shots in a row back to me.

"Good work!" I tell her.

A guy I know, Alex, who's a really good player, stops to talk to me. Emily, out of breath, invites us to play together.

"Sure," I say, acting cool and casual.

I stand at the service line, bouncing a ball up and down. Emily is watching me. A few brown tree leaves tumble across the court.

As I look across the net at Alex, sudden rage floods me, and all the good feelings vanish. I hate the guy just because he's not Michael. I bounce the ball again, tensing as I get ready to serve.

My first serve blisters its way over the net, practically spinning Alex around. *Point, Ryan.* I do it again, and then again, serving three aces in a row. When Alex finally does get a volley going with me, I push him back behind the base line, then tap over a little drop shot that he misses by a mile. I run him all over the court with my deadly topspin shots and end the match by ripping him a forehand that leaves a cloud of yellow fuzz in the air beside me and skitters the ball into a far corner of the court. He tries for it, but he's not even close.

"Jeez, Ryan," Alex says and leaves, scratching his head.

We kicked his ass, didn't we, Michael? Serves the guy right for trying to take your place.

"I can't believe how good you are," Emily tells me when I finish and walk over to her.

"Believe it, baby," I say, putting on a swagger and toweling off my face and neck. *Yes.* I have blown her away with my excellence.

As I walk around picking up tennis balls, Chrissie comes by in a short little tennis skirt. I haven't seen her since the funeral, but now she comes up to me.

"Wow, Ryan. You looked great just now!" Chrissie's accent is straight off a Mississipi mud flat. She has always reminded me of a Fourth of July sparkler, sending off light in all directions. She has blonde, curly hair and a blonde, curly personality.

From the side of the court, Emily is watching us. She has probably noticed that Chrissie merits a high score on the Hotness Scale.

Although Emily is the most beautiful girl ever, I still have to take an extra look at gorgeous Chrissie, who is pursing up her rosebud mouth in a way that makes me shift uncomfortably and think, Dang, Michael got a piece of that!

Neither Chrissie nor I mention Michael; it's like we've both decided that subject's off limits today. She starts to tell me a story about one of the club pros. Chrissie flirts as easily as other people breathe, tossing her hair, laughing, giving off sideways glances and little arm touches. She does this to every guy at the club, including our ninety year old half-blind garage cashier, Raoul.

Emily walks over to stand next to me. "Hi," she says to Chrissie in a friendly tone. She's low key about it, but I notice she's really close to me, her arm almost touching mine.

I introduce them, and Emily asks Chrissie where the nearest Ladies' Room is.

"Honey, you read my mind! I'll take you there."

As I wait for the girls to come back, a couple of the club pros walk by.

"Great match, Ryan. You should go back into training!"

"Thanks. Maybe I will." But I'm not serious about it.

The girls return, and Emily and I go out to my car.

"So she said she'll be quitting the club pretty soon," Emily says as she slides into the passenger seat.

"Who?"

"That girl we just saw. The blonde." Emily's voice goes neutral on the word *blonde*.

"What do you mean?" I start the car and begin backing out of our parking spot.

"I mean she can't play tennis much longer."

I turn my head to stare at Emily. "What are you talking about?

A second later, I slam on my brakes, throwing both of us forward, and just avoid sideswiping another car. The driver blasts his horn at me, but I barely hear him.

"*What* did you just say?"

Her eyes round with surprise from my reaction, she repeats the terrible piece of news as if it's nothing.

"Didn't you know?" she says. "That girl's pregnant."

• • •

I pull my car into an empty spot and sit there gripping the steering wheel. We've travelled a whole fifty yards or so in the tennis club parking lot.

"Ryan, what is it?" Emily's shoulder touches mine as she leans into me. Worry clouds her face.

"How do you know she's pregnant?"

"She was feeling sick in the bathroom, and she told me. Why? What does it matter?"

"The night of your party, Michael told me he slept with Chrissie. Once. At the tennis club." I'm staring straight ahead, my eyes burning. *I can't believe this.*

"What are you saying? That the baby's *his?*" Emily's voice hits the high end of the register.

I nod. "It could be."

"But he only slept with her once!" she says. "I mean, it could happen, I guess. But it just seems like … *that girl?* She could have a lot of boyfriends."

And she probably does, her tone implies.

"You don't like her, do you?"

"Well, it's just that…." Emily looks sideways at me, "She flirts a lot."

I can't deny it. "She flirts with everybody."

"Exactly. So she's got lots of men around."

"The thing is, Michael was worried about something that night. He said he had something bad to tell me, and I had to keep it secret. But he didn't get a chance to tell me." Guilt stabs at me. *He tried to tell me, and I wouldn't listen.*

"Really?" Emily sits very still, her hands folded in her lap, as she takes in this new information. "But you said he was slipping back into drugs, so it could have been that, too. And if it *were* his,

65

wouldn't Chrissie have gotten in touch with his parents, you know, after he...?" She doesn't finish her sentence. "She could have found them through the tennis club."

"I guess so." My hands loosen on the steering wheel, and I sink back in my seat, drawing in a big breath.

"Or she might even choose not to have the baby," Emily says. She puts her hand on my arm.

"Yeah." As always happens when I'm with Emily, a calm creeps over me. The tension drains out of my neck and shoulders, and my head clears.

"It shouldn't be my problem, but it feels like it is. Michael was like my brother, you know?"

"Well, I bet it's not even Michael's."

She's probably right. I relax even more. We sit in silence for a few seconds.

Then, "How does that happen, anyway?" Emily's studying the can of tennis balls in her lap. "To just sleep with someone *once?*"

A beat. The conversation has taken an interesting turn. "I don't know, Emily," I tease her. "How *does* it happen?"

I say it very suavely, as if I know all about it, when in fact I have not exactly had sex with a girl yet. It's on my list of things to do, but I haven't quite made it there.

She's turning pink now. "I mean, usually when you have sex with someone, you really like them, right? You plan to do it more than once."

A *really* interesting turn. But I can't be with Emily now. Not after what I did to Michael.

"He said it was in the Pro Shop. At the club."

"You mean, the *store?* Don't people come in?"

I give her a dry look. "I didn't discuss the logistics with Michael." A pause. "But knowing him, well.... He didn't exactly plan things out, you know? Especially not something like this."

"I guess."

I start the car again, then turn to her. "Thanks for coming with me today. It made it a lot easier."

Dimples appear in both of her cheeks. "You're welcome." We sit there smiling at each other, until I finally pull myself together and take her home.

Chapter Sixteen

"Please take the last fifteen minutes of class," Mr. Simpson announces in physics, "to pair up with one or two other students. You will be in these groupings for the rest of the year for lab work and the second semester physics project."

I stare down at my hands on my desk. Michael would have been my lab partner if he were still alive.

Get up. Go find someone else. But I can't think of who to ask. Maybe, if I behave as if Michael's still alive, I can make it true.

So I don't look for another partner. I sit there, while the other kids mill around, forming groups. When the bell rings, I finally get up and try to make my escape.

Jonathan stops me at the door. "Do you want to work with us? I'm with Calvin Yang, but we can take a third person."

"Yeah. Thanks, Jonathan." I know it's a pity offer, but I'll take it.

For a moment I consider telling him about the pregnancy. But I haven't heard anything about it from my folks or Michael's. Emily's probably right – it's not Michael's baby. I let it go.

A few minutes later, outside of Spanish class, Chase walks up to me. He's wearing this sweat-shirt that looks like he dragged it up off the floor after maybe walking on it for a month.

We haven't spoken since our fight by Emily's locker. I set my backpack down—better to keep my hands free in case he tries to jump me. As anger and grief rise again, I imagine a margarita-soaked Chase coated in sand like some giant breaded pork chop. It's a satisfying thought.

Chase starts this shifting thing he does, from one foot to the other. "You don't have any of Michael's stuff, do you?" he blurts out. "He was supposed to get something for me, but then he, you know…" His voice trails off.

"No. Like what? What was it?"

Chase shakes his head. "Never mind." He drifts off.

That was strange. I would just as soon not learn what Michael had for him.

• • •

It still burns me, the fact that Chase got Michael back into drugs after he'd been clean for three years. I remember the first time I saw Michael high. It was at our seventh grade school retreat, when we were taken off to this fancy resort place for three days to bond with our new classmates. I was sharing a room with Michael.

On the second night, I had gone to bed early. A hand on my shoulder woke me up.

"Get up." Michael sat on me, crushing my arm into my ribs.

"Go away." I pushed him off me and turned over.

A moment of peace, then, "You force me to take harsh measures." He yanked the pillow out from under my head.

Groaning, I grabbed some flip flops and followed him out of the room in my t-shirt and gym shorts.

"Man, what are we doing?" I was yawning and half-stunned by the bright light of the hallway.

"Just shut up, okay?" We walked as quietly as we could down the hall to another door. Michael knocked on it, saying to me in a low voice, "You're with Phoebe."

"Huh?" I did a double take. "Michael, what's going on?"

"Just trust me, man."

The door opened. In the room were another guy and three girls. It was a small room—and crowded. One of the girls gave me a meaningful look and walked over to me. This must be Phoebe. She was in my math class and had just moved here from some place like Houston. She wore skimpy shirts that rode way up on her belly and had this blonde hair that she flipped around while she talked. She talked a lot.

"Hi," she said.

"Hi." I didn't look at her.

"So I heard you know all these movie stars."

I grunted a reply.

"That must be *so cool*. Like, who've you met? "

I'd met plenty, as a matter of fact, but I would have eaten battery acid before I told her anything. "No one really."

I heard the striking of a match as this guy, Josh somebody, lit a joint and took a drag. Miss Anderson had warned us what would happen if we did drugs on a school retreat: "You will be immediately expelled." I was sweating, picturing myself thrown out of school after only three weeks. But if I left now, I'd look like a total wimp.

The joint started moving around the circle. Phoebe, standing next to me, inhaled noisily and handed it to me. I did the only socially acceptable thing and sucked in a lungful of smoke, and then more lungfuls as the joint kept working its way around to me.

Soon, I was in some kind of time warp. Just lifting the joint to my mouth took about five minutes, and it was taking me ten minutes or so to inhale the smoke. Phoebe was laughing very, very loudly, a high-pitched laugh that went into my ear drum like an ice pick.

My head turned very, very slowly and I registered, far away, as if through the wrong end of a telescope, Michael on the bed with Kayla, and three or four minutes later I realized that *he was lying on top of her!* They had their clothes on, but *still!* I started to crack up, then stifled my laughter, willing myself to be cool.

I was in a big armchair with Phoebe, who seemed very far away, even though she was right there in the chair with me. She was doing something wet and frantic to my mouth with her mouth. She must have popped a breath mint or something, because I caught this intense blast of peppermint.

I went with it. I didn't really like this girl, but her tongue was in my mouth, which made up for a lot.

I knew nothing about kissing at age twelve, but I did my best. Doing it with Phoebe was like wrestling with a suction hose. I was sure kissing had to be better than this – otherwise it wouldn't be so popular. But at the same time, I had a wicked hard-on and was sliding my hand lower and lower down her back until it was *almost on her ass!* She seemed fine with it. See, Michael? You're not the only one with game around here.

Then, someone said, "Heads up! I hear something!" We all froze. Phoebe's pointy elbow was boring into my ribcage. Footsteps walked up to our door and stopped. Then a soft tapping on the door, as if the person outside was testing to see if anyone was awake in there.

In absolute silence, we waited. I thought my heart would knock Phoebe off the chair, it was pounding so hard.

The footsteps started up again and disappeared down the hall.

"Okay, that's it, I guess!" I threw off Phoebe, peeled Michael off of Kayla, and dragged him down the hall to our room. Once safely back, I let go of his arm and said, "Dude! We could have got thrown out of school!" My lips felt huge and rubbery, and the room was slowly rotating around us.

"But we didn't." Michael was already climbing into bed.

I fell into my own bed, my head pulsing, thanking God we had escaped uncaught.

"Hey, Ryan." Michael's voice was muffled from his pillow.

"Yeah?"

"Phoebe's hot, huh?"

He could have her.

On the bus ride home from the retreat, the guy who had been in the room with us, Josh, was caught with weed in his backpack and was expelled from Pacific Prep.

"Bummer," was Michael's comment. After that, he started smoking dope and trying harder stuff too with this druggie crowd at school. "Come party with me, man!" he would say, and I did a few times, but finally told him I didn't like it and didn't want to get into trouble. We stayed best friends, though. What with our regular lunches and tennis games, schoolwork, and the closeness of our two families, Michael was too much a part of my life to be anything else.

As for Phoebe, I avoided her for the rest of the school year and was glad when she transferred to this alternative hippie school for eighth grade. I heard she thought the Pacific Prep kids were boring and uptight.

Chapter Seventeen

My folks have been talking to Nat and Yancy a lot since the funeral and have invited them over for dinner. It figures, I think with a flash of anger, that we kids aren't enough to make them stay home at night. They need a *good* reason, like the Westons coming over.

We're all sitting around our big dining table, with Nat on my right and Yancy across from me. It hurts me to see only seven places at the table. From the sad way that Maddy and Molly are picking at their food, I can see that they're feeling it, too.

Mom sits next to Yancy with an arm around her shoulder. People always say Yancy's beautiful, but I think if you took away the fancy clothes and hair, no one would ever look at her twice.

Tonight, she has this lost, sad look on her face. Both she and Nat look older and really tired. Nat's a handsome guy—Michael took after him—but now his face is puffy, like he's acquired an extra chin. He speaks only occasionally and his hands shake through dinner.

We sit for a long time at the table and share memories of Michael. I don't say much, since I still haven't forgiven my folks or the Westons for what they did when he overdosed.

"Remember that summer on Martha's Vineyard?" Mom says. Dad and Nat were filming a movie, and we were all living together in this big house we had rented. "When Michael and Ryan slept in a tent in the backyard every single night? They never used their bedroom at all, except to store their clothes!"

"During tennis matches," Maddy says, "any time Michael had to change sides, he would always do a crazy jump over the net instead of walking around. It was so funny!"

"And he put fourteen cherry tomatoes in his mouth one time!" Molly says.

"He did?" Yancy says. "I never saw him do that!"

"I think you were in Barcelona that day," I say in a bored tone. Heat crawls down my spine, as the room gets quiet.

"Ryan." My dad's voice holds a warning. He goes on, "*I* remember when he broke his leg snowboarding, and the Ski Patrol had to bring him down the mountain."

"Of course, he had to do it on the first day of our trip," Nat says. For the rest of the trip, we had all taken turns staying at the hotel to play Scrabble and Monopoly with him during the day, while the others skied.

All of a sudden, Yancy starts to cry. "We made so many mistakes." She twists her hands together, while my mom puts both arms around her.

Even I feel a little bad for her then. If that baby of Chrissie's were Michael's, it would mean everything to Nat and Yancy—to all of us, really. But it's not.

"We're suing the Breakers Club," she says, her lips set in a thin line. "For negligence. When the valets gave Michael his car."

"You're gonna win," Dad says.

I wonder what they think that's going to accomplish. It sure as heck won't bring Michael back.

She answers my unspoken question. "If it stops them from doing it again, it'll be worth it. Nadine, we're going to give any settlement we receive to the Teen League."

Mom nods her head, looking sober. "That's a great idea."

"What's the Teen League?" I ask.

"Yancy and I are on the Board there," Mom says. "They give support to disadvantaged teens, including counseling for drug and alcohol abuse. They help a lot of kids."

Too bad Michael didn't get any help.

Yancy tears up again and I wonder if she's thinking the same thing. She turns to me. "You were with him his last hours. What did he say to you? What was he thinking?" She digs in her bag for tissues. Even the candlelight on the table cannot soften the hard lines around her mouth and eyes.

They're all looking at me, waiting for my answer. She has to know the thoughtless, reckless way Michael spent his last evening on earth. What does she want me to say to her?

Then something comes to me: Michael's last five minutes of conscious life were in his Mustang, the car he loved, barreling down Pacific Coast Highway. For Michael, it didn't get much better than that. When he was thrown from the car, I was told, he had probably blacked out immediately. He never woke up.

"I think he was happy when he died," I say, "and he didn't suffer." It makes *me* feel better, anyway.

Nat reaches out and crushes my hand in his.

Chapter Eighteen

I'm driving up Laurel Canyon, with the top down and Emily sitting in the passenger seat beside me. Her legs are close to mine in the small front seat, and her hair whips around in the wind. If the karma gods weren't watching, I would reach out and take her hand, which is resting on her thigh.

Toby, her golden lab, sits in the back seat, warming our necks with his smelly breath. I enjoy maneuvering my car up the twisting road toward the top of the ridge, looking at the matchbox houses on stilts perched along the sides of the canyon. A few houses along the road sport scarecrows and jack-o-lanterns in honor of Halloween, which is next week.

We reach Mulholland Drive at the top, turn right, and wind our way along the ridge to the Runyon Canyon turnoff. On this beautiful afternoon, half of Hollywood is out walking its dogs.

I wasn't lying to Jonathan when I said that Emily and I were just friends. I've never held her hand or kissed her, although I've thought about it probably a hundred million times. But then I think of Michael and that giant worksheet in the sky. I don't want to spend my next life as an earthworm.

Toby trots along beside us as we walk on the road that winds high along the canyon wall. In all directions, we see steep hillsides and patches of trees intermingled with people's homes.

We stop for a minute while Toby digs under a bush, scratching up dirt with his paws. The freshly turned earth is darker than the dry, dusty stuff on the surface.

Out of nowhere a thought hits me. "She came to the funeral."

"What?"

"Chrissie. She came to Michael's funeral, even though she wasn't invited."

"Really?" Emily thinks about it. "Strange."

"Not strange if he's the father of her baby."

"There could be another explanation," she says slowly, as if her mind is racing in ten different directions, trying to find one.

"I don't know what it is."

"If it bothers you that much, maybe you should talk to her."

"What, just go to her, and say *Is Michael your kid's father?*"

"Something like that." She speaks slowly again, as if she's trying to figure out a puzzle in her mind. "Maybe then you could introduce her to Michael's parents. Wouldn't they be excited to have a grandchild?"

"I guess. They sure weren't the greatest parents."

"They might still be good grandparents. And they could help Chrissie out."

We round a corner in the road and stop to admire the combined city and canyon view stretched out in front of us. "It's so clear today," she says.

"Los Angeles," I tell her. "Greatest city in the world." She and I have a running argument about it, since I love LA, while she can't wait to move to the East Coast for college.

We start walking again. By now, I've learned that Emily has big plans for her life. For college and grad school, she wants to go Ivy League, then after that, live in Washington DC or Europe, working at a think tank or maybe as a diplomat.

"I'm not sure exactly what," she says. "But it would be nice to—I don't know—help make the world a better place." She looks almost shy. "It sounds ridiculous, doesn't it?"

"No." I feel about as deep as a piece of tracing paper. "I wish I knew what I wanted."

"You'll figure it out. You're really smart, Ryan." She slips her hand through my arm, and I press it close to my side with my elbow.

"You really think so?" I feel humble hearing Emily say I'm smart.

"Of course. You were smart about Michael that night. You took him off to a private place and took care of him. You knew he couldn't drive himself home. You told him to wait for you. It's not your fault that he ran off while you were gone for a couple of minutes."

My eyes get this prickly feeling, like I'm going to start crying like a big baby. Horrified, I stop dead in my tracks, which, since her hand is clamped under my elbow, makes her jerk to a stop alongside me.

I focus on a couple of little dogs that have run up to Toby, bristling and yapping to make themselves look scary. "You're not fooling anyone," I say to them.

Toby is rooted in one place, sniffing something interesting by the side of the road. I look down at Emily and her insanely kissable lips, and I know at that moment that she would let me kiss her—in fact, she wants me to kiss her—but I can't. If I do, I'll be lost—so in love that I'll never come back to my old self—and I don't deserve to have love when Michael is dead. And I killed him.

Besides I have a job to do, a debt to Michael that I have to repay. If he has a baby out there in the world, I need to know about it. My family and the Westons need to know about it.

I have to go see Chrissie.

We stand there looking at each other, and then the moment passes. Emily stares off into the distance, her mouth tightening a little in disappointment. We turn around and walk the road back to my car, not speaking.

I can't fall in love when Michael is dead. But the problem is, I think to myself, it's too late.

I already have.

Chapter Nineteen

I arrive at the tennis club, parking my BMW in one of the good spots marked "reserved." My parents are on the Board here, and the parking spot's one of the perks.

I can't get used to going to the tennis club without Michael. Like Camp Evergreen, the club and tennis—for me—are tied to him and his memory. I actually turn to him a couple of times, or rather, I turn to the place I expect him to be, and start to tell him something, then stop abruptly.

I am becoming strange.

Just thinking about the conversation I have to have with Chrissie sets my stomach on a roller coaster ride. Rather than deal with it, I load three hundred balls into a ball machine and adjust the settings. Every two seconds it will fire a ball at me in a random pattern: lobs, drives, slices with every kind of spin. I tell myself if I can return all three hundred balls to my imaginary partner, Michael will come back to life. On maybe the sixtieth or seventieth ball, the machine surprises me with a shot to my backhand. My feet are in the wrong place; *I'm* in the wrong place.

I miss the shot. Michael will stay with the dead.

After ten minutes, I reload the machine and start over. Maybe I can save Michael this time. Nope. A ball catches me in no-man's land and passes me by.

I do it a third time ten minutes later.

Nope.

Over and over, I reset the machine—I'm not sure how many times I do it. My legs start to shake, and sweat's pouring into my eyes, blinding me. I'm gasping for air, and my lungs are on fire. I'm missing every other ball now, tripping and stumbling.

I am back by the base line when the machine throws me a drop shot. My shoes squeak as I dig in for traction to sprint forward, lunging for the ball and missing by yards as I fall and skid on the court. Patches of skin separate themselves from my legs and forearms. I lie there, starting to bleed, while the machine continues to spew balls. A couple of them hit me.

Maybe I'll just lie here forever. It seems like a good idea to me.

I feel a cool hand under my arm. It's careful to touch only skin that's still intact. The hand helps me up, leads me over to a bench, and puts a bottle of cold water in front of me. I squint my eyes open. It's Chrissie.

"Thanks," I say, downing the water in one gulp. She leaves for a minute and returns with a medicine bottle and eye dropper. I sit there like a statue, while she douses my cuts with something that hurts, but is supposed to be good for me.

I start to say *thank you* again, but instead I say, "You wanna go to lunch?"

She walks with me as I limp into the club dining room. We find a booth. Chrissie's condition is now obvious to even the most clueless observer. Even I can see she's pregnant. Chrissie tries to exchange club gossip and small talk for a few minutes, but I'm not up for it. It's strange, after all the time I've spent with Emily, being with a different girl. But, I'm not really *with* Chrissie, of course. I'm just here because of Michael and the baby.

"So you holdin' up okay, honey?" she asks me finally. Her accent is so down-home I can almost smell catfish frying. She looks at me kindly.

"Sort of," I tell her. I realize my voice is shaky. "I think about Michael all the time. It shouldn't have happened. He shouldn't be dead."

"I know. It's sad," she says. "But his spirit's alive." She sips her lemonade from a straw and looks at me from under a fringe of blonde curls.

When the waiter comes, I order a burger, wondering why I'm even bothering. I'm not going to eat it. I'm still thirsty, though. I down half of my iced tea in one swallow. Meanwhile, Chrissie orders a club sandwich, extra mayo, with fries and extra ketchup.

I want to get to the real subject. "Michael talked about you. The night he died."

"What did he say?" she asks.

I try to make it sound better than Michael did. "He said the two of you were," I hesitate for a second, "seeing each other." I find myself looking out the window across the lawn toward the Pro Shop, then shooting my eyes back to her. Someone arrives with our food.

She bites into her club sandwich, then corrects me. "Michael and I had—a moment." Seeing my face, she adds, "What can I say? It was preordained."

"Preordained? What do you mean?"

"It was fate. It was meant to be." She touches her napkin to her lips.

I have the same thought I always get when I'm around Chrissie: maybe this girl's driving without a steering wheel.

"How old are you?" I look at my burger and push it away. Chrissie is working through her French fries, dipping them in ketchup as she goes. She seems to be taking this better than I am.

"Twenty," she says. So I guessed right. Chrissie's tiny, and with those blonde curls and blue eyes, she looks like an angel. But she eats like a lumberjack. She beams at me. She actually looks happy. A little corner of my brain thinks, I bet a camera would love her.

"It was Michael's idea. He came into the Pro Shop one night, right before closing. And, Lord, that boy could talk fish right up onto dry land." Her eyes are bright from the memory, then dim as a new thought hits her. "He told me he was eighteen, and I believed him."

I know she's telling the truth. Michael lied sometimes the way little kids do, like I've seen my sisters do. At that moment, he wanted to be eighteen. So he said he was.

"I told him that morning, the day he died. I told him I was with child."

I feel a cold finger go down my spine. So, I was right. That's what he was going to tell me that night in the stairwell. Michael knew that he'd gotten a girl pregnant and that, of all his many screw-ups, this was his worst.

When I can speak again, I ask, "What did he say? When you

told him?"

"He said he was only sixteen. And I said, 'A little late to be tellin' me that now, don't you think?'"

"What else did he say?" I'm hungry for anything about Michael on that day, his last day of life. What was going on with him?

"He wanted me to end the pregnancy. But I said, no, I was keepin' the baby." She grips her lemonade glass without lifting it from the table.

"He said his parents would kill him. He kept saying over and over again, 'I am so dead.'" Her face twists up over the irony of it.

I swallow hard, thinking of Michael grabbing my arm in the stairwell that night. *Stay here, man. Please. I'm not doing so hot.* And I just blew him off, like a total asshole. A complete, gigantic failure as a friend.

I feel like a raw, exposed nerve ending. I'm not eating, instead drumming my fingers on the table top.

"He said he would do practically anything to avoid tellin' his parents."

Cold chills are going up and down my arms. *Anything?* Like killing himself in a crash on Pacific Coast Highway?

"I felt so bad for him, but what was I supposed to do? End the life of my child for his convenience? I don't think so."

I can't take it anymore. I change the subject. "What happened anyway? Did the condom break?"

Her eyes down, she says, "We were ... caught up in it, you know? It just didn't feel like a condom moment."

I sit there, wondering if this girl's brains were accidentally sucked out of her head in some failed school science experiment. Chrissie has stopped eating, too, and is tearing her napkin into tiny pieces.

"*Excuse me?*" I say. "Let me be clear on what you just said. It didn't *feel like* a condom moment?" My voice is rising now, along with my temper.

At this, Chrissie kind of hitches her head back and gives me a long, hard look.

"Now, don't go gettin' your panties all in a knot, Ryan," she says in her deep fryers and hushpuppies accent. "I know how take care of a baby. I been baby sittin' since I was eight, and I practically raised my older sisters' boys. I got this one under control."

Time for the million dollar question.

"Do you know for sure it's his baby?" I watch her eyes, her face, looking for clues that will tip me off to the truth.

"Course I do! What, do you think I just sleep with everyone who comes along?"

Actually, Chrissie, that had occurred to me.

"So you're absolutely, totally positive it's Michael's baby? It couldn't *possibly* be anyone else's?"

"I do not appreciate your crass insinuations. Besides, my baby's none of your business." Chrissie looks at me like I'm a bug on the sidewalk.

But I persist. I need good news. If I keep asking questions, she'll eventually have to say something I want to hear.

"Do you have anyone to help you—parents, something like that?" I ask.

"My whole family's down South. I'll tell 'em eventually." But Chrissie doesn't seem particularly concerned.

"Michael's folks will help you."

Chrissie jumps a little and snaps out, "*No*. I'm not telling 'em. It'd just complicate my life."

Complicate her life? "His parents have to know! It's their grandchild."

She shuts me down. "I'll decide that. And don't you tell them! It's not your place to do that." Then she leans forward and adds, "Ryan, honey, don't worry about me. I been given this baby for a reason. It's not your problem."

I don't know what to think. I remember all the times Nat and Yancy jetted off, leaving Michael with the latest nanny, usually some airhead who spent all her time on the phone to her boyfriend. So do I let it go? Let Nat and Yancy spend the rest of their lives not knowing they have a grandchild?

What about me? Do I let Chrissie disappear with Michael's baby? Never see the kid again? Never get to know him, or even know where he is? For some reason, I think of four-year old Hector, the gardener's son. I'd like to know Michael's kid when he's four. Michael was as close to me as a brother.

"Give me your whole name and phone number," I say, passing

her a pen and paper. She looks like she's trying to think of a way out of it, but finally scribbles something and tosses it back to me. I try to make out what she wrote.

"Chrissie Valentino-Fellars?" I ask.

"Fellars is my real name, but I've taken Valentino as my stage name. I'm an artist," she says with dignity. "I came to Los Angeles to make a name for myself."

Great. She's an actress.

"Thanks. I'll give you a call," I say.

The waiter comes by to take my untouched burger away. Chrissie stops him.

"You don't want it?" she asks me. "I'll take it home for dinner."

"Be my guest." Yuck. This girl's grossing me out, going after my rejected food like a hyena.

Chrissie catches my vibe. She gives me a sharp look. "You didn't take one bite of this! Maybe you have twelve dollars to throw in the trash, but I don't."

Shame creeps from my toes up through and past my legs. I drive home, thinking this is some pretty grown up stuff Michael got himself into.

And now I'm in it, too, whether I like it or not.

Chapter Twenty

As I arrive home late that afternoon, my parents are just walking out. Judging by the relatively low poundage level of Mom's jewelry, I would guess they're going to a casual event. Also, Dad's wearing this leather jacket Mom talked him into buying, which they think of as casual, even though it costs as much as some cars. I try to arrange my features so I don't look as bad as I feel.

"Hi, sweetheart!" Mom says. They stop to give me a few minutes of face time before they take off for the rest of the evening.

"Sorry we have to leave," Dad says. "Business meeting." Since Michael died, it's almost as if they feel guilty about going out all the time. Not guilty enough to stop doing it, but guilty enough to apologize for it, anyway.

"How are you doing, honey?" Mom's using a fake-sounding syrupy voice that makes me want to kick over a lawn chair.

"Same," I say.

"All right, then." They wait another moment, just in case I might burst out with a confession or two. "So, we'll see you later on tonight," says Dad. They take off.

I walk into the kitchen. The girls are there, drinking apple juice. Being kids, they don't notice too much about my different moods. But when Rosario looks up from the board where she's cutting vegetables, her eyes darken. I can't hide anything from her. She doesn't ask, knowing I'll only tell her if I want to. And I don't. I say I'm tired and escape to my bedroom.

I lie in bed with my state-of-the-art noise-cancelling headphones, watching the Starship Enterprise perform maneuvers in space. The same thoughts run through my head, over and over. Michael is dead. This baby has no father. And it's my fault.

I try to push the thoughts away, but they return. Now, I hear not only the words Michael said to me, but the ones he said to Chrissie.

My parents will kill me. Stay here, man. Please. I am so dead.

I try to distract myself with homework. I should start that English paper that's due next week. I stare at my computer screen, my mind turning like a dog as he sniffs and circles for the perfect spot. I sharpen some pencils even though I never use pencils.

I picture myself down the road, keeping tabs on Michael's kid. For some reason, I've started thinking of it as a boy. I see myself checking in with him for birthdays and holidays, taking him to ball games and the beach. He would know Michael's parents and my family and would come over to our houses sometimes. Thinking of that relieves the sharp pain in my chest and makes it easier to breathe.

I go into video chat on my laptop, and a few seconds later, Emily's face fills the screen. I report to her everything that's happened and what Chrissie said at the club.

"So it's Michael's baby for sure," I say. "But she didn't want me to tell Nat and Yancy."

"Why not? They have a right to know!" On my computer screen, her forehead does that crinkle again.

"Yeah, but…"

"It almost makes me think she's not telling the truth. That's it's not really Michael's baby."

"*He* believed that it was." I know that now, looking back on how Michael acted that night in the stairwell. "I want to stay in touch with her. Keep track of the baby."

"How would you do that?"

"I don't know. Call her. Take her for coffee or something." I add quickly "I don't care about her. It's just about Michael's baby."

Emily's shoulders droop a little, but she doesn't say anything.

I repeat it. "It's her kid I want to hang out with. Not her." Somehow, I feel I have to explain this to Emily, even though we're just friends.

We sign off. Then I take a deep breath and call the number

Chrissie gave me.

"This is Chrissie's cell. Leave a message."

"Hey, Chrissie, it's Ryan. Gimme a call when you can, okay?" I want to get her address and maybe check in on her every once in a while. She's all alone in LA and maybe she'll need help one of these days.

Chapter Twenty-One

As I swing around the corner on my way to Emily's locker, I see Derek Masters standing there. Next to Emily. I haven't forgotten him hanging all over her at her birthday party. He is leaning against her locker with his hair spiked up in a studly kind of way and saying something that's probably incredibly witty.

Emily looks even prettier than usual today, her eyes sparkling and the hills and valleys of her blue sweater completely capturing my attention.

I forget that she's not my girlfriend, can never be my girlfriend. This guy's a total predator. I don't need his crap right now. Adrenaline surges through me, and I push forward.

"Derek. Wassup?" I say smoothly, signaling my mild surprise that he's sniffing around my girl, but also my full confidence that he doesn't stand a chance with her. "You ready to go to lunch, Emily?"

Derek's smile gets uncertain around the edges. "Hey, Ryan."

I stand there, mellow on the outside, but growing roots into the floor vinyl. After a minute, Derek takes off.

"So, you're friends with him?" I ask Emily, trying to sound cool and unconcerned.

"A little bit," she says as we head for my car. Since juniors are allowed off campus during lunch, Emily and I had made plans to have a picnic in the park.

When we get to the park, she tells me "I know exactly where to go!" She takes off running, me jogging behind her, and cuts diagonally across a big open area, dodging a few dog walkers and disappearing behind a hedge. When I come around it, she is spreading out a blanket in the shade under a tree.

"Our own private spot," Emily announces. She opens her backpack and produces sparkling cider and raspberries. I've brought turkey sandwiches that I made myself, refusing Rosario's offer to do it.

"This is *excellent,*" I tell her, trying to ignore the sudden dullness in my mind, the feeling that my head is full of cotton.

Michael will never get to eat raspberries in the park with a girl.

"I don't even care if I skip fifth period," she says. "I turned my homework in ahead of time just in case."

We eat our turkey sandwiches, and I try to show off by tossing a raspberry into the air and catching it with my mouth. But I miss, and it rolls away.

"Any missed raspberries must be fed to the other person by hand," Emily announces. "It's a rule." She locks eyes with me.

I hesitate. I can almost feel the dual weights of Michael sitting on one shoulder and Derek Masters on the other.

I look at Emily's lips. The karma gods are chattering in my ear.

Picking up the raspberry I dropped, I make a show of dusting it off.

I'm going to help Michael's kid, make sure he's okay. That should get me some positive karma points for sure.

Enough to earn me a little time with Emily.

Very slowly, I hold the raspberry out to her between finger and thumb. She leans forward, as I feed it to her, her lips just barely brushing my fingers.

Then it's her turn to toss a raspberry. She misses it. Wordless, she picks it up and holds it out to me. Barely breathing, I circle her wrist with my fingers and eat the raspberry off the palm of her hand.

For a long time, we send raspberries into the air and miss them, resulting in numerous penalty feeds.

"Did you know your eyes are different colors?" she says. "One of your eyes is half blue and half green."

Actually, I did know that, although it never seemed worthy of comment before.

"And you have this little chip in your tooth," she continues.

"You make me sound defective, or something."

"Oh, you're not defective. You're handsome." Emily blushes

watermelon pink again.

That's when I kiss her. Her lips are so soft and sweet—it's like kissing marshmallows. I'm taking it all in: her smooth cheeks, her satiny hair, a scent that makes me want to put my face into her neck and keep it there for about a century.

Her arms wind around me, and she kisses me back. Hot emotion rushes through me. I am powerful, sexy, masculine. She is all woman, responding to my slightest touch.

Emily pulls away. "You're a good kisser, too."

My cue to do it again. And in spite of everything, just for a moment, I'm happy.

This, I think, is what chemistry will do for you. Because Emily and I have mad chemistry. When I'm with her, I am no longer Ryan Mills, a nice, but ordinary guy who will always live in his father's shadow. With Emily, I am the great lover, Don Juan de Marco. I am Superman. I am Sir Lancelot, Knight of the Round Table.

Chapter Twenty-Two

I've been working with Calvin and Jonathan in physics lab, and with each lab, I feel like more and more of a dummy. Arriving at class today, I round the corner suddenly and catch the tail end of Jonathan saying "... didn't have anyone else," and Calvin replying, "Well, he needs to start doing something!"

"Reporting for duty," I say in a loud voice, and they both shut up.

For today's lab, they have found just the right role for me. I am standing at the top of a small ramp. My job is to place a ball bearing at the top, then let go of it at the right time. The ball rolls down a track, while my partners take measurements and snap out comments about velocity and constant acceleration.

I stare out the window. If Michael were here, we'd have a lab table in the far back, and I—by default—would be in charge. "Wake me up when it's over," Michael might say, and I would say "You wish" and assign him some slacker job.

It's not that I can't study hard and get good grades. It's just that I've never seen the point of it before. And I always felt like a super star, anyway, compared to Michael.

But compared to Emily and Jonathan, it's a different story.

"Okay, that's it," Calvin says, standing up. "You want to get together this weekend? Start making our study guides for finals?"

I start to answer him, then realize he's looking at Jonathan. But I'm a member of this group, too. "What are you talking about?" I ask. "Finals don't start for three weeks."

"Yeah," Jonathan says. "That's why we gotta get on this." At the moment, he's not my buddy, the Surfer Dude. He's in his alter ego, the Straight-A Science Geek.

"Count me in," I say. We divide up the work of outlining all the class material, and I demand my third of it.

"You sure?" Calvin asks me, probably envisioning his high GPA swirling down a black hole, never to be seen again.

"You bet," I say, stubborn. "I'll have it ready for our next meeting."

I'll show them, I think, as I walk out of the classroom. I'm sick of being the group slacker.

My outline's going to kick ass.

I gulp a little. It had better.

• • •

When Chrissie still hasn't returned my phone call after a day's wait, I start to worry. I call the tennis club and ask for her. I pace back and forth next to my car in the school parking lot, my cell pressed to my ear. A Corvette peels out of the parking lot with a screech of tires, drowning out the person on the other end of the line.

"Would you repeat that?" I ask, plugging my phoneless ear with a finger.

"She no longer works here."

I stop pacing. "She was working there last week!" I hadn't realized she was going to leave so fast.

"Well, she's gone now."

My stomach somersaulting, I ask "Do you have a forwarding number?"

They give me the same cell phone number I already have.

Don't worry. I tell myself that she's just been busy and she'll call me back. I leave a second message for her.

Another day goes by, and she hasn't returned that call either. I start to get that tight-chested panicky feeling again, but tell myself not to jump to conclusions.

The club ought to know Chrissie's address. I roll on down there and straight into the Manager's Office.

Becky, the assistant to the Manager, is there. Like me, she's in tennis whites, but she's got more muscles and a bigger mustache than I ever will.

"I can't give out her home phone or address," she rasps. "That's confidential information."

"Please? I think Chrissie needs help."

"If she needed your help, she'd ask you for it!"

I leave, muttering to myself about rule freaks. Standing outside the club, I text Emily to complain.

She texts me back. *Maybe it's for the best.*

But I don't feel that way. Why would Chrissie want to keep me away from Michael's kid? A steel band clamps itself around my head whenever I think of it.

When I get home, I consider calling Nat and Yancy about the baby, but something stops me. Instead, I call Emily on my computer. On my screen, she looks up at me from where she sits on her bed, cross-legged, surrounded by books and note cards.

"What are you doing?" I ask.

"English paper." It's obvious I'm interrupting her, but she puts down her pen and says, "What's up?"

"Should I tell Nat and Yancy about the baby?"

She purses her lips as she considers my question, a little vertical crease appearing between her eyebrows. "I think they're entitled to know."

"But I don't really have any information! I don't even know where Chrissie is."

She glances at her books. "Well, you don't have to tell them. You asked for my opinion, and I gave it."

I think about it. "I guess you're right. I'll do it."

"She hasn't left town, has she?"

I've been worrying about that, but didn't want to say it. A wave of panic starts to roll over me, but I push it down.

"I don't think so," I say. I sure hope not, anyway.

Chapter Twenty-Three

After I finish talking to Emily, I pick up a book, read a page, then put it down. I turn on the tube, pace around my bedroom, then turn it off.

Since I said I'd tell Nat and Yancy about the baby, I might as well do it now. Maybe they'll know how to find Chrissie's home address. It's about six in the evening, and I decide to drop in without calling.

Their house is this contemporary thing that's all white surfaces and right angles, both inside and out. Nat and Yancy wanted all those white walls for their art collection. Outside is a gigantic metal sculpture in the shape of a mobile, with arms extending out and circles and triangles dangling off them. Michael used to call it The Octopus.

The last time I was here, it was the night of Emily's party, when I went looking for Michael. I remember how stupidly relieved I was to find no accident along his route home.

Of course, Nat and Yancy hadn't been around that night. Even more than my folks, they specialize in disappearing acts. Those two wouldn't even know what to do with a grandchild.

I think back to all the times they flew to Rome, or had an opening to go to, or something better to do than spend time with Michael. The worst memory of all, the one that caused the split between me and both sets of parents, is the terrible day of Michael's overdose.

He and I were thirteen when it happened. My parents and the Westons were in Cannes for the Film Festival, having left Michael at our house, with Rosario in charge. Michael had been upstairs, supposedly doing homework, for a couple of hours. I was helping Ro unload the dishwasher when Maddy's voice came through the intercom from her upstairs bedroom.

"Molly says Michael's in the driveway." They can see the driveway from the upstairs windows of their adjoining bedrooms.

"Well, have Molly call down to Michael to come inside. We're having dessert," I instructed the intercom.

"Molly says he can't come inside."

"I'll go find him," I said.

Michael was lying in the driveway in a pool of vomit. He was on his side, looking almost peaceful, his face and t-shirt drenched and sticky. One hand was flung out to the side, the fingers slightly curled.

He must have wandered down the stairs and out the front door, stoned out of his mind, then blacked out.

Sitting there in front of the Weston's house, three years later, I still remember how freaking terrified I was that day. Seeing Michael lying there, my insides heaved, and for a brief second I thought I would throw up, too.

Instead, I screamed to Rosario to call 911. I remember my mind grasping for the little bit of CPR I knew. Putting my hand to his nose, I felt nothing, no air coming out. Frantic, I yanked at Michael, turning him over to let the vomit run out of his mouth.

"Somebody get me some paper towels!" I yelled, but by the time Ro came running with the roll of paper, I had already cleaned out Michael's mouth with my t-shirt. I prayed nothing was lodged in his throat.

I felt slow and stupid. All I knew was, I had to get oxygen into him. Molly and Maddy, five years old, were wailing and clutching each other, ignored by me and Ro as we struggled to keep Michael alive.

"Ro, help me!" We turned him over on his back, and I tried mouth-to-mouth, almost gagging from the taste of vomit. "Is his chest moving?" He just lay there, still and pale. Maddy and Molly had stopped crying and were holding each other, saucer-eyed.

"Keep trying!" Ro was kneeling beside me. She wedged the paper towel roll under his neck, so his chest arched out. "Try again."

I blew into Michael's mouth, and this time I felt the air go somewhere, and his chest went up, and Ro cried, "Yes!" I kept doing it, one breath after another, while Ro said, "It's working."

My back ached, but I kept the breathing going, over and over, thinking simply *stay alive*. Rocks in the driveway poked into my knees and calves, hurting me. Where was the freaking ambulance? Finally, we heard the sirens.

I remember Rosario's face, with its look of horror, the blinking ambulance lights, and the sight of my parents' open medicine cabinet, bottles of non-prescription and prescription drugs scattered across the counter. Four bottles had been opened, so, the paramedics had to assume Michael had taken all four.

"You're his friend?" one of the paramedics asked me. When I nodded, he said, "Was this a suicide attempt?"

"No." I was sure about that. Michael loved life. "He was just trying to get high."

Rosario blamed herself. "I should have watched him," she said to me in the ambulance, her eyes full of fear.

"You can't follow a thirteen year old around like he's a baby," I told her. Until it happened, we couldn't have known how our medicine cabinet would seem to Michael—like a candy store, irresistible.

We had to take my sisters with us to the emergency room. There was no one to stay with them. The ER was swamped. As we arrived, ambulances pulled up with casualties from a four car pile-up on Interstate 10. Bloody bandages, patients on gurneys, bottles of dripping chemicals, bags and tubes filled with blood.

My little sisters were holding onto each other and whimpering. Ro knelt and said, "This place looks scary, but it is a good place. The doctors here make sick people better." She smoothed back Molly's hair and touched Maddy's cheek. "You are safe here with us. But if you do not want to see, put your faces in my skirt." So both girls clung to Rosario's skirt, faces hidden, the whole time we were there.

A car blasts its horn, bringing me back to my own car, parked in front of theWestons' house. I shake my head, get out, and run up the front walk. It's Charlie who answers the door. He's been Yancy's personal assistant for as long as I can remember.

"They're not here, Ryan," he says, giving me this look of

sympathy. "But I expect them back soon."

"Do you think ... I could wait in Michael's room? Just see it for a minute?"

He hesitates. "They asked me and Clarisse to clean it out." Clarisse is Nat's assistant. "You're free to go through boxes if you want. Take whatever you like."

I follow him down the Weston's long hallway, still thinking about Michael, lying on a gurney while a crew of hospital people worked over him. As Charlie and I arrive at Michael's bedroom door, he gives me this apologetic look and reminds me, "They wanted it cleaned out. I think it's their way of dealing with the loss." He opens the door and my jaw drops.

The room's been gutted. All of Michael's personal things are gone, probably packed into the boxes stacked against one wall. The bed is stripped, the shelves are empty.

"Like I say, take anything you want," Charlie says. He leaves me alone.

I sink down on the bare mattress. I look at the boxes, which are all labeled. Fury boils up inside me.

As rage mounts, my mind goes back to how I sat in the Emergency Room that night, trying to reach the Westons, calculating the time difference and leaving messages at every phone number I had for them. By the time they finally called back, we were home and Michael was out of danger. The Film Festival, the working part of their trip, was over. Michael lay in my bed, still weak, but able to talk to them.

"I'm fine," he told them, his voice raspy. "No worries." I saw a flicker of some expression on his face, then, "That's okay. We'll be fine. See you next week."

So the Westons had no plans to interrupt their trip. They would stay in France another week, on vacation, just as if their son hadn't almost died.

Michael went to hang up, but I lunged for the phone and grabbed it from him. "Yancy! Can I talk to Dad? Or Mom?"

"They're not here, Ryan. They're tied up with something. I'll have them get back to you," Yancy told me, her voice small and tinny.

"I need to talk to them as soon as possible," I said. "Promise you'll give them the message?" She promised, and we both hung up.

I could not believe they were staying in France another week. Michael was leaning back against the pillows. "Hey, Ryan," he said, yawning.

"Yeah?"

"The nurse at the hospital said you saved my life."

I raised my eyebrows at him. "Yeah, well, the next time I won't, so don't do it again." He and I smiled at each other.

"You're such a dick," he said in a fond tone, and turned over and went to sleep.

I come back to the present, where I sit in Michael's empty room. Charlie had said I could look through the boxes, but when I check them out, I see they're all taped up. They have split up Michael's memory into tiny pieces and packed it away.

I can't stay here anymore. I have nothing to say to Nat and Yancy.

"Thanks, Charlie," I yell out, as I head for the front door.

"Okay, bye." He appears in a doorway, looking surprised at my taking off like that.

I leap into my car and start the ignition. The funny thing was, Michael got something good out of that day: he went off of drugs completely and stayed clean for three years. Until Chase came along.

For me and my sisters, it was different. It turned out Yancy's promise wasn't worth much, because we didn't hear from my parents for a few days, and then they just left a long machine message while we were off at school.

In the meantime, we were flipping out. Neither I nor my sisters could fall asleep. That whole week, we used air mattresses that Ro had put down in the library in front of the-fireplace—the five of us laid out in a row: Michael, me, the girls, and Rosario. It was the only way that Molly and Maddy—sandwiched in the center, between me and Ro—felt safe. Jasper was still alive then, and he slept at our heads, lying crosswise, so that each of us could reach up and put a hand in his fur.

Ro and I had gone through every medicine cabinet and cupboard in the house, gathering up pill bottles in a shopping bag, and hiding the bag under Ro's bed. We watched Michael nonstop, terrified he would do it again.

I remember the Westons arriving from the airport with my parents, the four of them pumped up from their Dealmaking Victories and relaxed from their nice vacation.

"Where's my baby?" Yancy called out. I walked up to her, steaming mad.

"Your baby's asleep upstairs, after being rushed to the hospital and almost dying." My voice was shaking with fury. "Ro and I scraped up the vomit and got him to the hospital and saved his life. But don't let any of us disturb your rest and relaxation."

"*RYAN!*" My mother stared at me.

I stalked away.

"Apologize!"

"NO!" I shouted. And I never did. A wall grew that day between me and my parents. And, until Michael died, I never spoke directly to the Westons again.

Chapter Twenty-Four

Another day passes without hearing from Chrissie, and I'm going nuts. There has to be someone at the tennis club who will give me her address. I do a mental run-through of possible targets and come up with Marge, who works in the Admin office. I smile to myself. *She's perfect.*

She's the type who wallpapers her cubicle with postcards of celebrities and spends all her off hours standing in line for free tapings of TV reality shows. I usually avoid her because she bombards me with questions about my dad. My plan is to offer Marge something she wants in exchange for what I want.

My dad can get tickets to practically any event in town. I almost never ask for stuff like this, but today I will.

I stick my head into his office suite at our home to find Phyllis, his assistant, juggling three blinking phone lines. She shakes her head at me, but I say "Please? I only need a minute."

Dad, in the office behind her, catches sight of me through the open door. "It's okay, Phyllis," he calls, waving me in.

I sit down across from him, noticing the surprise on his face. It's been more than three years since I came to visit him in his office. It has taken this Chrissie problem to bring me back.

I used to spend hours here. When I was young, I read a lot of Dad's scripts and gave him my notes on them, and he'd teach me stuff like how a story should be structured and how to write dialogue.

Dad still uses paper more than he does electronic gadgets. His desk is piled high with scripts, mail, and messages. His list of Things to Do, covering two typed pages, is in front of him, lying on a large month-at-a-glance calendar that's black from all the inked in meetings, auditions, lunches, events, and other things he does with his life.

His eyes are red and tired, and the three lines are still blinking on his phone, all on hold, waiting for him. But there's a pleased smile on his face. "What's up?" he asks me, leaning back and putting his hands behind his head.

I'll have to tell Dad some version of the truth; the man can detect bullshit from a distance of a thousand yards.

"I want give two tickets to someone at the tennis club. It's kind of a thank you, cuz she's been nice to me."

His face goes expressionless when he realizes why I'm there. I know he's disappointed, but he'll do this favor for me. He should, after all the times he's waltzed out of the house with Mom, leaving us kids behind.

He leans forward, putting his elbows on the desk. "Jared Abernathy's new film comes out in two weeks." Dad has just signed Jared to star in his next project, *Mystery Moon*. "You want tickets to the premiere and the party afterwards?"

"That'd be great! Thanks." I stand up as the number of blinking lights increases to four.

He gives me a nod and picks up the phone as I leave.

The next day, I go to Marge and make her my offer. "All you have to do it get me some information, okay?"

Faced with the option to do her job right versus blowing it off to hang with Hollywood celebrities, Marge's choice is clear. An hour later, she calls me with Chrissie's home address and phone number. *Yes.*

I start to call Chrissie's number, but then reconsider. I don't want to scare her off. I decide to go pay her a visit instead. It's now late in the afternoon, and I've got a date with Emily tonight. I'll go up to Chrissie's first thing tomorrow morning.

• • •

I justify my date with Emily by the fact that I've been working to find Michael's baby. If Jonathan's right, the good deed will cancel out the bad one on the karma worksheet. She and I are going to the Santa Monica Pier, and I want to have fun.

Ever since that kiss with Emily in the park, I've been a goner. I can no more resist her now than I could stop breathing or swallowing. And she seems to feel the same way: we have become the Make-out Maniacs.

On the Pier, we ride to the top of the Ferris wheel and exchange fantastic, face-sucking kisses. She's a little freaked out, though, by being up so high. I distract her by telling jokes, then French kiss her through the last two cycles of the big wheel, until our little car finally shudders to a stop on the ground.

The ride over, I walk with her along the pier.

"I haven't seen you since noon yesterday," she says, putting her lower lip out in a cute way. For us, that's a long time.

"That's because you went home with your carpool," I say. "You should let me drive you home every day." She and I grab every chance we can get to be together.

"You're practically already doing it! My afternoon carpool has barely seen me in two weeks."

"Quit it. I'll take you home in the afternoons."

"What about on Wednesdays?" Emily stays late for Songbirds rehearsal that day, but her friend Chloe, who stays after for debate, takes her home.

"I can wait for you on Wednesdays. Tell your carpool and Chloe that you've got a new ride."

I put my arm around her as we lean against the railing and look down into the water. Her warm body presses up against mine.

Although I know it's wrong to be with Emily after what I did to Michael, I sometimes think he would have understood in his own way. As he would have put it, *Never pass up a chance for some booty.*

In my case, it's a little different. I'm not getting any actual booty from Emily, although I fantasize about that nonstop. But I *am* completely, gonzo, out-of-control in love.

"Ryan?"

I come back to earth. Emily's next to me, her hair flying and cheeks red from the wind. She has this amazing way of knowing exactly the right thing to do for me. She stands there, calm, saying nothing, waiting for me to come back to her. Mentally, I mean.

"Michael and I used to come to this beach all the time," I tell her. "We'd bring my dog Jasper and play Frisbee."

100

"How long did you have him?"

"For eight years, starting when I was six. He was the coolest dog."

I start to tell Emily a story. "You want to know the best thing Jasper ever did? He ate my homework once. It was awesome, to be able to say to a teacher 'The dog ate my homework'."

"He did? He really ate it?"

"Swear to God," I say. "It was in Mr. Randall's algebra class. He was such a dick. I had to tear the assignment up into tiny pieces and mix it with canned food. But Jasper ate it all. And I went to school, told Randall the dog had eaten my homework, and I got detention. But it was totally worth it."

"You *fed* your homework to the dog?" Emily's eyes are warm as she rests her chin on my chest and looks up at me. "What am I going to do with you, Ryan?"

"I don't know," I say. "What *are* you going to do with me?" We exchange a long, steamy look.

"I guess you'll just have to wait and see." Her voice strokes the words.

By now, we are facing each other, and Emily's leaning against my chest. Right here is one form of going to heaven, holding Emily in a full frontal body press. But I am having a male problem. I'm growing a boner, and it's probably my biggest ever. I mean, I could hit a home run with this boner or whack a hockey puck the entire length of an ice rink. I am making small, but relevant body adjustments, hoping Emily will not notice there are now three of us in our little huddle.

Leaning her body against mine, she says, "I can feel your heart." After recovering from the shock of what I *thought* she was going to say, I think to myself, *no wonder.* My heart's beating like a jungle drum. Damn. I've been trying to maintain my aura of coolness, yet now my heart has betrayed me, with its wild, passionate pounding for Emily.

She suddenly straightens up and moves away from me. There we go. She has finally become aware of my trusty appendage. Caught, I give Emily a guilty look.

"I'm a guy. I can't help it." Given the crowds around us and the bulge in my pants, I'm glad we've turned toward the railing again. I am a ship, with my mast facing out to sea.

"I'm sorry," she says. "I was being a tease, wasn't I? I'll stand two feet away from now on."

"No, be a tease! I'd rather get a little action than none."

Emily's giggling. "Ryan, do you ever, you know, screen your words before you speak?"

I think about it. "Not really. It's unfortunate." I pause. "And now, I've got to walk to the car like this."

"Walk behind me," she says, and that's what I do.

• • •

That night I dream I am riding on the Ferris wheel, but somehow it's really a roller coaster. I am jammed into a little car with Michael and Chrissie. Michael is trying to hold this baby and come on to Chrissie at the same time. But the baby keeps making weird noises. My whole family—Mom, Dad, and the girls—are in cars behind me, and I want to crawl back to them, but I'm too scared. So instead I move forward on the roller coaster, and it turns out my new seat partner's Mr. Randall, my eighth grade math teacher, who gave out detentions like they were sticks of gum.

Then, Mr. Randall grabs my arm, with this creepy expression he always got when doling out punishment, and says "Soldier Rock!"

I wake up with a tight feeling in my chest, gasping for air.

It's so unfair that Michael will never see the ocean again, will never kiss another girl.

"Soldier Rock," he had said in the stairwell that night. I'm the only person in the world who he would have said that to, who would have known what he meant.

I tell myself that wherever Michael is now, he can kiss as many girls as he wants. But I don't believe it. I know he's just rotting in the ground.

I lie in bed and stare at my shutters until finally the night is over and cracks of daylight are filling up the room.

Chapter Twenty-Five

Chrissie lives in a crummy walk-up apartment in this armpit of a neighborhood in the Valley. I pull up at ten o'clock the next morning in my impossible-to-miss red sports car and look out on the dead grass and peeling paint of her apartment building. So much for traveling under the radar. Chrissie's probably already spotted my car and is making her escape out a back window at this very moment.

The building's designed like a truck-stop motel, with each apartment door visible and facing the street. To get to the second and third floor apartments, you climb stairs and use exterior walkways that run along the face of the building. I reach Apartment 206 and see that the door has a peephole, which I try to look through. But it's made only for looking out, not in. I ring the bell and wait.

No answer. I ring the bell again, leaning on it a little, while the hairs rise up on the back of my neck. I have the strangest feeling I'm being watched. But there's total silence on the other side of the door.

"May I help you?" Two guys holding full grocery bags have just walked up. They're older, like maybe in their early twenties. Their eyes are raking me over from head to foot.

"Do you live in this building?" I ask.

"Yeah. What do you need?" The guy talking has a goatee and small wire-rimmed glasses. His friend's wearing a pink button-down shirt.

"I'm looking for a girl named Chrissie. I know her from the Palisades Tennis Club."

The goatee guy is still looking me over. "She moved out of the building."

I freak. "Moved out! When?"

"Just recently." He shifts the grocery bag in the crook of his arm.

"That's right," the second guy says. "She moved out really recently!"

"Do you have a forwarding address for her?" I move my shoulders around as nervous tension floods my body.

"No. She left in a hurry."

Why? What is she so afraid of? "What about a phone number?"

"Sorry." With an annoyed expression, the goatee guy glances down at the bags in his arms, full of cans and wine bottles.

Flipping out, I find a piece of paper and scribble my name and phone number on it. "If she calls you, or if you get any information, would you let me know? It's really important."

"No problem."

I follow the walkway to the stairs, go down to the ground floor, then look up over my shoulder, to see them continuing along the second floor walkway with their grocery bags. I hop into my car and sit there, wanting to smack my head against the steering wheel.

I can't believe this. That one conversation with me drove her into hiding? My car peels out of its parking space with a squeal of tires. The whole way home, my mind turns this way and that, but keeps hitting dead ends. I don't know anyone else who knows her. She's from the South, but where? She never said.

Then I have an idea. She's an actress. Maybe she's a member of SAG or AFTRA, one of the acting unions. She would probably send them any new address or phone number she had.

Hah! I'm on it. I'll track her down. I'll make sure of it.

As I walk down the hall at school with Jonathan, we run into Derek Masters. He is striding along with a couple of other guys from the basketball team. They're shouting and high fiving each other, putting on a masculine display for all of the females lucky enough to be in the area.

When he sees us, Derek stops. "Takahara! I've gotta get with you about that history project."

"I know—I'll call you," Jonathan says.

We walk on. "You have history with him?" I ask, getting a sinking feeling. That would be Hellman's European History. The one Emily's in.

"Yeah, he's in all those classes."

"You mean the AP classes?" I ask, although I know that's exactly what he means. English, math and history. "He's in there with you and Emily?"

Jonathan nods.

I can't stop myself from asking, "Does he talk to Emily a lot?"

He nods again. "Affirmative."

"Do you think he's after her?"

Jonathan hesitates. "Affirmative."

I knew it. I knew Derek was on the prowl for Emily. But I didn't know that he was a star student sharing numerous AP classes with the Girl I Love.

"But you and Emily are just friends, right?" Jonathan looks at me sideways.

"Well, I guess we're more than just friends now." I stare at the floor tiles, noticing a couple of cracks beginning. Things are going great with Emily, but how great? Does she love me?

We arrive at the door to my Spanish class.

"Very interesting." Jonathan puts his hand on the doorframe, leaning on it. He gives me a knowing look.

"You can take Masters down."

"You think?"

He points at me. "But not if you wimp around. You have to go for it." Having delivered his opinion, he leaves.

I wonder what Jonathan would know about winning over women. All he ever does is surf and blow things up in home chemistry experiments. Still, he has a point.

I go into Spanish and sit there thinking about Emily, about how beautiful and smart and amazing she is. More than anything, I want to tell her that I love her. I want to tell her that I love her eyes and her smile and her gorgeous ass, and I love the way she makes me feel, that there's hope for me, that I will make my mistakes up to Michael, and that maybe, despite all my screw-ups, I'm still entitled to have some kind of a life. I love Emily absolutely and without end. I want to tell her all of that.

But I need to know she'll love me back. To win out in the long run against a guy like Masters, I have to be smart, successful, accomplished. I have to make a plan. I pull out a piece of paper and start to write.

"Mr. Mills?"

My head jerks up.

My ancient Spanish teacher Mrs. Witherspoon points to a sentence written on the whiteboard. Her eyes are like little pieces of hard, black flint. They gleam at me.

Ellos _____ que yo soy adicto al chocolate.

"Which verb correctly fills in the blank: *saben* or *conocen*?"

Easy. *"Conocen."*

The eyes brighten as she realizes she's found a victim. "Mr. Mills, did you do last night's assignment?"

I squirm and glance at my watch. "Most of it." I think.

"Class! Why is Mr. Mills' answer incorrect ?"

Hands shoot up, while I slump down in my seat and wait for the bell to ring.

• • •

That night in my room, I throw darts and brood about Derek. I've hung the dartboard so I can hit it from anywhere in the bedroom. I lie on my bed and aim for the bullseye.

I must outmaneuver Derek with my suaveness and expertise. I need a plan to make Emily fall in love with me.

I sink one dart right in the center then, overconfident, send the next one into the wall. It glances off and falls to the floor.

In Phase One of the plan, I decide, I have to impress her. I have to show Emily—and myself—that I deserve her. This means I have to kick ass in my semester finals, which are only a week away, just before the winter holiday break.

As another dart hits the target, I decide to start right away. I locate all my textbooks without too much trouble, but reading them is another matter. My history book is like a force field of gray text, impossible to penetrate. I sit at my desk and stare at it blindly, trying to concentrate, but I find myself worrying instead about where

Chrissie's gone. Throwing down my book, I google her and try to find a website for her, but there's nothing.

I go back to reading, but I can't get worked up about the Louisiana Purchase. Ace the class—what was I thinking? Between Michael's death and meeting Emily, I've done even less work this semester than usual. Right now I'm headed for a C.

I look at my watch. It's 8 o'clock, too soon to go to bed. As I stare at the history book, I notice bits of bold print floating around in the sea of gray.

Cool. The bold print's the most important stuff, the material I need to know. I spend the rest of the evening jotting down all the bold sections on color coded flash cards. I'll learn the flash cards cold and pray that's enough.

The next day I move from studying history to Spanish, but I can't concentrate. I find myself calling SAG and AFTRA, only to learn that Chrissie's not a member of either. I eventually learn my vocabulary by making lists and getting Ro and my sisters to quiz me.

I meet with Calvin and Jonathan. Using my bold print approach, I've produced my section of the study guide for physics. Calvin looks it over and says "You got the main ideas, but none of the fine points."

"I'll do it over," I try to say, but they shake their heads. Ashamed, I swear to myself I'll do better in the spring.

Why doesn't Chrissie call me back? Two days before exams, when I should be jamming on my books, I drive up to her apartment building again and try to talk to the manager. He's not there, so I leave him a message, which he doesn't answer.

Taking my finals, I think I did okay, but I'm not sure I got the A's I wanted. I'll have to wait for my grades.

As I leave school for the holidays, my mind runs over what I have to do next. Chrissie's building manager must have a forwarding address for her. I'll go up there tomorrow morning and look for him. But this afternoon, it's time for Phase Two of my plan to win Emily.

I drive to the bank and plunder my savings account. It holds money I've been given over the years, for birthdays and graduations, which I've never spent. Pockets stuffed with hundred dollar bills, I take a deep breath and drive into Beverly Hills.

I am a man, fighting for what I want. Derek Masters may have good grades, but I bet he doesn't know how to show a woman she's special. It's time for me to sweep Emily off her feet.

Chapter Twenty-Six

Tiffany's is on this fancy pedestrian-only shopping street they've constructed off of Rodeo Drive. The first thing I notice as I walk into the store is the walls are red. This throws me, as I don't remember red walls from the one time I came here with Dad. It must be a holiday thing. They have pine branches and gold and silver Christmas decorations all around – as if Tiffany's doesn't have enough gold and silver in it already.

I walk in with my jeans and high-top sneakers, wondering if I should have dressed up a little.

A human mountain in a guard uniform moves toward me. "May I assist you?"

I'm thinking he may soon assist me out into the street, where he decides I belong.

"I need a present for a girl – a piece of jewelry."

He takes me over to a round-faced lady with scary fingernails. Her name is Stephanie.

"What's the occasion?" she asks.

I'm already jumpy and irritated, a sure sign that I've entered a Place of Shopping.

"It's for…. well, she's kind of my girlfriend. Starting to be, anyway. So, I want to… give her something." Ten minutes, I think, ought to be enough to find something nice.

Stephanie eyes my old t-shirt and my backpack, where Emily has made these cool doodles with Sharpie markers. "How much were you thinking to spend?"

I have no idea. I plunge my hand into my right jeans pocket and unearth a roll of C-notes, which I drop on the counter.

"Oh!" She counts them. "I think we can help you!"

"Wait—I'm not done." I produce another wad of bills from my left jeans pocket.

Giving me a warm smile, she counts those, too. "I can show you a number of things in your price range." One at a time, she pulls things from cases, laying them out on a black display tray. "For a sixteen year old girl," she says, "I think either a short necklace or a bracelet."

All I know is that I want something simple and classy. Stephanie has just gotten started showing me all my choices when I see it—a plain, but interesting-looking chain with a heart.

"Is this silver?" I ask.

"White gold. And the stone in the center of the heart's an aquamarine." The stone is this perfect blue, kind of an Emily blue. The heart's very simple, but it looks elegant to me.

"This looks like Emily," I say. "I'll take it."

"That's it? So fast?" She almost sounds disappointed.

"That's it." I wonder to myself if I'm nuts to do this, to spend this kind of money on a girl I've only known a few months. *Don't wimp around. Just go for it.*

After handing over my fat roll of cash, I wait for whatever piddling change Stephanie can throw my way. She packs the necklace up for me in an aqua box and slips it into an aqua bag.

"One suggestion," she says. "Give her a card along with the necklace, and write something romantic on it. Win her with words."

"I will. Thanks a lot." And Ryan-as-Sir Lancelot rides off into battle.

Following instructions, I buy a heavy plain white card. In my neatest block printing, I write:

> *Dear Emily,*
> *I studied hard for exams this time. I think I did well. I*
> *think you are a good influence on me.*
> *I love you. A lot.*
> *Ryan*

I read the message over. I sound like a moron. But I only have one card; I didn't think to buy a back-up. I seal it into its envelope and drop the card into the aqua bag.

Now, I just need to set up the perfect moment to give it to her.

• • •

Arriving home from Tiffany's, I garage my car and head for the house, thinking about what I'm going to do at Chrissie's building tomorrow. If I can't run down the manager, maybe I can find those two guys again and ask some more questions.

Our gardener Alberto is trimming a hedge. He has brought Hector and even put him to work watering pots. Hector stands with his short legs apart, holding a hose with both hands, his mouth all scrunched up like he's really concentrating. He checks a pot and asks, "Enough water, Papa?" He's barely tall enough to look over the edge of those huge pots and has to stand on his toes to see.

My brain flashes back to when I would hang around my dad's movie sets, watching him work. I always asked a million questions, and dad would take the time to answer them. "Hey, Hector. So you helping your dad? Way to go, man."

He's focused on getting the stream of water into the pot just right. "Thanks, dude," he manages to say.

For the millionth time, I think about Michael's kid. *I want to know him.* But to do that, I have to find him.

Losing him would feel like losing Michael all over again.

• • •

The next morning, I pull up in front of Chrissie's building and sit for a minute, studying it. It's easy to pick out her door, Apartment 206, on the second floor, six over from the left.

Walking up to the staircase, I notice the mailboxes for the first time. The name on mailbox 206 is Fellars. Funny that whoever moved in after her didn't change the mailbox name. Maybe the place is still empty.

Nobody answers my knock at Apartment 206. Same thing at Apartment 101, where the manager lives. I decide to stake out the building, private detective style, and go back to wait in my car.

Anyone going in or out can see me parked there in my bright red Beemer, but I'm just hoping I'll see them first. I've brought some tennis magazines, but the articles are too basic to be interesting. Also, it's hard to read when I'm looking up every five seconds.

An hour goes by. I shift around in the car seat and get out a couple of times to stretch my legs. Every once in a while a door opens to let someone out, but it's never anyone I know. That's when I realize I'm not even sure who I'm looking for. Chrissie's gone. I don't know what the manager looks like.

I can look for those two guys and talk to them again. Another half hour passes. The sun is straight overhead, baking me, and I have a dentist appointment.

I'm just about to leave, but when a van pulls up and a guy gets out. He's short, carries a toolbox, and has a big circle of keys attached to his belt. Seeing him walk toward Apartment 101, I head him off.

"Excuse me. I'm looking for a forwarding address for Chrissie Fellars. It's very important."

He throws me a suspicious look. "Why you want Chreesie?" he demands.

"I need to reach her. I need to know where she went."

He pulls his head back, looking even more suspicious. "Where she went? She don' go nowhere."

"What do you mean? I thought she moved out."

"Nah, she no move out. You haf bad information!" He stomps off.

Thank God. I find myself with this huge, stupid grin on my face. *She and the baby are still here.* Until now, as relief floods me, I hadn't realized how worried I really was.

Those two guys lied to me. I wonder why. What is Chrissie so scared of?

She's obviously not going to answer the door for me. I'll have to catch her coming or going. I'll come back, and I'll stake this place out until I find her.

Chapter Twenty-Seven

I get one A on my fall report card.

One. And a bunch of crummy B's.

It's just because you started studying so late, I tell myself. This semester I'll stay caught up and learn the stuff as I go along.

I look down at the assignment sheet from my physics teacher, Mr. Simpson. It says: Your project will analyze the motion of an object with regard to displacement, velocity, work, force, power, and energy. Example of object: a billiard ball. I must approve your choice of object before you start.

Jonathan, Calvin, and I are going to research possible topics and present ideas to Mr. Simpson next week. I'm determined to walk into that meeting with a good idea.

I don't know anything about physics, but I do know how to find things on the internet. I sit down at my computer. After checking for emails from Emily, I type into the search box: *eleventh grade physics project: movement of objects.*

Sweet. A whole list of project ideas pops up. Something catches my eye: golf clubs. When they're not talking about physics, Calvin and Jonathan are talking about golf. Apparently, Calvin's a fantastic player, and Jonathan's just starting to learn. I've only played golf a couple of times, but these two are obsessed.

I read up on it for a while, then write an email.

Hi, you guys—

What about golf clubs? We could film both of your golf swings and do a frame-by-frame analysis. I have all the camera equipment and editing skills to do this. It would make a very cool video presentation.

I hit "Send," hoping I haven't missed anything really obvious. I don't want to make an idiot out of myself.

• • •

I park in front of Chrissie's building, prepared to camp out for a few hours if I have to. But I get lucky. After about half an hour, someone comes through a door with a plastic laundry basket full of clothes.

It's Mr. Pink Shirt. I sneak up the stairs, follow him down the walkway, and come up behind him as he opens the door to his apartment.

"Excuse me."

He jumps a foot in the air.

"I'm sorry," I say. "I just want to talk to you."

He tries to shut me out, but I step into the doorway.

"You said Chrissie moved out!" I cross my arms across my chest and glare at him.

This guy isn't as smooth as his friend, who did all the talking last time. He is fanning himself with one hand and taking deep breaths. He has almost white blond hair and a bunch of rings on his fingers.

"I'll call the police!" he yelps. From inside the guy's apartment, I hear music—a bunch of woodwinds piping a New Age tune— and smell candles scented with orange and cinnamon.

I try to calm him down. "I just want to help Chrissie. Her baby's father was my best friend."

"You mean the guy who died?"

"Yeah. He and I grew up together."

He looks me over. "You better not be making this up!"

I raise my hand. "Scout's honor."

"Hold on." He disappears. The sound of whispered arguing drifts my way, then he reappears. "Jay'll be here in a second. I'm Spencer."

Jay comes out holding a baseball bat, looking as threatening as he can manage to be in a bathrobe and flip flops, his hair wet from the shower.

I put up both hands in a surrender position. "I come in peace."

We all sit down, Jay continuing to hold the baseball bat, while I explain everything. I end by saying, "Michael was like my brother. I can't let his kid just disappear."

They look at each other. "It's so sad," Spencer says.

"Lemme get dressed," Jay says.

A few minutes later, we walk over to 206. Spencer knocks. "Chrissie, honey?"

Chrissie opens the door, and I can tell from her face that she knows about me. Jay must have called her when he was changing.

"You got me," she says flatly.

I'm so relieved to have found her that I almost can't be mad. Her belly's gotten bigger, and I'm glad to see she looks healthy. Her blond curls are piled up on top of her head, and her lips and cheeks have something pink on them.

Sweet. Michael's kid is here and doing fine.

I ease my way in. Chrissie's place is the opposite of her dingy and depressing building. Sun pours in onto plants that sit on the windowsill. The crayon-yellow walls are covered with family photos and old posters from "I Love Lucy," and a large bed in a corner has a green and blue patchwork quilt on it. Other than a tiny table by the kitchen, with two chairs, the only place to sit is on big floor pillows.

"I like your place," I say, partly to warm her up a little and partly because I mean it.

"Thanks." She nods to Jay and Spencer. "We're okay."

"You sure?" Jay looks like he wants to hang around, but Spencer pulls him off.

We sit on the two small chairs at the table, and I say, "Why'd you try to lose me, Chrissie? What did you think was going to happen?"

She suddenly blinks back tears. "Have you told Michael's parents?"

I wasn't expecting that one. "No."

"Well, please don't!"

"Chrissie, they're the grandparents."

"Just don't." Chrissie turns red as she says this, looking at me defiantly.

"You have to eventually. It's not fair to them."

"I don't have to do anything! And don't you *dare* tell 'em

yourself." Chrissie frowns at me. "Don't even think of doin' that!"

"Chrissie, they could help you," I say cautiously. "It's *hard* to have a baby."

"Not as hard as your life's gonna be if you tell 'em!" All of a sudden, she's like a skyrocket with a lit fuse, ready to blow at any minute. "You came here lookin' for me. You wanna see me again, then promise me you won't tell!"

When I hesitate, she says it again. "Promise me, or I'll *really* disappear!" Her cheeks flush bright pink.

If she wants to play stubborn, I can match her. I sit back, arms crossed. "I'll promise, but you have to tell me why. And it better be good!"

"All right." Chrissie picks up a paper napkin on the table and begins to tear it in little pieces. "I'm afraid they'll take my baby away from me!"

She has caught me by surprise. "What are you talking about?"

Her lips tremble. "People like them can do anythin' they want to people like me."

"You don't know anything about them!"

"Yes, I do! I checked 'em out." Her eyes widen. "You can't tell 'em, Ryan!"

"What are you scared of?"

Her voice gets thin and high-pitched. "Fancy rich people like that, with their lawyers, they'll tell a judge I'm nothin' but white trailer trash. They'll say I knew he was only sixteen. *Which I didn't!* They'll say I'm ignorant, that I'm a bad mother. And the judge'll believe 'em."

Noticing my surprised look, she snaps, "I seen it happen." Chrissie is shivering as if the room's cold. "Back in South Carolina, my momma works for this family, the Mayfairs? Well, the son, Beau—he got a girl pregnant—a white trash girl from the South Side. I knew her a little. Judge Mayfair had the orders signed before that baby was even born."

She gets up, takes a throw blanket off the bed, and wraps it around her shoulders.

"They took the baby out of her arms in the hospital, and it was all legal! There was nothin' she could do. They said she was a druggie and an unfit mother. She came by the house to see her child, and the Judge got a restrainin' order against her."

No wonder she was afraid of me coming around.

I sit there for a moment, thinking. Finally, I say, "Chrissie, you're not trailer trash," although the truth is, I don't know her at all. But I do know Nat and Yancy. I think again of them living it up in France while Michael recovered from his overdose.

"I won't tell them," I say, "but you have to promise to stay in touch with me."

"I will." Now that I've said I won't tell, it's like she feels she can relax a little, taking a deep breath, sitting down, and stretching her legs out in front of her.

"How are you doing? Do you need money?"

Her chin goes up. "I'm good. I have a cashiering job. SaveWell Pharmacy."

"Cashiering," I say. "Why d'you choose that?"

"Well," she drawls, "I 's offered the lead in a film, but I said, no, my dream is to cashier at the SaveWell."

Okay, so it was a dumb question. "Do you have any money saved up?"

"A hundred forty-nine bucks. I'll be fine. I always am."

Jeez. Chrissie's in deep trouble, and she doesn't even know it.

"Do you need any help?"

She nods her head. "My car blew out on me, and the mechanic says it's not worth payin' to fix. So I'm stuck takin' the bus everywhere."

As she talks, I realize how tired she looks. She has black stuff smeared around her eyes, like she didn't have the energy to wash her face.

"It's okay," she goes on, "'cept for my doctor's appointments. It's really hard for me to get to the medical clinic. It's 'bout twenty minutes from here by car, but an hour by bus, with two changes. And I have to walk six blocks from the bus stop to the clinic."

"When do you have to go?"

"Once a month. The next appointment's a Wednesday at four."

"Wednesdays are bad for me…" I start to say. Actually, the truth is, I'm booked every day after school, since I've started driving Emily home in the afternoons. On Wednesdays, I stay late to get her after Songbirds rehearsal.

Chrissie droops. "Alright then," she says. "Just thought I'd ask.

Jay and Spencer would help me, but they have a conflict that day, too."

I think fast. Chrissie needs the help. Emily will understand. She can catch a ride with her friend Chloe that day, the way she did before I came along.

"I'll do it," I tell her.

"Really? Thanks!" She sounds so grateful that I'm glad I said yes. Her next appointment is in twelve days. But there's something I have to tell her first.

I say it very smoothly and casually. "Just so you know, I have a girlfriend."

Chrissie bursts into laughter. In fact, she laughs so much that I'm a little put off.

"Lordy!" she says, wiping her eyes. "Who is it? That one little girl I met who was just a teensy bit jealous?"

"Well, yeah," I say, maintaining my dignity.

"Honey, tell her don't worry. I don't pick apples off other girls' trees. Besides, you're too young for me."

Michael wasn't.

She reads my mind. "Don't even start with me. He said he was eighteen."

"Okay, then, I'll see you next Wednesday."

As I leave, in spite of my new problems and worries, I feel like a giant load's been lifted off my shoulders.

Chapter Twenty-Eight

"I can't believe you did this, Ryan."

Emily and I are having dinner at Afterworld. It's one of those pretentious restaurants on Melrose Avenue that I usually avoid, except that I tolerate this place because the food's great. They know my dad and were willing to reserve me a nice private table by the window. Just what I wanted for tonight.

Emily looks at the necklace in the aqua Tiffany's box. My card lies on the tablecloth next to it. She's put her hair up on one side with something sparkly, and her lips are a shiny red. She's the hottest girl in the whole place, and she's with *me*.

I've already decided that this is not the time to tell her that I've located Chrissie, and that she's going to have to find another ride home next Wednesday. Luckily, I know she's got Chloe as a back-up.

A waiter comes with our desserts and takes several lifetimes to scrape the crumbs off the tablecloth and refill the water glasses before he finally goes away. I pleat my napkin over and over, waiting for him to leave.

"*Nice*, girlfriend!" he says to Emily, nodding at the Tiffany's box before he sweeps off.

"Do you like it?"

She reaches out and touches it. "I *love* it. It's incredible." Her forehead creases. "It's just that—Ryan, it must have been so expensive!"

"That doesn't matter. It's for you."

"Did you mean what you wrote in the card?"

"What, that you're a good influence on me?" I'm stalling for time. What if she doesn't love me back?

"No, you said you loved me. Did you mean that?"

"Yeah. I meant it. That's what the necklace is for. To tell you that." I take a sip of water, set the glass down, then pick it up and take another sip.

She puts it on, latching it and letting it fall on her neck. It sparkles like the thing in her hair and lights up her skin and eyes.

"Wow." I stare at her. "You look amazing."

I'm trying to read her expression, waiting for the response I want. As usually happens in places that are full of themselves, they've cranked down the lights so low that we're basically functioning on candles. She reaches across the table and takes my hand.

"Ryan, this is the sweetest thing anyone's ever done for me."

I wait.

"I love you, too."

"You're not just saying it because I bought you a necklace?"

"No. I love you, Ryan. I really do."

She loves me. This beautiful, incredible girl loves me.

I'm a stud. I have total game.

Hah! In your face, Derek Masters!

We hold hands across the table, while I fight off guilt, reminding myself: you're allowed to have a life.

"I have something exciting to tell you," she says. "Remember the summer program in England? The one I was interested in?"

I nod.

"Well, I can go after all!" She waits for my reaction, looking at me closely.

My brain slowly creaks into gear. Emily's going away this summer? "How come?"

"Aunt Liddy offered again to pay, and this time my mom twisted Dad's arm until he said yes."

That must have gone over well with The Man of the Family. From what I know about him, it must have felt like losing his left nut.

"So you want to go?" I ask, knowing the answer.

"Yes, but Ryan, they have space in the program." Emily traces a finger along my wrist as she waits for me to speak. "If you're interested."

"Are you inviting me to go with you?"

"I guess I am."

I put a credit card on the bill and lay it on the edge of the table for the waiter. "What kind of program is it?"

"You study English history and travel around, visiting all these historical sites."

Visiting castles and reading about wars and royal proclamations—I don't think so. On the other hand, a summer traveling around with Emily in England could be major. And those summer programs are usually pretty chill. I'll bet I could slide by without learning any actual history.

Michael's baby would be born by then, so I'd be all done with my job of taking Chrissie to the doctor. It wouldn't be uncool or anything if I left town.

"Where would we stay?"

"In student housing." She meets my gaze head on.

Meaning frequent access to Emily with no parents around.

"Sounds like a really interesting program," I say.

She clasps her hands together. "I hope you can go!"

"I'll talk to my folks." I know my parents would let me, once they got over their shock that I, their son, would be willing to give up a summer of beach and boogey boarding to study history in England.

I squeeze her hand. "They should be okay with it."

"Really? You'll go?"

When I nod, she says, "Ryan, it'll be so great!"

I can hardly believe my luck. Emily loves me, and I'm going to England with her. But a thrill of fear runs through me. I wonder how many good deeds I'll have to do to repay the karma gods for a summer of love and lust in England with Emily. I'm not sure there are that many good deeds in the entire world.

• • •

Jonathan and Calvin reject my golf club idea. We are standing outside Mr. Simpson's office, waiting to see him.

"Naw, man, we have a really cool object in mind to study," Calvin tells me. "A car!"

A car? The example Mr. Simpson had given us was a billiard

ball. Now that I think about it, Simpson kind of *looks* like a billiard ball. His head does anyway. Round and smooth and shiny.

"I thought he wanted us to pick something simple."

"Yeah, but a car's way cooler. We can get into some really advanced concepts with it," Calvin says.

So I follow them into Simpson's office, feeling like the dummy they already know me to be, and Simpson blows their idea out of the water.

"A car's way too complex for this project. I wanted you to select a simple object and evaluate its movement from a number of standpoints." He looks back and forth between the three of us. "So what's your back-up proposal?"

Jonathan and Calvin look blank.

"I had expected you to be prepared for this meeting." Simpson taps his pencil on the desk.

I jump into the void. "We were also thinking about golf clubs. You know, using physics concepts to evaluate our golf swings."

"Excellent suggestion!" Mr. Simpson booms. "For example, you can evaluate how your body positioning and the type of club you're using affect the distance that you hit the ball. In that alone, there's a wealth of physics concepts for you to consider!"

"Yes," I say, as if I know what he's talking about. "Calvin and Jonathan are the golfers, and I have the film-making equipment and expertise." I figure all those thousands of hours spent hanging around Dad's movie sets when I was younger should help me out now.

"Way to save our ass, Ryan!" Jonathan says afterward. "Now what do we do?" The two of them look at me for direction.

In a matter of minutes, I've gone from group outcast to group leader. I flail for a few seconds, then finally say "Why don't I put together some script ideas, and then we'll meet on the golf course?"

I better not blow it now, I think. This project is thirty percent of our grade.

Chapter Twenty-Nine

I'm holding a bouquet of flowers and standing on the Wintraubs' front doorstep. Having decided it's time to check me out, Emily's parents have asked me to dinner. They're way ahead of my parents, who have barely even figured out I'm seeing someone.

I've arrived right on time. Although I just showered, my shirt's already pitted out from the prospect of meeting Mr. Wintraub. I'm glad I wore a jacket.

The Wintraubs have a Spanish-style house in a neighborhood where you can see the houses from the street, and the kids ride their bikes and walk to school. I like it better than my neighborhood in Bel-Air, where there are no sidewalks and all you see as you wind along are privacy hedges and security gates.

As the front door opens, I hear a raspy bark and the scrabbling of toenails on hardwood. Toby bursts past Emily and her mother and launches himself in my direction.

"Hi, Mrs. Wintraub. I'm Ryan." I hand her the flowers as Toby throws himself against me. He must weigh a hundred pounds, but I withstand the blow. "Hey, there!" I say to him, scratching his ears.

"Why, thank you. These are lovely!"

I had expected Emily's mother to be a hot Momma, kind of a cougar type. Instead, she's this plain woman with a wide, pale face. When she smiles, though, her eyes shine and she's almost pretty.

"Please call me Eleanor. I'm so glad to meet you, Ryan." She and Emily take me to sit in the living room. Eleanor gets me a Coke, saying "My, Toby really likes you!"

Way to go, Ryan. My plan tonight is to win over every member of the family, and I think I've already gotten Eleanor in my corner.

Emily's mom is a schoolteacher, and Mr. Wintraub is an accountant. Emily has told me her dad's goal in life is to put his three kids through private school. "He's doing it," she had said, "but there's never any money left over for anything else."

As Mr. Wintraub walks in, I leap to my feet, displaying my perfect manners.

"Dad," Emily says, "This is Ryan."

He looks me over. "Hello, Ryan." With his super short salt-and-pepper hair, steely gray eyes and ramrod posture, it's all too easy to picture him in commando gear with an assault rifle, using me for target practice.

"It's very nice to meet you, sir." I put out my hand to shake his. "Thank you for having me."

After letting me stand there for a second with my hand out, he shakes it as if he knew I had head lice or maybe a social disease.

"That your car out there?" He nods toward it, looking out the living room window. My sports car is parked in between a VW Beetle and a van with a sagging bumper.

"Yes sir." I even got it washed before I came. The perfect red paint and silver chrome glitter obscenely at us from the Wintraubs' curb.

"*My* first car was a rusted-out ten-year old Chevy Impala. Worked for two years to save the money for it."

I stare at a corner of the living room ceiling. "Yes, sir."

We go into the dining room, where the table is set with a cloth, flowers, and candlesticks. The Wintraubs sit down to dinner like this every night. In addition to Emily and her parents, the younger kids are at the table—twelve-year old Julia, and my telephone friend, Ethan. He's ten.

Julia has her dad's steel gray eyes and, Ethan, his mom's smile. Emily, I can't place in this family. She must be a throw-back to some long lost ancestor.

I turn to Julia, who Emily has told me goes to the same school as my sisters.

"You go to Elsie Williams, don't you?" I say. "My sisters go there. They're in second grade – Molly and Madison Mills."

"Molly's my second grade buddy!" At Elsie Williams, each little kid gets paired with an older student for the school year. The pairs get together for reading and other projects.

"You're *that* Julia?" I ask. "Molly loves you. You're practically the only good thing that's happened to her this year, since she ended up getting…" Julia and I say it in unison. "Miss Cruella!" Julia clutches her throat, making gagging noises.

"I had Miss Cruella in second grade, too," she says. "She sucks!" Two down, I say to myself. Eleanor—and now Julia—are in the bag.

Ethan begins to grouse about his soccer coach. "He only plays me if we're totally winning or totally losing."

I find myself looking at Emily. She's facing her brother, giving me a view of her profile.

"And he plays Jackson Schwartz twice as much as me, even though I'm better than him."

She's so beautiful. I admire her forehead, the way her hair falls, the dimple in her cheek when she smiles. She wears this red sweater that sets off those perfect round …

"Ryan?" I jump and crush my knee against a table leg. It's Mr. Wintraub. He has gone from cold to glacial, having caught my lust-filled inspection of his daughter. His expression is about ten percent *I've-been-there* and ninety percent *don't-even-think-it*.

"Yes?" I croak. I attempt to shove my acute knee pain down into my subconscious brain, so that I can pretend to myself I don't feel it.

"I understand your father's in the film industry?"

I've avoided bringing this up with Emily, but it looks like they all know anyway. I don't know why he's being so cutesy about it. Saying to me *I understand your dad's in film* is like saying to the President's kid *I understand your dad's in politics.*

"Yes, sir," I say. When no one says anything, I add, "He directs films, mainly, now, but he used to write all his own screenplays, too."

"I just read an article about your father in *The American*," Eleanor says. *The American*, a national magazine, did a cover article on my dad, something about his influence on American cinema. Dad's assistant Phyllis has it framed and hanging in Dad's office with all the other magazine covers he's been on.

"Are you planning on following in his footsteps?" Mr. Wintraub has a mean glint in his eye.

"I haven't made any decisions yet." *I will never be anything more than a gnat, a nothing, compared to my dad.* I got used to the idea a long time ago.

"So, no goals or plans for the future?"

"I'm still working on that."

Mr. Wintraub nods, as if to say, *it figures.*

Emily's passing around plates of warm peach cobbler with ice cream. She leaps into the conversation, speaking directly to her dad. "Ryan's an amazing tennis player. You should see him."

"Ethan's getting interested in tennis," Eleanor says.

I see my chance. "Ethan, if you want, I'll take you to my club some time. Knock a few balls around?"

His face lights up. "All right!" Third one in the bag, I think.

Emily hands me the cobbler pan, and for a moment we make sizzling eye contact in front of her entire family. I spoon out a second helping, thinking to myself, God I love this girl.

As I raise a forkful of cobbler to my mouth, I happen to catch Mr. Wintraub's eye. I give him a weak smile as I read his expression. *You'd better look out, boy, because I'm watching you.*

• • •

I tell Emily I want to take Chrissie to her doctor's appointment next Wednesday. "She has to change buses twice and walk six blocks, and it's really hard for her," I say, hoping to generate some sympathy.

"But then I've got no way to get home," Emily says. She is giving me this look that says *thanks a lot, buddy.*

"I thought Chloe could take you, like she used to." We've been walking Toby in Emily's neighborhood, while we hash over the subject of Chrissie.

"Not anymore. Her schedule's changed."

I hadn't known that. "What about someone in Songbirds?"

Her hand slips out of mine. "Are you going to take her to every doctor's appointment?" She corrects Toby as he barks at a terrier across the street.

Now that she mentions it, Chrissie did say something about monthly appointments. "Just once a month."

"That's only in the beginning of the pregnancy. My neighbor, who I babysit for, is due next month, and she goes to the doctor every *week*."

Every week. I gulp.

"This doesn't make any sense," she says. "Michael's parents should help her, not you." Toby has wound his leash around a lamppost, and she stops to untangle him.

"She's totally scared of them."

"But why does it have to be *you* helping her? And why do you have to drive her to doctor's appointments?" She finally unwinds Toby and leads him away from the lamppost. "I mean, don't you think it's strange for us to be caught up in something like this? We're only sixteen!" She stands there in the middle of the sidewalk, breathing in and out really fast, like she's having a panic attack.

I stop, too. "Emily, *I'm* caught up in it. Not you."

"I *am*, though. If you're going to stop driving me home on account of her."

"It's just a few times!"

She takes a few slow, deep breaths, calming herself down. "Okay." More breaths. "I understand. And I can find another ride home on Wednesday."

"Thanks." I have the coolest girlfriend in the whole world.

"Derek Masters will do it. He's offered before."

"What!"

"He has basketball practice on Wednesdays, and he doesn't mind driving out of his way to drop me off." Emily's mood seems to have mellowed, because she's looking almost calm.

My nice, neat plan concerning Chloe has exploded, and chunks of it are falling down all around me. Now I'm the one having a panic attack. "Wait a minute! Why does it have to be Derek?"

"I need a way to get home. What do you want me to do?"

"But why Derek?"

"There's nothing going on between me and him."

"But Derek's after you! He's only doing this to get you away from me. Don't you see that?"

She doesn't answer, but steps to the side to bypass a hole in the sidewalk.

"Hah!" I say. "You know I'm right."

She still doesn't answer.

"Chrissie knows I have a girlfriend. We've agreed nothing's going to happen. But Derek's interested in you. If you ride with him, you're encouraging him. You're leading him on."

"Derek knows I have a boyfriend," Emily says in a quiet voice. "I need a ride every day, not just the days you feel like doing it. Derek's willing to help me out."

"But Emily...."

We've reached her house. She stops by my car. "I've gotta go in now. I'll see you tomorrow, Ryan."

Chapter Thirty

The subjects of Chrissie and Derek are now these two hard, sensitive little spots that Emily and I have to avoid, or we'll start to argue. Since I can't talk to her about them, I find myself venting to Jonathan, sitting with him on a bench during a free period at school.

"A baby! That's intense," he says. "That was Michael's secret, wasn't it?"

"Yeah." We sit there contemplating Michael and all the ways he had of getting himself into trouble.

"How are you helping her?"

"Taking her to doctor's appointments, for one thing."

Jonathan lets out a bark of laughter. "Oh, so, up in the stirrups, huh? Is she hot?" He leers through his black-framed glasses.

"Shut up, man! It's not like that." Jeez, this is bad enough without Jonathan acting like an infant.

"Just stand by her head," he says, looking wise.

"Thanks, I'll remember that." After a second I add, "The worst part is, Emily's getting rides from Derek Masters now."

Jonathan whistles, his eyebrows arching up over his glasses.

"But no worries," I say. "Emily and I are officially an exclusive item."

He cackles. "Not for long!"

"Cut it out!" I brood for a minute. "And on top of it, Emily doesn't think I should be helping Chrissie. She thinks Nat and Yancy should do it."

Now he's stern. "What does it matter what Emily thinks?"

"Well, she's my girlfriend."

"So? It's none of Emily's business!"

"It's not?" The bell rings, signaling five minutes to get to class. "Dude. Your bitch doesn't tell you how to live your life!"

Again, I wonder how he would know. Although he *has* taken Samantha Morton out a couple of times recently, his first dates ever. She's a fun girl who's on the debate team with him.

"But this stuff with Chrissie affects her."

It's time to go to class. Jonathan stands. "This isn't about her. It's about Michael." He slings his backpack over his shoulder.

"Just remember, man," he says, "bros before hoes. Every time."

He takes off, and I'm about to go, too, when my ring tone floats out of my shirt pocket. The display screen on my cell shows a number I don't recognize at first.

"Ryan, it's me, Yancy."

"Oh, hi!" For a minute, I freak, thinking she's found out about the baby. How can I explain keeping this little thing from her, the fact that she's going to be a grandma?

"I have a favor to ask."

I breathe easier. I grab my backpack and start walking to class while I talk.

"Miss Anderson from school called us about Michael's locker. She needs somebody to empty it out." Her tone is as smooth and easy as if she were asking me to pick up their mail for them.

It's been four months since Michael died. A cold prickle goes down my back as I think of his locker sitting there all that time, with his stuff in it. It figures that Nat and Yancy never thought of it, just as they never thought of anything else Michael might have needed when he was alive.

"Nat and I are leaving for Rome, and you're there every day. Would you just scoot by and throw the contents into some shopping bags? We can pick them up from you next time we come over."

I can't believe her. She's acting all casual, like it's no big deal.

"I don't have the combination," I say, not wanting to make it easier for her.

"Oh, I have it! Got a pen?" Then, "Take your time," she says, making this big show of being patient, while I fumble for a sales receipt in my pocket, and repeating the numbers twice while I write them down, holding the receipt against a wall. She's a regular fountain of generosity.

If Nat and Yancy can't even pick up their dead son's things from school, they don't deserve to know about a grandchild. From now on, I've got no problem keeping Chrissie's secret.

"All right, I got it," I say, pocketing the number. My resentment spills over. "I'll do it for *Michael*."

A silence on the phone line, like she can't speak.

"Thanks." She chokes the word out and clicks off.

• • •

On the day of Chrissie's doctor's appointment, I run up the two flights of stairs on the outside of her building and arrive at Apartment 206 right on time. I'm mentally cursing my fate that I have to be here when Emily is hanging with Derek Masters.

"Wow, some car!" Chrissie says when she sees it.

I hadn't realized how big her belly was: I have to pull back the passenger seat a couple of notches for her.

"Lord, I can hardly wait to get my shape back!" she says.

I'm not sure what to say to that. "So, what's gonna happen at this appointment?"

She shrugs. "Nothin' much. They wanna check on you all the time, just to make sure the baby's behavin' itself."

"Don't you have to eat special foods and take vitamins, and stuff?"

"You betcha. I eat all organic. I'm not infectin' *my* child with deadly toxins." She breaks a Kit Kat bar out of her purse. "You want some?"

"Sure." I take a piece and we chew in silence for a minute. I pull my car into the lot of her seedy medical clinic, and we go in and sit down to wait on plastic chairs.

I shift around on my seat as I think about how unfair life is. Not only have I never once gotten naked with a girl, but now I have to take a pregnant one to the doctor.

Somehow, I've managed to miss out on sex and go straight to its consequences.

I picture flashing lights and ringing bells as I enter the waiting room. *Attention, patients! First virgin ever to cross the threshold of an*

131

obstetrician's office!

I drum my hands on my knees, shooting to my feet when Chrissie's name is called.

"You're stayin' right here," Chrissie says without missing a beat. I sink back down immediately, happy to sit in the waiting room.

I sit there, staring at the wall, and as has happened so many times these past months, I'm thinking about where Michael would be if I hadn't killed him. He'd be here, in my place, I think. Or more likely, in the examining room with Chrissie.

Or would he? Michael had a way of quietly checking out when he came up against something unpleasant. I was always better than he was at doing the hard jobs.

After Chrissie's done, she says she wants to take me to dinner. "It's the least I can do."

I check my watch. Emily's rehearsal should have ended fifteen minutes ago. She's probably with Masters right now.

"Hold on," I say to Chrissie. I whip out my cell. Thumbs flying, I send Emily a text. *Hey baby what up?*

Hi

That's all she's got for me? *How was rehearsal?*

Fine

I can't help myself. *Hows Derek?* She's probably in his car right now.

Don't be like this Ryan

Instantly, I feel bad. *Sorry. Its just that im crazy for you*

I know

I'll call you when I get home

Okay

Love u, I write.

But she has already signed off.

Chrissie is waiting. "One more," I say. I call home and tell Rosario I'll be home late.

We go to Sal's Diner. It's one of those places where the waitresses wear fifties uniforms and each table has its own jukebox. We slide into a pink vinyl booth.

"A jukebox!" Chrissie takes a quarter from her wallet and starts leafing through the song list. "I'm gonna splurge and get a song!"

I'm moping about that text from Emily. *I know?* I say *I love you* and she says *I know?*

"How about *Baby Love?* That seems fittin'."

I watch her slide the quarter into the slot, taking care to punch in the right code, so she gets *Baby Love* and not the song next to it.

"Just think if I got *The Monster Mash* by mistake!"

"Hang on." I say to Chrissie, pulling out my cell again.

"Checkin' in with the little woman?"

I don't answer. I text Emily. *U there?*

Yes

Lets not fight

I don't want to either

Ill be home soon.

Where are you?

Oops. I hadn't planned to tell her about dinner with Chrissie.

Got delayed

Delayed???

Double oops. *Stopped for a quick bite*

No response. I can't take this. *Gimme a break Em. Tell me u love me*

Of course I love u. but I disagree with what you're doing.

But u luv me?

I already said I did. Gtg

She signs off.

My pride won't let me text her again. "I'm up for some tunes!" I say. "You wanna pick them?" I dig in my pocket and spill a pile of quarters onto the table.

Chrissie gasps. "You bet!" She flips through the song list. "I'm gonna get all songs with "baby" in the title!"

The waitress, wearing a name tag that says "Ethyl," arrives with our water. "Top o' the marnin' to ye," Chrissie says to her.

Then, to me: "You don't mind if I practice my Irish accent, do you?"

"Go right ahead."

It turns out Chrissie can do a dozen accents, and has invented a cast of whacked out characters: a stoned out surfer astronaut who can't drive his space shuttle; a new age yoga teacher from Brooklyn, and—in honor of her pregnancy—a Lamaze instructor from New Delhi. She begins hollering out birthing instructions in an Indian accent, making me laugh.

"You're great at those voices."

"You know who my idol is?" Chrissie says. "Lucille Ball. She's my Instructor of Comedy."

I remember the posters on her apartment walls. It turns out Chrissie can do a wicked Lucy impression.

"You sound just like her."

"I should. I watched 'I Love Lucy' my whole life. Or at least, I did when we had a TV." She says it so easily that I figure I'm allowed to ask.

"What do you mean? You didn't always have a TV?"

"Honey, sometimes we didn't have *food*. We used to pick dandelions by the side of the road and cook 'em up for dinner."

"Really?" I think of my uneaten hamburger, the one she took home, and shame sweeps over me again.

"Yeah. But then we moved in with Judge Mayfair and his family." Chrissie is matter-of-fact about it. "My momma's a Domestic Engineer by profession. Housekeeper," she adds when she sees me looking at her.

"For six years I lived at the Mayfairs' house with my momma. In their maid's room."

"That must have been interesting." I signal Ethyl for the bill and check my watch. Emily should be home by now. Unless Masters has sweet talked her into running away with him.

"It worked out. I started helpin' their cook, Jessie, all the time."

"So you learned how to cook and play Lucy Ricardo?"

"*And* I learned how to play tennis. Beau taught me. The Mayfairs' son. He's two years older 'n me." Chrissie pulls a mirror and lipstick out of her purse and paints a pink mouth on herself.

"What happened to him?" Besides fathering a baby.

"Ole Miss and then law school. Meanwhile, I left home when I was eighteen to find fame and fortune in Hollywood!" She sweeps her arms out.

"But you don't wanna get out there and act, Ryan?" she asks. "I mean, you've lived in LA all your life."

"Not me." I'd rather be shot execution-style than perform in front of people. I speak without thinking. "If I did anything in film, I'd go behind the camera."

"Like how? You mean directing?"

I backtrack immediately. "Nah. I mean, I don't really know." It's not something I think or talk about much. When your father is God, King, and Emperor all rolled up into one, you don't usually assume you can follow in his footsteps.

"So what *do* you like to do?" she says.

That's a good question. What I've done most of my life is drift around with Michael. After a minute, I say "I like to play tennis."

"Yeah, you're really good, too," she says. "I've seen you." After a minute she asks, "Ben Swanson told me you used to train with him. How come you stopped?"

"I dunno. Got tired of it, I guess."

"You'd be incredible if you worked at it."

Ethyl brings our bill, and I grab it.

"Hey, I asked *you!*" She's digging in her purse for her wallet.

"I'll pay." I think of Chrissie's hundred and forty nine dollars in the bank.

"Well, thank you." Her hand comes out of the purse holding a piece of paper. It's a grainy out-of-focus picture of something unrecognizable.

"It's my ultra-sound picture. And look!" She points to a tiny nub protruding from this larger thing. "It's a boy!"

"Really?" I had already decided that, but it's nice to have proof.

"I'm naming him Michael."

That chokes me right up. As we walk out, I try to stop the burning behind my eyes by blinking my eyelids a bunch of times. I drop her off saying, "I'll be in touch."

She's naming him Michael. Wherever he is right now, I bet he liked hearing that.

Chapter Thirty-One

By now, even my parents have figured out I have a girlfriend.

"So tell us a little about this young lady!" Dad booms. He and Mom stand in the doorway to my bedroom. Mom's purse is over her shoulder, and Dad's wearing a jacket, holding his car keys.

I put on my most sarcastic voice. "Don't let me keep you from your important plans."

Dad counters with his determined-to-ignore-my-sarcasm face. "We have a few minutes before we have to leave."

They barge on into my room, Dad sitting in my desk chair while Mom perches on the edge of the bed.

"Spill the beans," Dad prompts.

"Well, I'm getting good grades because of her." I just got A's on a Spanish quiz and a history assignment.

"I like this girl already!" Dad says.

I figure this is my chance to ask them. "She's gotten me really interested in English history. As a matter of fact, there's this summer program." I describe it, stressing the intellectual discoveries and historical insights that await me in Merry Olde England.

"Ryan, what a wonderful opportunity!" Mom claps her hands, while her bracelets clank together. She's wearing *leather pants*.

Dad nails me with a look. "And this girl's going to England, too?"

"Her name's Emily." I stare off into the distance.

"Okay, so you're going to be... studying history... with Emily? In England?"

"Yes."

I catch a knowing look in his eye.

"Alright, give us some information on this program, and we'll think about it." He's onto me, but I can tell it's a yes.

"And we'd like you to bring Emily around for dinner one night."

"I'll check our calendar and give you a date," Mom says.

"No problem." All right! England here we come. I wait for them to leave, but they just sit there.

"This is nice, having a chance to chat a little," Mom says.

Spare me. I stare at my framed poster of *The Godfather*, my favorite movie of all time. It's personally autographed by Francis Ford Coppola. He's friends with Dad. *Ryan,* it says. *A chip off the old block. You'll be giving me a run for my money one day.*

Yeah, right. I'll probably be an unemployed derelict, lying around on my ass.

"Well, I guess we'd better go." Mom and Dad stand up. Of course, they'll be gone all evening, while we stay with Ro.

"Bye." I turn my back on them, and after a minute they leave.

• • •

Mr. and Mrs. Wintraub have won four theater tickets at a raffle, and they've invited me and Emily along. I arrive in a sports jacket and tie and stand, chatting with them in their entry hall, while we wait for Emily. Eleanor smiles at me. "It's good to see you again, Ryan."

I'm looking forward to an evening with Mr. Wintraub about as much as I would boot camp, or maybe oral surgery. I'm just hoping to get through the evening without pissing him off.

Then, Emily comes down the stairs. I gawk at her. In this light, her eyes look intensely blue. Her dress has a low, round neckline, and her hair is up, showing off the back of her neck and her creamy, perfect shoulders.

I hate how weird it is between us now. I wish things felt easy and simple again.

Emily gets to the bottom of the stairs, and there is The Necklace. It's the first time I've seen her wear it since the night I gave it to her.

It glows against her skin. The simple white gold links pull your eyes toward them, while the heart, with its aquamarine in the center, points to the most kissable part of Emily's throat. It looks rich and elegant. It looks *expensive.*

She turns, smiling, to her parents, and so do I, and we both register the expression of shock on their faces.

"Emily!" Eleanor says. "Where on earth..." She glances in my direction, then away.

"Ryan gave it to me." Emily's smile fades as she looks from her mom to her dad and back.

"What was the occasion?" Mr. Wintraub asks, his voice tight.

Emily turns to me, a question mark on her face.

I fumble for the right thing to say and don't find it. "I don't know, I just wanted to give her something," I bleat.

"How much did this cost?" Mr. Wintraub demands. We are still standing in their front entry. Mr. Wintraub's practically standing toe-to-toe with me, jabbing his face into mine.

"David! It doesn't matter!" Eleanor puts a hand on his arm, but he pulls it away.

"It does!" he says. "Emily can't accept something like this. I don't want her owing him."

"Mr. Wintraub," I say. "Emily doesn't owe me anything. It's a gift. I paid for it from my savings account."

My eyes meet Eleanor's, and she smiles at me in an encouraging way. She's a cool lady. I wonder what she's doing with this guy.

"You wanted to give her a gift, so you went out and spent a small fortune from ... what, your *trust fund?*" The way Mr. Wintraub says it makes it sound dirty, shallow. I can see myself through his eyes—a spoiled rich boy who uses money to buy people.

And isn't that in fact what I did? I wanted Emily to love me, so I bought her a crazy-expensive necklace, something that Mr. Wintraub could never afford to give Emily, or Emily's mother, for that matter. And I did it with a four-figure wad of cash I had lying around, through no work or effort of my own. Ten minutes earlier, I had been proud of myself, proud that I had done something to show my girl what she meant to me. Now I'm ashamed of myself. I look at the floor, humiliated.

"Dad!" I hear Emily now. "I know how Ryan meant this. He

was telling me I mattered to him. That's all. And it's not his fault that he comes from a wealthy family. That's your hang-up!"

"I think I should go," I say. I can't believe that anyone wants to sit and chat at a restaurant right now.

"Oh, so that's your response?" Mr. Wintraub says. "Run away?"

All of a sudden, I am looking at him from a great distance. He is edged in red.

I force myself to take a deep breath, several of them. I count to five. Then, I speak carefully, choosing each word.

"Mr. Wintraub, I really love your daughter, okay? She's special to me."

I pause for a second, then continue. "She's a beautiful person, and she deserves to have a beautiful necklace. If I can afford to give her one, *what's the harm in that?*"

A silence follows, while I have one of those weird moments where you think *That was really awesome. I wonder who said that?* And then you realize that it was you. I get over my shock and stare Mr. Wintraub down, defiant, no more polite-bowing-and-scraping Ryan. Now I'm giving him man-to-man-tell-it-like-it-is Ryan.

I glance over at Emily, who sends me a look so scorching hot I'm afraid she's going to ignite the draperies. Mr. Wintraub looks like he's been sucking on lemons.

"Well, shall we get going?" Eleanor's voice is high and strained. Wordless, we walk out to the Wintraubs' car to go to dinner.

Should be a fun night.

At the restaurant, Emily takes every chance she gets to hold my hand and gaze at me adoringly, which she knows will send her dad into fits of rage. His face is dangerously red, while a vein or something throbs in his temple. I can see it from across the table.

Eleanor and I, the peace makers, make small talk like two lunatics, smiling too much and laughing too much. It's a relief to go to the theater, and more of a relief to say good night and finally escape home.

But Emily and I are back on the high burner again, hotter than ever.

Chapter Thirty-Two

She and I go out to Venice Beach on a Friday afternoon. It feels so good to just be alone with her. We pull off our shoes and walk along in that uneven way you do down by the water, when the beach is slanted. Our fingers are interlaced and our feet sink deep with every step. I love the squawks of the seagulls and the beach sand between my toes. I feel myself relax, the nervous tension draining out of my neck and shoulders.

It's warm for January, but because it's winter and the sun's going down, the place is almost empty. We walk away from the water, find a patch of dry sand, then end up lying down. We kiss, and she presses her body against mine. My hand slides up under her shirt. We lie there for a while, fooling around, my hands moving under her clothes.

As the sky darkens and we start to get cold, we walk back up the beach toward the boardwalk, with its stores and restaurants. I ask her "Are you hungry yet?"

"Not really," she says.

"You want to get out of here? We'll find a place to eat later."

My BMW's in the shop, so I'm driving the extra car my family keeps for just such circumstances—a three year old Lexus sedan that Mom replaced with a new Jaguar.

Mom's Lexus is all alone in the deserted parking lot. I open the door to the back seat so we can throw in the sandy shoes we're carrying.

Emily gives me a playful push, saying "Climb in." I do, my heart leaping like a jackrabbit.

• • •

We are lying together in my Mom's sedan, on its wide back seat with its soft, expensive leather. I have my arms around Emily. I touch her shiny hair and put my face against her neck. I smell lavender and the salt of the ocean, as well as the leather of the car seats. A seat belt digs a hole in my hip, but it's a small price to pay.

I'm on my back, and she's lying on top of me. We're fully dressed, but I can feel her breasts, soft against my chest. I'm so turned on, I can hardly think.

"I want to see you. I want to take off your clothes." I can barely get the words out. The entire length of her body is pressed against mine, making coherent speech difficult. I close my eyes and try to think of a total turn off. Mr. Wintraub's unsmiling face comes to mind.

Light is shining in the windows onto Emily's face. She looks like one of the angels they have in those paintings I've seen at the Louvre. She pulls back a little to look into my eyes.

Almost out of my mind with wanting her, I slowly, painfully count to ten. I wonder if Mr. Wintraub owns any firearms. As I slide my hands up her back to unsnap her bra, our eyes meet.

"I've never done this before," she says. She looks as nervous as I've ever seen her.

Taking a deep, shaky breath, I begin to count to one hundred, picturing armed guards around the door to Emily's bedroom.

"Neither have I."

We kiss some more, very tenderly. She lays her head on my chest and I put my arms around her.

"Maybe you need time," I say. I stroke her hair. We have light from the lamp posts in the parking lot, but we've steamed up all the windows, giving us a feeling of privacy.

"Are you … uncomfortable?" she asks me. My boner from the Pier was nothing. This one's like the state of Florida.

"I'll survive," I say, hoping it's true. "Anyway, we don't have any condoms." We untangle ourselves and start to sit up. Emily is silent, then mumbles something I don't catch.

"What?" I ask. She mumbles again, and I could swear she's saying *I might have a few in my purse.*

"You have *condoms in your purse?*" I am riveted by this new piece of information.

She turns red as a traffic light and tries to reach for her purse on the floor of the car, but I, with my tennis player's lightning reflexes, am faster. Grabbing it, I slide away from her on the car seat. Emily bursts into laughter and clutches my arm.

"Hey, that's private!"

"Oh, no." I hold the purse out of her reach. "It is written in the Code of Dating when a girl brings condoms on a date with a guy, he's entitled to open her purse and take them out." I turn my back on her and unzip the purse. Seeing a condom package, I pull out a strip of some four or five and wave it in the air.

"Not just a condom, folks, but multiple condoms!"

Emily's laughing helplessly. She gets control of herself. "Those were in there for months. Just in case something *good* came along."

"Were not," I say. "They're, like, *shiny*, they're so new. And they were *on top*. I mean, on top of the keys, on top of the wallet. These condoms have my name written all over them!"

She laughs again, but will admit nothing. So after a brief stand-off, I realize that I'm right back to being what I was five minutes ago – a beggar, hoping for crumbs.

"It's okay," I tell her. "Let's go to dinner." But now that Emily has thoroughly established who's in charge here, she relents. She gets a gleam in her eye.

"You can take off my clothes if I can take off yours first. But I can't promise I'll do anything more than that."

"Deal," I tell her.

So I have to go first, and we are laughing and nervous, and then I'm naked, while she is fully dressed, and I'm a little embarrassed, and she says, "Wow," which I hope is a good thing, and then I slowly take off her clothes and see her neck, her shoulders, and then, God, her breasts, and, God, she's so freaking beautiful, and we are nervous and laughing and awed and serious, all at the same time.

Emily has such a warm, womanly body. I am touching her, but our bare skin sticks to the leather upholstery, and the seat isn't long enough for me, and a couple of times we freeze, conscious of car headlights passing over us. And then we laugh and kiss, and at some point we start to really fool around and get serious. I have

142

fantasized about this moment, wanted Emily, thought about touching her so many times, that in the end, I just do the things from my fantasies and hope it's okay. We don't laugh anymore, and we look into each other's eyes and go to a place where we are totally, insanely into each other, but then it's time for that comedy of errors which is the condom and then, after more laughter and finding places for our arms and legs in the crowded back seat, we finally Perform the Act, with me saying "Are you okay?" every twenty seconds, and it is awesome and awkward and tender all at once.

And after we are done, I tell her it will be better next time, and she says "No, it was interesting," and I say "I love you," and she says "I love you, too."

Just as we realize it's eleven o'clock and I have to get Emily home, I start to see alternating bands of blue, orange, and red light. I look out the window and there, looking in, is a big man with a blue shirt and a badge, and I hear the words, "Open up. Police."

• • •

Right in a row, Emily screams, I toss her my sweater, she pulls it on, and I, clutching a wadded up t-shirt over my private parts, lunge for the window to lower it an inch or two. The cop is standing there, trying to keep a straight face. I feel like yelling "Very funny!" out the window at him, but I decide against it. I hear the sounds of Emily behind me, whipping her clothes on.

"Get outta here, you guys," he says, letting a big grin escape.

I am half-dressed as I drive Emily home. I've managed to locate my pants, although my briefs are somewhere in the back seat, and my shirt's on, but unbuttoned. Emily has pulled on most of the basic clothing items, but her usually smooth, sleek hair's running wild, curling out in all directions. She's got one sock in her hand, but can't find the other.

"Do you think he saw us, like, naked?" she asks me.

"Definitely. It's okay. We just won't ever go to Venice again."

"*Omigod.*" She's looking in a mirror. "Why didn't you tell me about my hair?" It's completely matted in the back and frizzing out in the front.

"I like it. It's so...post-intercourse," I say, feeling very sophisticated. Then, I pull up in front of the Wintraubs' house, look out, and see Mr. Wintraub standing in the open front door. He's just a dark silhouette in the lighted doorway, but I think I see the outlines of a semiautomatic weapon. I am sinking below the dashboard trying to button my shirt without seeming to. I look at my watch. It's five minutes to midnight, so we're right on time.

"I'll handle this." Emily acts brave, but as she runs her fingers through her hair, I can see they are shaking. She's wearing more clothes than I am, though, and we know that, unlike me, Mr. Wintraub will let her live.

"You're okay," I tell her. "You've been walking on the beach. That explains the hair and the bare feet." I give a jaunty wave in Wintraub's direction, while Emily sprints across the lawn toward her waiting father.

As I peel out of there, a thought pops automatically into my head. *Wait 'til Michael hears about this.*

"Awesome, dude," he would have said. "Took you long enough."

Well, yeah, compared to Michael, who lost it just before his fifteenth birthday. But Michael's dead, and I'm not the type who would tell anyone besides my best friend. So I will have to keep my big news to myself.

Chapter Thirty-Three

The next morning, as I stand with Calvin and Jonathan at the first hole of the Beverly Crescent Golf Course, my mind's back on last night, in the car with Emily. I still don't know what happened with her dad. I hope she's not locked up in a tower right now, growing her hair into long, rope-like braids.

I set up a tripod and video camera, while Calvin and Jonathan choose golf clubs and pull out their data charts. If we need to, we're prepared to step aside and let other groups play through. But it's a really slow day at the course.

I wonder whether my physics partners are still virgins. I'm not, I think, feeling proud. Not anymore. I have had sex one time. I've moved over to the other side, passed into manhood.

I wonder if I look different. Can people tell by looking at me that I Did the Deed last night for the very first time? *There's one,* someone might say upon seeing me. *A brand new non-virgin. You can spot 'em by the stunned gratitude on their faces.*

Calvin and Jonathan are checking over their data recording sheets. Calvin's saying. "If we keep the club length and the rotational velocity constant to begin with, we can determine the range at different launching angles."

"Speak English, Calvin," I say.

Jonathan jumps in. "It just means if we use the same length club and swing it exactly the same way each time, we can discover how far we can hit the ball using different angled club heads."

"Right, and I'll film it all, so we can analyze your swings in slow motion, or even frame by frame."

"This is gonna be cool, Ryan," Calvin says.

I should be glad Calvin's happy with me for once, but instead I'm worried. "We need to find a way to spice it up though, make it interesting."

What if we called it something like "Physics Nerds Go Golfing"? I look at Jonathan and Calvin. As physics nerds go, these two are the dream team. Calvin could be the show-off golfer, and Jonathan the new guy on the course.

I grab a pad and write out some ideas. This thing will not go to Sundance or Cannes, but it might make a boring high school science project into something you could stay awake through. Then, I pitch the idea to my partners.

"You want us to wear costumes?" Jonathan looks fearful.

"And act?" asks Calvin. To my surprise, he sounds more fascinated than horrified.

"It would be very low-key," I say. "It could be funny."

They promise to think about it.

• • •

It's time for Emily to meet the family. I have picked her up from home, driven through our gates, and pulled up our long driveway. I park in front of the house. A few other cars are in a guest parking area off to the side.

"Are they having a party?" Emily asks as she fidgets and checks her hair in the rearview mirror.

"No," I tell her. "I don't know who those cars belong to."

We walk into the entry hall to see my parents talking with Nat and with Dad's casting director, Mitzi. Dad's still deep in pre-production for *Mystery Moon,* and it looks like he brought some of his work buddies home from the studio to eat with us.

My parents have forgotten Emily's coming to dinner.

This massive, weird bronze sculpture stands in one corner, dwarfing the humans, and on the other side a wide staircase goes up to the second floor. I put my hand on the small of Emily's back and walk her up to them.

"Emily, this is my dad, my mom, Nat Weston, and Mitzi Travenor." Mitzi, who's one of my favorite people, has been casting Dad's films for as long as I can remember. Mitzi's six feet tall and broad shouldered, with this wedge of frizzy orange hair. She's from New Jersey but tends to dress from wherever she took her last vacation. There's this sari-like thing wrapped around her, and a red dot on her forehead, although the Indian effect is undercut by the Nike running shoes.

"Gimme a hug, gorgeous!" Mitzi screams, and I hug her hard. Mitzi turns to Emily and says, "Sorry, honey, but I got to him first. When he was five, he promised to marry me, and I'm holding him to it." Mitzi's in her mid-forties and has been with her partner, LeeAnne, for the last twelve years.

Before Emily can answer, the star of *Mystery Moon*, Jared Abernathy, walks in. Blessed with good genes and a good plastic surgeon, Jared's a guy who is best described by the word "chiseled." With a superhero jaw line and insanely cut shoulders and arms, he doesn't so much move as strike poses for those fortunate enough to have him in their line of sight. He has black hair and the kind of blue eyes that leave a streak of blue behind when he turns his head.

"Yo," he says to me. He knows I'm the son, but I can tell he can't quite remember my name.

"Hi Jared. I'm Ryan," I say. "This is my girlfriend, Emily."

"Well, hello," he says. He seems to think he's entitled to give Emily a really obvious appreciative once-over, checking her out from top to toe. Emily would ordinarily wither a guy who acted like that, but here in my parents' house, meeting a major movie star, she's a little off her game. She bites her lip and looks down.

"*Jared.*" Mitzi gives him a push.

"I should never have discovered him," she says to Emily, sounding apologetic. Five years ago, Jared served Mitzi a latte at a West Hollywood coffee bar. He's now recognized in thirty eight countries.

Emily looks around her, glassy-eyed. Our front entry hall is the size of her family's combined living and dining rooms. Through an archway you can see into a room with a grand piano and, behind it, a long wall of glass and mirror cabinets full of Oscars, Emmys, SAG awards, Golden Globes, and every other prize on the planet. Every week, one of the maids cleans all the glass and mirrors and hand polishes each award.

Dad jumps into the conversation. He knows he messed up, but

there's no problem my dad can't fix.

"Emily!" He takes her arm, giving her the Doug Mills twinkle-eyed smile. Waving a hand at the others, he announces, "You derelicts know where the bar is. Go make yourselves drinks. Emily, may I give you a tour of the garden? It's nice this time of day." He takes her off.

Mom walks up. "Emily seems very sweet."

"Yeah, she's cool."

"Would you ask Ro to get some bottles from the wine cellar?" Our wine cellar's bigger than a normal-sized bedroom and is outfitted with all this high-tech stuff to keep wine bottles happy and comfortable. "And also ask when dinner's going to be ready?"

I go to the kitchen, where Ro's working and Maddy and Molly are, as usual, sitting at the counter in the center island. After a while, Dad brings Emily in to us. The two of them are talking and smiling, although Emily still has this glazed over expression. Dad says to me, "You two sit next to me and Nadine at dinner, OK? It'll give us some more time to get acquainted with Emily." He disappears.

"I saw your fountains," Emily says. She has that look of a deer suddenly caught in the high beams of a car. It's a natural reaction for a first timer to our house.

"But did you see the waterfall and the sculpture garden?" I ask.

Emily gets a big laugh out of that one until she realizes I'm not joking.

I introduce her to Ro and my sisters.

Ro takes both of Emily's hands in hers and kisses her on the cheek. "Such a lovely young girl," she says. The twins smile at her. I know they are mentally gearing up to tease me later.

Mom comes into the kitchen and walks up to me and Emily. "I get to have her now, for a few minutes," she says to me, taking her arm. I look at them standing together, my mother and my girl. Mom's jewelry weight looks approximately equal to her body weight. She's pretty, or she was before the Botox and the starvation. Her eyes have that scary I-shouldn't-have-had-that-last-facelift look to them. But she is smiling at Emily and trying to be nice to her.

Emily smiles back. She looks like a rose from our garden, fresh and pretty. Her shiny hair swings as she talks, and she's big compared to Mom, but in an awesome, sexy kind of way.

They both look a little shy around the other. Finally, Mom says she wants to show Emily something and hauls her off to another room. I wonder what the two of them could possibly say to one another, but a few minutes later I see them with their heads together.

When Emily gets back, I pull her into the library, where we can be alone for a minute. "What did she show you? What did you talk about?"

"You," she says. Mom had taken her to what I call the Wall of Woe, that is, the wall with all the family photos, including those that document my dorky developmental stages.

"So you saw the buck teeth and the braces?"

"Yep."

We hear a knock, and Ro's face peeks in. "It's time to eat!"

"Did you check your email?" Emily asks me as we walk out to the dining room. "They sent a bunch of information about the England program. I'm so excited!"

I try to feel excited, too. I wonder if Oxford has a tennis court somewhere that I could use.

At dinner, the conversation turns to work, as always. We are sitting at the huge dining table, which Ro has loaded up with platters of roast beef, mashed potatoes, green veggies, and salad. I'm grateful to Dad for being so nice to Emily. He has her seated next to him and is explaining what went down at the studio today.

"We're auditioning for the role of Roxanne," he tells us. "It's a small role, but it's an important one. All her scenes are with Jared, and they've gotta be red hot together to make it work. So Jared's been coming to the callback auditions to read with the actresses."

"How's it going?" I ask.

Mitzi makes a face. "We called back ten girls," she tells me and Emily," and not one of them really did it for us. I saw five hundred to get down to the ten."

Dad passes Emily the salad. "We don't need her until September. Mitzi'll find her. She always does."

"Darn tootin,' Mitzi says, reaching for her glass."That's why he keeps me around."

"Emily," Mom says, "would you like to come to Doug's birthday celebration?"

Emily turns to me with a question on her face, but I love Mom's idea.

"You've gotta come to Dad's party."

My dad will turn fifty at the end of this month, and Mom's planning a blow-out. We're talking two hundred people—Dad's friends and people he works with. Because of who he is, most of them will be Hollywood A-listers. I give Emily the date, and she says, "But that's the day of the Madrigal competition in San Francisco." She'll be performing up there with the Songbirds for the state championship.

"I'm so sorry." She gives me and my parents a regretful look. "I would have liked to come."

I think she and I both feel kind of bad that we won't be there for each other that weekend, what with me missing Emily's performance and her missing my dad's party.

The talk continues, and someone asks me and Emily about college applications.

"We apply next year," I tell the group, "but this year, the junior class is traveling to New York and Boston in May, to check out schools there." I've been signed up since October, mainly because it'll be fun to go traveling with my class.

"Are you going on the trip, Emily?" my mom asks.

She nods. "I've always wanted to go east for college. And then study in Europe after that—history and international relations."

"Europe is so charming!" Mom says. She stops, as if she's not sure what to say next.

Emily continues. "Yes, but I think I'd like to end up in D.C. in a foreign policy job."

Everyone nods their heads and makes murmuring noises.

"What about you, Ryan?" someone says. I'm not so sure I want to move to the East Coast, even for a few years. I've been to New York a lot. It's okay, but I'll take the beach, sun, and ocean any day over some dark concrete canyon.

"I guess I have to think about it," I say. Once again, I feel like a wash-out, an aimless rich boy just floating along. Everyone I know has dreams, plans, accomplishments. Except for Michael, and look where that got him. I think suddenly, what am I good at? What have I done with my life up to now? Diddly squat, that's what.

Chapter Thirty-Four

"Way to go, Ryan!"

I'm at the tennis club. I lean over, my hands on my knees, gasping for breath. Sweat drips from my hair and forehead onto the surface of the tennis court. A hand pounds my back.

"Awesome match!"

I stand up, taking a towel someone hands me and wiping off my neck and face. I've just almost beaten Mason Ronson, the number twelve seeded player in my age group in California.

He beat me by one point in the last game. It was a fluke that I played him at all; his partner for the practice match called to say he had car trouble, and no one else was available.

A couple of dozen people are standing around, part of the crowd that began to gather at our court when people caught on to the fact that an unknown player was running neck and neck with Mason Ronson in a practice match.

He's approaching me now, hand outstretched. I shake it, feeling the hard calluses on his palm and fingers, even worse than mine.

"*Who* are you?" he asks, as if he can't quite believe such a nobody almost took the match away from him.

"Ryan Mills."

"Who do you train with?"

"No one."

His mouth shuts in a thin line. "Good match," he says in a clipped voice, turns on his heel, and stalks off.

My old tennis coach, Ben Swanson, walks up. "Don't get a swelled head," he says. "You just played the match of your life, and Ronson's coming off a torn hamstring."

"No chance of my getting a swelled head with you around," I tell Ben, grinning.

"You should come by the club more often. I can throw you some more practice matches, if you want."

"Sounds good," I tell him. "I will."

• • •

I'm at Sal's with Chrissie. Her eyes are red, and her curly hair looks dry and limp.

"You look beat," I say.

"It's just havin' to take the bus everywhere—to work and for all my errands," she says. She pulls out two quarters and puts them in the jukebox. "I shouldn't be spendin' money on this, but I can't resist."

"Here." I pull out my wallet.

"Thanks, but I'm not your charity case."

"This isn't charity. It's helping."

"Whatever. I mean, thanks, Ryan, but I don't need handouts. I need more money."

"Explain the difference."

"I need a better job," she says. "One that pays more."

"Like what?"

She shrugs. "Maybe there's a role out there for a Great White Whale."

"Have you had any auditions lately?"

She shakes her head. "Are you kiddin'? I look like Wife of Moby Dick."

An idea pops into my head and out of my mouth, without any intervention from my brain.

"You want to come to a party this Saturday? It's my dad's fiftieth birthday, and we're having a thing at my house." Emily can't come with me, but there's no reason why I can't take Chrissie.

Chrissie takes a huge bite of her sandwich. "I work Saturdays. Thanks, though."

"Can you get out of it?"

She eyes me with suspicion. Her face is practically drooping with fatigue.

"You want me to change my schedule to go to some fifty year old birthday party? Honey, I just *got* this job. Some of us peons gotta *work*, you know."

"I'd like you to meet my dad," I insist. I give her my most persuasive smile. "Do it for me, Chrissie?"

Too late, a thought hits me like a splash of cold water. Emily's not going to like this.

Chrissie is focused on her plate. "Who's your dad? Friggin' Elvis Presley?" Her mouth's full.

"Doug Mills." I wait for the reaction that's sure to come. What am I going to do? Not tell Emily? She'll find out and be even more pissed off.

Chrissie stops chewing. She puts down her fork. "You mean *the* Doug Mills? The filmmaker, Doug Mills?"

I nod, wondering if Chrissie's going to get weird like some people do and never act normal around me again. A trickle of sadness runs down my back at the thought of it.

"Sweet Lordy, why didn't you say so?"

"I just did. And trust me, I don't do this very often." My voice sounds cranky, even to me.

Chrissie looks down. "Well, *thanks*, Ryan." When I don't reply, she says again, "No, really, thanks. You've been great. I really appreciate your trying to help me like this."

She rebounds from her initial awe. "So your dad's *Doug Mills*? How come you're not an asshole?"

"I'm a genetic mutant," I tell her, hoping that our relationship stays normal. I'm also hoping that Emily never finds out I did this.

"I think I'll wear my lime green chiffon, with the lime green sandals. That'll have an impact."

I don't doubt that it will.

• • •

It's a gray Thursday afternoon, and I've confirmed that Mom has back-to-back appointments with her nutritionist, trainer, and hair stylist, while Dad's at the studio and Ro is taking the girls to ballet, gymnastics, and French.

Arriving home from school with Emily, I drive my car through the security gate, but instead of going up the driveway, I take an access road along the edge of the property back to the two-bedroom Mills family guest house. It's hidden from the main house by a stand of trees.

"This is so much better than that back seat," Emily says.

"No kidding," I say. "Now I know the real reason kids go away to college. They need a place to have sex."

Near the guest house door, I fish out the key from its hiding place. I hang a baseball cap on the door knob, which we tell all our visitors to use as a "Do Not Disturb" signal for the staff.

Once inside, we attack each other. This is the part in the movies where the kissing lovers fall hard against the door or the wall, then roll along the wall, still making out, and managing to remove all their clothes while never disentangling their lips.

But I can't imagine falling against a hard door with Emily. No cinema sex for us, I decide. I unbutton her blouse. I take her hand and lead her into the bedroom, where we lie down on the bed.

"Show me what you like," I tell her.

"I don't know. I can't. I'm too shy." It's true, I've realized. When it comes to sex, Emily's this funny combination of shy and modest, yet ready and willing. I see a clear Opportunity for Leadership.

"I have a few ideas." But I'm finding the harsh overhead light's not to my liking. It's messing with my mojo.

"Hold on." I get up, find some matches, and light a couple of candles. I flip off the mood-busting light, then walk back to the bed where Emily's lying, propped up on an elbow, watching me.

Emily and I are creating a film of our own where I, Ryan, play the role of Don Juan de Marco. She's looking at me in a way that almost makes me turn around, to see the person behind me she's really looking at. All that adoration, awe, and total lust cannot possibly be for me. But they are.

Very slowly, I lie down next to Emily. I smell lavender on her skin and feel her breath on my face as she turns toward me. I put one hand in her hair and very gently pull her head back. Her eyes close, while I kiss that incredible place where her neck meets her shoulder.

Chapter Thirty-Five

"Lemme get this straight," Jonathan says. "You asked Chrissie to your dad's birthday party in Emily's place?" We are sitting outside our classroom talking in low voices.

"She needs to get work. This way I can introduce her to people."

"Did Emily gripe about this, too?"

"She sorta doesn't know I asked Chrissie to go."

"Just like she sorta doesn't know you take Chrissie to Sal's for dinner after doctor's appointments?"

"Kinda."

Suspicious, he says "You're not hooking up with Chrissie, are you?"

"No! Jeez man!" I scowl at Jonathan.

"I get it. So you're hooking up with Emily then!"

I don't say anything.

"Hah!" Jonathan says. "I knew it!"

"Yeah, well, what about you? Are you hooking up with Samantha?"

Jonathan has been taking her out for a while now. He avoids my eyes.

"Hah!" I say. "I knew it!"

We sit there for a minute.

"It's pretty awesome, huh?" Jonathan says.

We crack up, like a couple of twelve-year olds.

• • •

School has ended for the week, and I'm standing at Michael's locker. I have a couple of big shopping bags under my arm and Michael's locker combination in my hand. My stomach feels queasy and my mouth dry.

The hallways are quiet, as a lot of kids have finished and taken off for the weekend. Emily's gone, too, since her mom picked her up early for a doctor's appointment.

I look around. Nobody knows I'm here. I should have just told Yancy to do this herself.

When I swing the locker door open, something that I'd forgotten about Michael comes back to me—how tidy and organized he kept his things. You never expected that from the wild and crazy Michael. The sight of his textbooks, lined up from shortest to tallest, makes me want to bawl all of a sudden.

I pull out the heavy textbooks and put them in a double strength shopping bag. Given that Michael died after only the second week of school, it's likely none of them were ever opened.

There's a spiral bound notebook with dividers, for each class, where Michael took his class notes. My chest burns, and I try to breathe. Again, I'm about to become this big crybaby at the sight of his familiar handwriting. There isn't a lot of it, as note-taking was not one of Michael's strengths.

Michael has put in one of those locker dividers to create an extra shelf. On the shelf are a square box—a white gift box with a lid—and a big, lumpy manila envelope. I drop the envelope into the second shopping bag, then take out the box. Curious, I lift up the lid and look. Inside are wax paper baggies containing white powder.

My whole body goes hot.

Jamming the lid back on the box and stuffing it into my shopping bag, I whip shut and relock the now empty locker. As I turn to hightail it for my car, I expect any minute to hear police sirens and megaphone-amplified voices ordering me to give myself up.

A hand grips my arm.

I have that feeling you get on a roller coaster where the bottom drops out from under you, and you free fall, while your guts do a pop-and-lock in your abdominal cavity.

It's Ballbuster Anderson. I never even heard her coming, but she's famous for that. She wears special shoes designed for stealth and speed. She looks pissed as hell.

"What are you doing, Mr. Mills?"

I don't know how she manages to be intimidating when she has to crank her head back at a right angle to look up at me, but she does. I'm quaking inside, thinking of the illegal contents of my shopping bags.

"Just emptying Michael Weston's locker." For one brief, horrible moment, I see Anderson sniffing my bags, like those dogs at the airport, then realize I am hallucinating.

She puts her hands on her hips. "I asked his parents to do this!"

"Oh. Well, they kinda passed the job on to me."

"They had no business doing that. Are you all right?"

I nod. "I'm fine. Really. I haven't even gone through this stuff. I'm just giving the bags to the Westons."

"Okay then." Miss Anderson is checking me out, probably looking for signs of impending violence. I can't blame her, since I assaulted Chase and all.

"Mr. Mills," she says. "I've been talking to some of your teachers."

I comb through my memories of class but can't think of anything I've done wrong.

"Your classwork and test scores have improved enormously this year. Excellent job!"

I'm averaging an A minus on my school work this semester. "Thank you." I move to the right, hoping to better block her view of my drug stash.

"If you continue at this rate, you'll qualify to do a Senior Honors Project next year."

"*Really?*" Jeez. Alongside Emily and Jonathan. "I didn't think my GPA was high enough."

"Qualification is based on either total GPA or significant improvement during the junior year. You could potentially qualify based on improvement."

"Really?" I say again, broken-record style. *Me*, qualify for the Senior Honors Project?

"But you'd need to get straight As for the rest of the term. You think you could pull it off?"

"I can try." I'll do it.

"That's the spirit! All right, then, keep up the good work!" She moves on.

I drive home, stopping at every stop sign and staying under the speed limit. A potential qualifier for the Senior Honors Project cannot get busted for drug possession.

I should have just flushed the white powder at school, I think, but I can't make myself destroy anything from Michael's locker. At least, not yet.

I avoid the kitchen as I enter the house and, thinking I'm in the clear, head for the stairs to my bedroom. *The Senior Honors Project.* The thought blows me away.

"Ryan!"

I jump about three feet into the air.

"Oh, hi Mom."

She's curled up on a sofa in the library with a magazine and a cup of tea.

I'd like to just wave and blow past her, but at the moment I feel like I should be on my best behavior. I stop to chat her up. I'm standing beside this special imported chair of hers that we're not allowed to sit on. I slide the shopping bags down behind it.

"How're you doing?" I ask.

"Fine." She gives me an actual warm smile. "I'm giving myself a break after the Teen League Annual Dinner Gala. It was this past weekend."

"Oh, yeah? Was it a big deal?"

She nods. "Fund raising is so stressful!"

I vaguely remember her talking about the Teen League one night when the Westons were over. "Are they the ones that do the drug and alcohol counseling? For teenagers?"

Speaking of which, I think, I just happen to have a whole shopping bag full of cocaine. Right here, hidden behind your Louis the Eighteenth Ming Dynasty chair.

"Yes, among other things."

I have a community service requirement to fulfill before graduation. "Is that a place where I could volunteer? Maybe work with the kids with substance abuse problems?"

"They have a program for high school students," Mom tells me.

"I could get you in there for an interview, if you want."

"I think I'll check it out myself—thanks." Should I tell her about what Miss Anderson said? Maybe I'll wait until I've actually qualified.

"Okay, so, see you later!"

I take the stairs two steps at a time up to my room. Even though there's nothing but trees outside my window, I lock my bedroom door and close the shutters. Opening the box again, I stare at the pile of baggies.

This is what killed Michael. I knew he had started doing blow again this summer with Chase. I should just flush it, but there's so little left connecting me to him. Even something like this, I hate to get rid of.

I open up one of the bags and sniff. There's a faint smell that I can't place. I close the bag up again.

I wonder what Michael saw in this stuff. I've smoked weed half a dozen times and, not seeing the point of it, never tried anything harder. But I never had a stash of drugs fall into my lap before, either.

I call the Westons' house and get their machine. "Hi, it's me, Ryan. I went to Michael's locker. Nothing there except books and a notebook. I'll give them to you next time I see you." I hang up. I will never tell them, or anyone, about the cocaine. As for the big manila envelope, it's mine now. Whatever's in that envelope is a piece of Michael, and I'm not letting it go.

The envelope is unsealed, but closed with a metal prong. I undo the prong and stick my hand down inside. It closes on something that I pull out and see are photographs. I never saw Michael take any photos of his own, but here are twenty or so that people must have given him at different times. They go back as far as eight years, and I recognize many of them, or the people in them.

Here's Michael at a birthday party, Michael on Halloween dressed as a pirate, Michael and me getting on the bus to go to camp. There's a strip of four photos from one of those photo booths with Michael and Anna Ferguson—they are making faces, and in the last shot, he's kissing her. Anna was the only girl Michael ever really fell for. Maybe she could have saved him, but her parents split up and she moved away in the middle of tenth grade.

Then I see a Polaroid of Michael and me coming out of Lake Evergreen together, arms raised in triumph, grinning widely. I remember someone taking the shot, but Michael nabbed it, so I haven't seen this photo for six years. I turn it over and there, in Michael's neat printing, are the words "Soldier Rock."

I feel that pain again, that feeling that I am being torn down the middle. Can a sixteen year old have a heart attack?

I stuff all the photos back into the envelope. I will deal with this later. I stick both the envelope and the box way in the back of my ski clothes drawer. People don't ski a lot in Los Angeles. I don't think anyone will be looking in that drawer soon.

Chapter Thirty-Six

Torches line the long driveway of our house, lighting up the grounds and gardens. Cars are arriving—Mercedes, Jaguars, Rolls Royces, sportscars, and limousines—while valets scurry to open doors for passengers and move the cars to a parking lot at the other end of our property.

Emily's in San Francisco, performing with the Songbirds in the state Madrigal competition. I've told my parents that an actress friend of mine is coming instead of Emily. With everything that's going on, though, they probably don't remember.

A black towncar that I arranged for Chrissie pulls up, as I stand waiting in front of my house.

She steps out, wearing a fluffy little dress. It's lime green. Even with her big belly, she's hotter than I've ever seen her. Men are checking out her blond curls and pink rosebud mouth and cleavage and legs that look like they go on forever in her short dress.

I told my folks she was expecting. They probably don't remember that either. Well, they'll know soon enough.

She sees me and drifts in my direction. "Lord, get me into a chair."

I steer her up to the house, but at the door, Chrissie hangs back for a minute.

"You okay?" I ask.

"Pinch me," she says. "This can't be real." Our massive art-filled entryway is packed with internationally known actors and film people. A few feet away, three Oscar-winning actors are laughing uproariously over something. After a minute, they stumble off to refill their drinks. Chrissie stares after them.

"Oh, it's real," I say.

She takes a deep breath, straightens her spine, and grips my arm as we move forward. Mom's got one of her eclectic party music mixes going in the background. Trays of champagne flutes and appetizers show up beside us, carried by more of those Hollywood wannabes who hope to be discovered and leave the field of catering forever. Chrissie stays close beside me, while a path automatically opens up in front of us.

I know everyone at the party, of course. Famous heads turn to stare at us. There are a lot of raised eyebrows and shocked looks, while a huge producer that Dad has never liked gives me a knowing leer and a thumbs up. I smile and look away.

Crap. I should have known that people might get the wrong idea about me and Chrissie. As usual, she's handling our situation better than I am. She's smiling and nodding at people as we walk along.

"How you doing?" I ask.

"I need a nice, hard chair," she drawls. "Either that, or a crane to get me up again."

"There's a chair." It's perfect. It's right next to good old Mitzi. Since Mitzi's a top casting director, Chrissie needs to know her. The only problem is: someone's sitting in that chair. In his black jeans and white t-shirt, he could pass for one of the caterers.

"That's Jared Abernathy…" I start to explain.

"Jared Abernathy! My friend Raylene'll kill me if I don't get his autograph." She starts to dig in her bag for a pen, but I stop her.

"Seriously uncool. I'll get you an autograph later."

"Thanks," she says meekly, dropping the pen back into her bag. "You ready?"

Chrissie's head goes up. "Ready!"

I've never seen her in a setting like this, where she's really working it. She's an actress, and she's onstage. She almost begins to glow, like something inside of her is emitting light through her skin. She approaches Jared, with me trailing behind. He looks up, and his eyes widen as he takes in the fertile and fantastic Chrissie. She stops in front of him.

Every part of Jared – his body, teeth, profile, and hair – is a product of the Hollywood Magic Machine. What the stylists, surgeons, and trainers can't fix, the airbrush artists will. He has just made the "Ten Hottest Hollywood Bachelors" List, and his photo has been everywhere.

Chrissie flashes him a dimple. "You look strong and healthy."

"Thank you," Jared says, a smile beginning at one corner of his mouth.

Chrissie's Southern drawl does a slow molasses drip. "What I *meant* was, you look strong and healthy enough to get up and offer your chair to a lady in need."

Jared jumps to his feet, flashing Chrissie his famous devastating smile. He helps her sit down.

"And is there anything else the lady needs?"

She gives him an angelic face. "I'd love some o' that bubbly water. I'd ask for a bourbon, but I'm tryin' to preserve my son's brain cells." She points to her belly. She is batting her eyelashes shamelessly at him.

As Jared takes off through the crowd, Chrissie waggles a couple of fingers at him.

"I think he likes you," I say.

She shakes her head. "I know his type. That boy would make eyes at a fire hydrant."

I introduce Chrissie to Mitzi. "Chrissie's an actress." I see Mitzi's eyes slide down to Chrissie's waistline. Tonight Mitzi's got these rhinestone eyeglasses on a stick. She brings them up to her face, squinting through them, looking from the belly to me, and back to the belly.

"Well, haven't *you* been busy?" Mitzi glares at me through the glasses. I'm standing by her chair, as there are no other seats.

Chrissie announces cheerfully, "*I'm* the one who's been busy. Don't go lookin' to Ryan on this one!"

Mitzi gives a startled yelp of laughter as Jared returns.

"Your water." He shoots Chrissie a look that heats up the room by about twenty degrees. Beyond his perfect profile, an older former A-list actress grips the stem of her martini glass until I'm afraid she's going to snap it in half.

Chrissie accepts the water from him. "Thank you," she says sweetly, putting it down without even taking a sip.

Jared pulls up an ottoman next to Chrissie. When he sits on it, he's looking up at her. "How do you know your baby's a boy?" he asks, picking up from where they left off.

Chrissie pulls the ultrasound photo from her bag and points to the evidence of little Michael's manhood. I've seen Chrissie flirt before, of course, but it's been with the busboys at Sal's Diner, amateurs who she could paralyze with a single look. Now, up against Jared, she's competing in the Flirting Olympics. She gives him a downward, sideways glance.

"My boy's a Taurus. Taurus men make great lovers." She looks him over. "When's your birthday?"

"March 29."

"Aries," Chrissie informs him. "You're passionate, but selfish. What do you say to *that*?"

"Me, selfish? I battled my way through a long drink line for you!" Jared makes it sound like he just swam the English Channel. "And I don't even know your name."

"Chrissie Valentino."

"Jared Abernathy."

"Very well then, Jared Abernathy, I *might* buy the unselfish part. The passionate part you still have to prove to me."

"I'd be happy to prove it to you." Jared looks like he's ready to prove it right now.

I notice that Mitzi has been watching the two of them. In fact, a lot of people are sneaking looks at the big-bellied and beautiful lime-green girl who has Hollywood's It-Boy sitting obediently at her feet.

"She's really talented," I say in a low voice to Mitzi. "She needs a break. Can you find her some work?"

Before Mitzi can answer, I see my parents making their way through the crowd toward me at warp speed. Dad's face is red, his mouth set in a thin line. Behind him, Mom sways along on her stilt shoes, trying to keep up with him. They pull in beside me and stop, Mom's long earrings swinging like a pair of tether balls.

"People keep giving us the good news," my dad says.

I stall. "What do you mean?"

"We understand we have a grandchild on the way?" Mom and Dad both look at me as if to say, *we're waiting*.

I can't resist. My evil twin takes over. I step back, so my folks can look across Mitzi, to where Chrissie is sitting. "That's Chrissie," I say. The two of them inspect her with expressions of horror.

She looks about twenty months pregnant. She's telling a story. Her hands move through the air, and her face changes from one expression to the next, while Jared leans back on the ottoman, looking at her in this lazy, admiring way. Then she takes Jared's hand, palm up, and traces her finger across his palm, apparently describing what she sees there. He throws his head back and laughs out loud.

Dad's head whips around in my direction. *"Who is that?"*

"A friend of mine. I told you I was bringing her."

Mom, who is fuzzy on things under the best of circumstances, now looks like she's moving into panic mode. "Where's Emily? How long have you been seeing this other girl?" She cannot take her eyes off Chrissie's belly.

"Emily couldn't come tonight. She…"

"Who *is* this girl, Ryan?" Mom looks so upset that I step over and put my hand on her shoulder.

"See, that's what I'm trying to tell you…"

Roman Brandeis walks up. He's a talent agent who reps probably a quarter of the people in the room. "Doug!" Roman pumps Dad's arm. "I hear congratulations are in order!" My mom looks like she's going to faint.

Seeing us, Chrissie somehow manages to stand up. "Mr. and Mrs. Mills, it's a pleasure to meet you." She is sweet and bubbly, the perfect young lady. She sends a shower of sparkly energy in the direction of my father. "Mr. Mills, now I see where Ryan gets his good looks!"

Dad looks momentarily distracted, while Mom gives Chrissie the stink eye.

Then, although I wouldn't have thought it possible, the evening plunges even deeper into surrealism. Nat and Yancy walk up. They're looking back and forth from my parents to Chrissie.

"You're having a *grandchild?*" Yancy's voice scales up into incredulity.

No, you are, I think. But I can't tell them. This is another thing I didn't think of, that Nat and Yancy would be here tonight and would meet Chrissie.

Mom is twisting her hands together. "I can't believe you broke up with Emily!"

"No, see…."

"She was such a nice girl!"

"Mom…"

"I want an explanation," my dad yells.

"Well, I…"

"Now!"

"Dad…"

"It's not Ryan's baby!" It's Mitzi, who is looking disgusted. We all stare at her.

"How the heck would *you* know?" Dad asks.

"I've been paying attention!"

"To *what?*" It's the first time I've ever seen my dad look confused.

"Just forget it. It's not Ryan's baby."

Mom and Dad visibly relax, but Mitzi has other things on her mind. "Now, listen to me!" She grabs Dad and Nat by the arm and whispers to them. They look at Chrissie and Jared like they're totally checking them out. Nat's nodding. Meanwhile, Chrissie turns a little pale and sits down suddenly, while Jared quickly hands her the water glass. He grabs a magazine from the coffee table and fans her.

"It's just the heat in the room," she says.

"I'll take you out for some air." Jared navigates her through the crowded living room, leaving a huge wake behind them. They disappear through some French doors out to the patio.

"Where'd you find this girl?" Mitzi says in my ear.

"The tennis club," I tell her. "She can do any accent you ask for. She can do comedy. She's hilarious."

"When's she due?"

"May 12."

Mitzi has already inspected Chrissie from top to toe. "All her size is in her belly. She should be thin again by September."

"Without question," I tell Mitzi, even though I'd never given it a second thought until this moment. Then I ask, "What's in September?"

"That's when we shoot the scenes with Roxanne in *Mystery Moon.*"

"Roxanne?" I am trying to remember. They had talked about it at dinner one night.

"The role I've been trying to cast, the girl in *Mystery Moon*." Mitzi half-turns to include Dad and Nat in the rest of the conversation. "I want to audition Chrissie for Roxanne."

• • •

The next morning, Emily calls me from San Francisco. "We won, Ryan! We won the state competition."

"You're kidding! That's terrific." It's Sunday morning, and I'm in bed, half awake. I sit up, running my hand through my hair and yawning.

"We go to the Nationals in June! You're still picking me up at the airport, right?"

"Oh! Yeah, sure." I confirm it's three o'clock at LAX and hang up.

That afternoon, I pull up to baggage claim curb at LAX to find Emily waiting. Her cheeks are really pink, and she starts right in talking as soon as she sees me.

"It was so much fun! I wish you could have been there." She tells me about it on the way home, while I listen, saying things like "Uh huh," and "Sounds good." I can't focus right now. I'm trying to figure out how I'll get my Spanish paper written and get Chrissie to her next check up on the same afternoon.

"So how was your dad's party?" she asks finally.

"Good."

I can sense that she's waiting for more. "That's all? I mean, who was there? What happened?"

I can't make myself say that I brought Chrissie. So I tell her what I can, which isn't much, thinking that I hate this. I hate keeping stuff from Emily. *So don't do it. Tell her,* a voice inside me says. I finish with, "I'm sorry I couldn't fly up to hear you sing. But, you know, my dad's birthday..."

"It's okay. I'm sorry I couldn't make the party."

There's nothing more I can say after that, so I drop her at her house and drive home.

Chapter Thirty-Seven

Emily and I are in the guest house, studying after an hour of hot, heavy breathing sex. I'm in a pair of old sweat pants, and she's wearing one of my t-shirts.

"I like wearing your shirt. It makes me feel like I'm your girl," she says.

"You are." I run my hand down her bare leg.

Since we discovered the guest house, we've spent almost every afternoon holed up there—during the week anyway—alternating between doing our homework and fooling around.

I think of those rockets that travel up into the sky, silently and almost invisible except for the tiniest trail of light, and then explode into giant sunflowers of color, with later explosions of different colors careening away in little squiggles, and deep reverberating booms. That's what sex in the guest house is like.

It's the most fun I've ever had indoors.

Lucky for us, both Wintraubs work, and my house is usually empty during the week. Weekends are different, but on weekdays, work, appointments and lessons keep my parents, Ro, and the girls away until close to six o'clock. I hang the baseball cap on the front door knob of the guest house to ward off the cleaning and maintenance staff.

I'm studying, and Emily's curled up in a corner of the sofa with her laptop. Outside, rain falls in heavy sheets. It pounds the roof over our heads. Emily loves the rain, but I think rain belongs in places like Michigan and the Amazon. I must have been born under a sun sign.

"Ryan?" Emily says to me, "How come you're so distant with

your folks? I never see you act that way with anyone else—so, kind of, cool and withdrawn."

"Where did *that* come from?" It isn't like we'd been talking about them, or anything.

"I've noticed it. And, well, your parents asked me about it, too."

I jump to my feet and start pacing back and forth. "They *did*? When?" It doesn't take much to get me going over Mom and Dad. Heat rushes to my forehead and temples.

"The last time I was here for dinner." Emily's been over a few times now.

I can't believe they've been bugging her about this. Like, *hello*, I live right here in the same house with them. What about having a conversation with *me*? "Yeah, well I'm pissed off at them!"

Emily is waiting, wearing her *I'm listening* expression.

"First off, they totally shafted us three years ago, when Michael overdosed." My finger stabs the air as I make each point. "Second of all, they're freaking *never* home. It's like they're doing us a favor to have dinner with us!"

Emily has put aside her laptop, her expression sober.

"You should tell them how you feel," she says. "Because, your parents are two sad people."

"They oughta be. They oughta be two *sorry* people!" Anger is boiling up through my belly and chest and into my face. I feel myself flush red, and I take a few deep breaths.

"You really should talk to them," Emily says again. "Clear the air."

"I'll think about it." I sit down next to her, and we try to work. As usual, I'm diddling around with my easy homework from the regular classes, while Emily's writing this intense essay for her AP English class and studying for another hard-core AP History exam.

She yawns and stretches her arms toward the ceiling. Her hand goes through my hair, and a minute later she pulls me toward her and really plants one on me—a serious soul kiss that has me thinking it might be time for another study break. But a question bubbles up from some dark part of my subconscious.

"Emily? Why do you love me?"

She pulls away from me a little and gives me this teasing look. "You want to know the exact moment when I knew I loved you?"

I nod my head. I definitely want to know that.

"It was the time you made me laugh so hard that I fell off the couch."

I do make Emily laugh. A lot. And most of the time, it's on purpose. And she did fall off the couch that one time, when I really got her going, but I didn't think she would love me for it.

"I need something better than that."

"Okay, let's see. I love you because you're fun. And because you're good to me, and you're always there for me."

She pauses. "And because you're really, really hot."

I don't know if *I'm* hot, I think, but Emily and I are definitely hot together.

"And so now *I* have a question," she says. She starts to put the cap on her pen, then fumbles and drops it.

I wait for her to pick it up off the floor, cap the pen, put it away, and finally face me.

"How do I know that you love me for *me*, and not for my looks?"

There's a good answer for that question, but it's hard to put into words. I finally say, "I feel good around you. I can be myself." I think some more. "But the other part is, you make me better than I am. I can't describe it. When I'm with you, I feel like I can do anything. Does that make sense?"

"Yes," she says. She puts her head on my shoulder. I pull her close and curl up with her on the sofa, thinking *this is as good as it gets.* Right here. Now. This moment.

We sit there for a long time, listening to the rain.

• • •

That evening, my cell rings, and it's Chrissie. "I'm in the hospital."

"*What!*" I jump up from my sprawl on the bed. "Why? What happened?"

"I started to bleed. Jay and Spencer brought me here," she says. "But the baby's fine."

I look at my watch. It's seven o'clock on a Tuesday night. "Which hospital? I'll be right there."

Forty-five minutes later, I'm standing beside her hospital bed. A blue curtain cuts across the middle of the room, giving us privacy from Chrissie's roommate, who's by the window. Jay and Spencer, in ratty t-shirts and gym shorts, take up the only two chairs in sight.

"*You* tell him," Spencer says. He fans himself with his hand.

"We were in the laundry room of our building, and Chrissie comes in," Jay says. "And we were talking about how to get chocolate stains out..."

"Because they're the *worst*," Spencer says.

"And then I started to bleed on the floor," Chrissie cuts in. She's propped up in bed in a hospital gown, her blond curls spilling across her shoulders. She has one arm around her pregnant belly, like she's protecting it.

"Why? What's wrong with you?"

"The doctor called it a ... an eruption," she says.

"An *abruption*..." Spencer starts to say, but Jay cuts him off.

"It's called a placental abruption. It means the placenta has separated from the wall of the uterus."

"How serious is that?" I ask. I sit on the edge of the bed, since there's nowhere else available. Jay has his arm across the back of Spencer's chair.

"Mine's a small separation." Chrissie raises her chin. "It might even heal on its own. I'm fine. I'm goin' home tomorrow."

"*Excuse me,* may I get a word in?" Spencer says. "She has to go on bed rest."

"What? For how long?" I demand.

"Not long," Chrissie announces. Her voice is calm, but her arm tightens around her belly.

"For as long as it takes!" Jay says. "Could be for the rest of the pregnancy— as much as ten weeks."

"Ten weeks?" I say. "That's two and a half months!"

"But it could also heal, in which case I could get up," Chrissie says. "I don't want to miss the audition, Ryan!"

"We'll see. Until it does heal, she *has* to stay in bed," Spencer says, giving her a meaningful look. "All the time!"

"So, you can't work?" I ask her. "Or go out of the apartment?"

"No!" Jay and Spencer say it at the same time.

"That doctor was over-reactin'." Chrissie waves her hand in the air.

"Look, we talked to the doctor," Jay says to me. "This is really serious."

"What do you mean?"

"I mean, if she doesn't stay in bed and this abruption thing gets worse, she could die, and so could the baby."

Did he say *die*? Panic swarms me. I'm a sixteen year old kid. I didn't sign up for this. Or maybe I did sign up for this, but I didn't know what I was doing. I start taking deep breaths, trying to stay calm.

"We'll help you, honey," Spencer says to Chrissie. He moves over and sits on the edge of the bed beside her, putting his arm around her shoulders.

My thoughts are racing. *The baby could die.*

It would be like Michael dying twice.

"How will you pay your rent?" I ask.

"I got it covered. I have a call in to our landlord, Mr. Park."

"Good luck with that," Jay says in an ominous tone.

"No, I can sweet talk him." Chrissie sounds very sure of herself. "He likes me. I just paid this month's rent, and I'll tell him to keep my security deposit. I'll hold him off for anythin' else I owe with fried chicken and banana cream pies. He loves my cookin'!"

There's a plan. Pay your rent with banana cream pies.

"Chrissie, you have to tell Nat and Yancy." I try to catch her eye, but she avoids me. "This is serious. You need their help."

"I told you before – NO!"

"But, Chrissie…"

"I gotta get outta here!" She throws off her sheet and blanket and tries to move past Spencer to get off the bed, but he pins her down. "You're not going anywhere, Missy!"

I just know it—she's going to run off and die and kill the baby, and it'll be my fault, just like with Michael. "I won't tell them!"

She sinks down. "You promise?"

"Swear to God." I'm thinking frantically. It looks like she's got her rent covered for now. I get a big cash allowance every month from my parents. It could go for some of her other expenses.

"Ryan?" Chrissie asks. "My place is only five minutes away. These guys have been here all afternoon. Would you mind picking up a few things for me? The clothes I was wearing are ruined, and

I need something to wear home tomorrow."

"No problem." I walk out with Jay and Spencer. "I don't know what to do," I tell them. "I live a half hour from here, and I have school and other stuff."

"We'll help. We love Chrissie," Jay says, while Spencer nods his head.

I get their phone numbers and follow them to the apartment building, where I let myself into Chrissie's place with the key she gave me. It's nine forty-five by now.

I flip on a light and look around. It's weird being here all by myself. In my jeans pocket, I find the list she wrote for me. Pants, blouse, underwear, bra. Jeez.

I go through her drawers. I am numb, unable to think about what all this means, how it will affect me, what might happen if I mess up. The last time I messed up, a friend died. Now it could happen again.

I focus on the job in front of me. Chrissie wears tiny, lacy little thongs in pink and red and black. I try not to look, but of course I do. Seems like she needs something to sleep in, but I don't see anything that looks like that. No nightgowns or even a big t-shirt. Maybe she sleeps in the nude.

Too much information. In my back pack I have a size extra-large Pacific Prep athletic shirt – a clean one. I'll give her that.

I'm in Chrissie's little bathroom when I see the clock on her wall. I get a prickling sensation on the back of my neck. At the exact moment that my mind registers that it's ten o'clock, my cell rings.

I don't have to look to know it's Emily, for our regular good night call. For a split second, I consider not answering it. But I don't want to sneak around and lie. I pick up.

"Hi." Her voice is warm and breathy in my ear. I stand there in the bathroom, looking at Chrissie's perfume bottles and trying to sound normal as I speak.

"Hi. What's up?" I say.

"I'm in bed already," Emily says. "What about you?"

"Well, funny thing," I say, eyeing the shelves. "I'm at Chrissie's place."

Silence greets me on the other end. I rush to fill it, explaining what happened and what I'm doing. As I talk, I look around. I've never been in a girl's bathroom before, except for Mom's, which doesn't count. Chrissie's got this arsenal of girl products: lipsticks, bottles of nail polish, and glass containers with cotton balls, nail files and cruel-looking pointy little scissors.

"You're packing up *clothes* for her? Like *personal things*?"

"Just a few things." I try not to think of that purple bra and panty set that caught my eye.

"Ryan, this is getting really weird."

"Tell me about it." I'm looking at Chrissie's nail polishes, which are at eye level.

"Why do *you* have to do this? Talk to Nat and Yancy. They can get her a nurse."

"I'm afraid what Chrissie would do if I did." Some marketing dude must have been hungry when he made up the names of these polishes: *Raspberry Mist, Strawberry Swizzle, Peachy Keen.*

"Honestly, Ryan. She's holding you hostage."

"She doesn't mean to. She's just scared. The neighbors are going to help."

"What a mess! It's too much responsibility!"

"Maybe, but what am I supposed to do?"

"Get a grown up to handle it!"

"Well, I can't, Emily, okay?" I'm losing patience now. "I gotta finish here. I'll talk to you tomorrow."

"But, Ryan...," she is saying as I hang up. I didn't mean to hang up on her, but I had to go. I still have to take this stuff to Chrissie, and I've got a test tomorrow that I have to study for. Chrissie can't even get up for a glass of water, and it could go on this way for a couple of months. And she or the baby could *die.*

Emily's right. It's too much for me to handle.

What am I going to do?

Chapter Thirty-Eight

That night I lie in bed trying to breathe. It feels as if something bigger and heavier than me—like one of those giant Zamboni machines at the ice skating rink—is moving across my chest, crushing it.

My life is spinning out of control. I can't help Chrissie with this. I'm too young. I'm not ready.

I throw off the covers and go to the drawer with my ski clothes. I'm looking for the big manila envelope full of photos, but the box of drugs is on top. I pull it out and put it on the bed. After a minute, I open it and sit with it in my lap, looking at the envelopes of white powder.

Did Michael use to feel the way I do right now, that everything was screwed up and that it was all because of him? Is that why he did drugs? To make himself feel better?

In one minute, I could feel better. It's right here, relief in a bag, courtesy of the drug cartels.

I force myself to set aside the box and grab the envelope, pulling out the photographs and going through them. All those memories of Michael. I'm in a bunch of the shots, too. I find the one that Michael had labeled "Soldier Rock," showing me and Michael, dripping wet, coming out of the lake. Our fists are raised in the air, and giant grins split our faces in half. I hold the photo for a long time, thinking and remembering.

Soldier Rock. It was one of the best moments of my life. And it happened because of Michael.

• • •

It was the summer we were eleven. A bunch of us at camp had broken the rules and sneaked over to Soldier Rock, which stood in Lake Evergreen, just far enough from the shore that you had to swim to get there. Most of us had climbed up to a ledge we used for diving that was probably a fifteen foot drop to the water.

But Michael had climbed to the top. He was maybe forty feet up from the lake. If a counselor had caught him up there, he would have been in big trouble.

"Come on down, Michael!" I yelled to him. "Dive from down here."

"It's awesome up here!" he yelled to me. "You gotta see this!"

As so often happened, I followed his lead. I half-crawled, half-climbed my way up, grabbing small outcroppings of rock and gripping with my toes, like some humanoid-gecko life form. Too late, it occurred to me that it would be awfully hard to go down the same way.

We could see the entire lake, the surrounding forest, and a backdrop of saw-toothed mountain peaks. An eagle floated by, very close, and Michael and I stared at it, following it with our eyes until it arrived at a messy bunch of branches and twigs in a tree some two hundred yards away.

"Look, it's got a nest!" Michael said.

The others were yelling to us. It was time to go. One by one, they dove into the water and swam to the beach where our backpacks lay. I looked at Michael, and he was laughing at me.

"Only one way down," he challenged me. We peered over the edge. Huge boulders surrounded the rock, poking up out of the water. It looked like we were a million feet in the air. I leapt back from the edge, gasping.

"*Jeez*, Michael!" I was practically shouting. "What're we gonna do?"

"We're gonna jump," he said.

"We can't jump! We're gonna *die!*"

"Look." He pointed down. "All we have to do is aim for that patch of deep water. See?"

I followed where his finger was pointing. "There are *big rocks* down there!"

"So, we jump past them. We can do it." Michael said it like he was suggesting a walk on the beach. He stood there in his swim trunks, with his sunstreaked hair, already starting to look studly at age eleven, while I pictured our lives coming to a swift end on the boulders down below.

"I can't do this," I said.

"Sure you can. You're a beast."

There was no choice, other than waiting to be helicoptered off the rock by a rescue squad of grown-ups. I decided I would rather die.

"On the count of three," he said.

I tensed up. The rock felt hot and rough under my bare feet.

"One, two, three..." Together, we ran across the top of the rock and jumped. I remember the rush of air, the slap of my legs hitting the water, plunging down, down, down into the green depths, then fighting my way to the surface, breaking free of the water with a huge intake of breath, Michael bobbing up beside me, and then the cheering of campers on the beach as we paddled for shore and struggled out of the lake. One of the guys took a Polaroid of us, arms raised over our heads, exhilarated by our incredible leap.

The word spread between the kids at camp. No one that we knew had ever been brave enough to jump off the top of Soldier Rock. For the rest of the summer, Michael and I were gods, secret heroes among the campers, unbeknownst to the counselors.

And I owed it all to Michael. When I tried to tell him that, he brushed it off. "I knew you could do it," was all he said.

For me and Michael, "Soldier Rock" became our mantra for those times when life really sucked, or when it seemed like we were completely screwed. When we got caught toilet papering the Hathaway's cactus garden, that time we got lost hiking on the mountain up at camp, and even when my dog Jasper died, one or both of us would say, "Soldier Rock!"

It meant *If you can jump off Soldier Rock, you can handle anything.* But it meant more than that, too. Although we didn't say it, Michael and I both knew that when you jumped off of Soldier Rock with someone else, you were going to be friends forever.

Soldier Rock. They were the last words Michael ever said to me.

Feeling suddenly really tired, I slide the photos back into the envelope. I replace it in the drawer along with the box of white powder and climb into bed. But I still can't sleep.

I lie there for hours, looking at the ceiling, while the giant Zamboni machine returns and does a slow parade across my chest.

Chapter Thirty-Nine

Jay and Spencer meet me outside Chrissie's door late the next afternoon. This morning, while I was at school, they brought her home from the hospital. When Chrissie opens the door, Spencer screeches at her.

"What are you doing out of bed?"

"Lettin' y'all in." Chrissie looks as tired as I feel. Four hours of sleep has turned my brain into oatmeal.

"I gotta to go to the bathroom," she says, leaving us alone.

"She's still on her feet!" Spencer moans.

"We've gotta make a schedule," I say. Someone has to check Chrissie every few hours to see what she needs. All errands, shopping, and food preparation have to be done for her.

"Where do you guys work?"

"I go to Cal State Northridge during the day," Jay says. "and tend bar at night. Spencer works at Bloomingdale's."

"Fine linens and towels. Afternoons and evenings," Spencer says.

"Don't worry," Jay says to me. It turns out one of them is usually home in the morning, so they can check in on Chrissie regularly and help her up until about two in the afternoon.

Chrissie comes back from the bathroom and climbs into bed. "Juanita in 401 said she would help, too."

We call Juanita, who's a nurse at the same hospital we took Chrissie to. She can take weekends. The three of them will help with Chrissie's groceries and errands.

Which means that I'm responsible for Chrissie Monday through Friday, from whenever I can get there until bedtime.

I go into shock. *Every day during the week.* Images run through my mind. The guest house. Hot sex in the bedroom. Spooning together on the sofa. Emily, her hair ruffled, padding around bare legged in one of my t-shirts. Studying together side by side.

The hours we spend after school in the guest house are our favorite times together. We can't go there on weekends, because my family's usually home then.

Gone. Emily will kill me. *I'll* kill me.

"I can't do this." It takes a minute before I realize I've spoken aloud.

"You don't have to," Chrissie says. "I'll be fine in the afternoon by myself."

"You will not!" Jay says. "You need someone here."

"It's okay. I'll be here," I say. I can still take Emily home after school. I'll just have to drop her, then go straight to Chrissie's. The fact that Emily lives south of school and Chrissie lives north of it, and that dropping Emily will add an hour every day to my travel time, are not important.

I'm glad I can get her home every day. I try not to think about the other part, that all trips to the guest house are off, at least for now.

• • •

"So you're just going to let it all go?" Emily says. "Us? Our relationship?" We are sitting in my car, parked in front of her house.

"No! We'll still have lunch together. I'll still take you home from school. And see you on weekends. And on the East Coast trip in May. And this summer in England." *Please understand.*

She crosses her arms in front of her. "You'll take me home from school, then five days a week go off to play nursemaid to some *blonde flirt* you barely know?"

"Who means nothing to me. Emily, she could *die.* The baby could die. How can I walk away from that?" My hands clench and unclench themselves on the steering wheel.

"How are you going to help her? You're not a doctor. You're not her husband. You're practically a stranger to her." Emily shakes her head in frustration. "She should be asking her friends and family to help her—or a medical person. Not *you*."

Chrissie's other options don't matter to me. *I'm* the bad karma guy. *I'm* the one with the debt to repay.

"What about us?" Emily asks again.

"It's just for a few months. And then we have England." I put my hand on her shoulder and then touch her hair, but she pulls away.

"You think this is going to end with the pregnancy? What's she going to want from you next?"

I don't know. I'm just trying to get the baby born. But I can see why Emily's mad at me. I'm a bad friend. I failed Michael, and now, in trying to make it up to him, I'm failing Emily.

I'm a loser, a person who means well and tries hard, but who in the end messes up everything he touches. I'm bad news. No matter what I do, I hurt people.

I sit there, paralyzed, unable to speak.

"Ryan, say something!"

My whole life I've never been anything much. A guy with average talent who doesn't work very hard. A person who slides by.

Emily's voice continues, but only random phrases pierce through the fog around me. *Nat and Yancy need to know. This girl's manipulating you. Too much responsibility. You're only sixteen.*

Only one thing is clear to me. *No one is ever again going to die because of me.* This baby—and Chrissie—are going to live. Or if they don't, it won't be because of anything I did or didn't do.

"I'm sorry," I finally tell Emily. "I'm sorry for everything."

Chapter Forty

I'm driving with Emily after school, thinking how much it sucks that I have to take her home. When we pass the turn-off to go to my house, I can almost feel my steering wheel try to veer in that direction, as if my car wants to go to the guest house as badly as I do.

"So how was your day?" I ask.

"Fine." She's looking out the window.

"Did you see my note?" Since we have each other's combinations, I've started leaving notes and cards in her locker, trying to cheer her up. Today I taped a hand printed piece of paper saying "I heart you" to the inside of the door.

A dimple shows in her cheek for a second then disappears. "Yes. It was sweet."

Silence. A minute goes by.

"Oh, come on, Emily, talk to me!" I can't stand feeling awkward and uncomfortable with her, when it used to be so easy.

She pushes out a sigh. "Okay. I was looking online. Didn't you say Chrissie's starting her third trimester? Of the pregnancy."

"Yeah."

"Well then she's going to start seeing the doctor twice a month, instead of once."

"Oh." More bad news. Just what I need.

She looks at me sideways. "I'll have to get Derek to cover those days, too."

"Okay." Does despair have a taste? There's a bitter flavor in my mouth that's new to me. Maybe it's depression.

We reach her house, and I grab her hand before she can get out of the car. "Emily, come with me to Chrissie's! You can bring your books, and we'll study together."

She pulls her hand back. "I don't feel comfortable doing that! I don't have the time. And I've got all these extra Songbirds rehearsals for the Nationals."

"Maybe just once or twice? You could get to know Chrissie."

"No! There's no point, Ryan, and I feel really weird about it."

"But Emily—"

"I need to go now." She gets out of the car and leaves me there alone.

• • •

I bring my books and laptop to Chrissie's every day.

"I have to study while I'm here," I tell her, and she agrees.

So I do study, in between getting Chrissie snacks and glasses of water, doing her laundry, running to the post office, and keeping her entertained. The last thing is, for her anyway, the most important.

"I'm goin' nuts, Ryan! If this abruption doesn't kill me, the bed rest will!" She shifts around in her bed, stretching her arms and legs, and staring out the window to the sunny day outside.

"You can do it." I try to sound soothing, but I know I'd be pathological if I were stuck in here every day, unable to move.

I try to find ways to make Chrissie less miserable. I bring her library books, as well as DVDs from my dad's huge library containing almost every movie ever made. I download game software onto her laptop and help her find a cheap long-distance telephone package so she can call home to South Carolina as often as she wants. I bring her take-out food and play cards with her. I bring her jokes.

Just stay in bed and don't die.

Then I arrive to find her climbing up on a step stool to catch a spider.

"You've got to stay in bed!"

"But the spider…!"

"I'll get it for you."

She doesn't want to hurt it, so I have to capture it and put it outside. When I come back in, she says, "Ryan, do me a favor. Take a picture of me so I can send it to my momma and show her my bump." She's wearing her bed rest uniform—my extra-large Pacific Prep t-shirt, which used to be huge on her, but now grips her belly like sausage skin.

I use my cell phone to photograph Chrissie, standing sideways in my t-shirt, then take another shot of her from the front, and hand her the phone. She sends them off by email.

"There we go," she says. "To Darnell Fellars in South Carolina!" Then, as the phone vibrates in her hand, "I'll answer it for you!" She starts to punch the "Talk" button.

I dive at her and grab the phone away. Is she crazy? How does she expect me to keep her secret if she starts answering my phone? Scowling at her, I take the call.

"Ryanito?"

"Oh, hi, Ro." I hate lying to my family, but I have to if I want to keep the news of the baby from Nat and Yancy. "It's gonna be another late night. This project's a bear."

"Mmm." She clearly doesn't believe me.

"I wanna talk to him!" It's Maddy in the background. A few seconds later, she's on the line. "You're copying Mom and Dad now," she says. "When are you gonna be home for dinner?"

"One of these days soon," I promise and sign off.

Chrissie's still standing next to me. Why won't she just do what the doctor says?

"Get back into bed! Chrissie, you're totally freaking me out."

"I don't know why y'all are making such a fuss," she says, settling herself against her pillows, "I'm gonna start gettin' up. I don't care what those doctors say."

A slow burn starts in my chest. I'm losing my girlfriend over this. And not just any girlfriend – it's The Only Girl I Will Ever Love. I haven't had sex for three weeks, which bothers me ten times more than all those years of virginity ever did. It's amazing how fast I got used to having regular sex. For a while there, I was ranking it right up there with oxygen.

Not only that, but I'm busting my tail to earn the A's I need to qualify for the Senior Honors Project. I stay up until one and two in the morning studying, and it's harder and harder to concentrate. I missed a math assignment yesterday and will have to do double work tonight to make it up.

And now Chrissie's being a pain in the ass. The slow burn speeds up.

"Hey," I demand. "How come your mom or one of your sisters can't jet out here and help a little?"

Chrissie's eyes get big and round. "For your information," she says, "Poor people don't jet around much. My sisters have more children and more problems than they know what to do with. My momma has a good job, which she *needs*, because she's helping the other girls right now. I've always been the one who didn't need help."

"But now you do."

"I know, and she *will* help me. But not right now. She knows I can manage for a while without her. I always do."

"Yeah, you're managing because *I'm* giving up my life to help you!" I'm standing in the middle of her one and only room, towering over her as she sits on her low bed.

She launches a volley up in my direction. "Well, don't do it if you don't want to!"

"You asked for my help!"

"Just drivin' me to the doctor. I didn't ask you to come here every day."

"But you needed the help."

"True. But I only want help from people who wanna give it. If y'all are gonna start fussin' with me, forget it. I don't need that negativity in *my* life!"

We glare at each other.

"So, go!" she says. "Go to your girlfriend!"

I can't. I'm tied to her by Michael's death and by this little unborn kid.

"I mean it! Go on!"

"Don't be ridiculous. You're way over-reacting." I sit down on the edge of the bed. "I brought you a new mix," I say, handing her a CD. "Country western."

I stay at Chrissie's that night until eight o'clock and study until two in the morning. Emily calls me, but we only talk for a minute. I've got two missed assignments to make up and a test to study for, when all I want to do is fall into a coma and sleep for twenty-four hours straight.

185

Chapter Forty-One

Emily and I still have lunch, but not every day. "I need to see my girlfriends, too, sometimes," she says. We are mainly silent during our rides home in the afternoon.

On Friday I leave a card in her locker that says "I love you this much" over a picture of the Grand Canyon.

A lot of good it does me. She cancels our date Saturday night, because she has a headache.

Then, going home Monday in my car, she lobs a grenade at me. "My carpool will let me rejoin," she tells me. "They had replaced me, but the VanderBergs just bought a seven-seater, so there's room for one more."

"You don't want to ride with me anymore?" My whole face is numb, which is good, because otherwise I'd cry and make an ass out of myself.

She smooths her hands down her skirt, as if she's smoothing out wrinkles, although I don't see any. "It's just that they have an opening now, and who knows what else Chrissie's going to ask for? Maybe next week you'll tell me you can't take me home at all anymore, and then I really be stuck."

"I'll keep taking you home," I say, but then I think, what if Emily's right? What if things get even worse?

"Also," she says, "This makes no sense. You're driving an hour out of your way every day to take me home."

"I *want* to spend that time with you! I love you!" Then, I wait, hoping. A long moment passes until....

"I love you, too," she says.

In a rush of emotion, I jerk my steering wheel and pull over to the curb, almost clipping a pickup truck in the lane next to me. The truck fishtails as the driver punches his brake to the floor, trying to avoid me.

"Sorry!" I call out.

The truck, which has slid by my parked car, starts to back up. Fast.

Crap.

The driver pulls parallel to me, screaming in a voice straight from a horror movie. *"You cut me off, freak!"*

"I'm really sorry, man!" I know better than to mess with a guy in full-blown road rage. If I antagonize him, he could pull out a machete and slice me in half.

He's still screaming, spit flying from his mouth, while his face turns the color of a ripe tomato. He claws for his door handle.

Emily and I sit there, not moving so much as an eyelash. With cars on three sides of us, we can't drive away. That's one thing about convertibles. When you've got the top down, it's hard to escape a guy like this.

Fortunately, rage seems to have reduced his fine motor abilities. He still hasn't gotten his car door open.

Seeing the fear on Emily's face, I think fast.

"You got any bags?" I say. "My girlfriend's about to throw up!"

His rant comes to a stop as his eyebrows knot together in confusion. "Bags?"

"Yeah. Or like maybe a bucket?"

He peers over at Emily, who claps a hand over her mouth. That decides him.

"Learn how to drive, dude!" He floors it, peeling out of there with a squeal of tires.

Emily and I sit there for a long moment, treasuring the fact that we're still alive. Finally I turn to her. "What a prick."

She starts to laugh, and so do I. "I can't believe you asked him for a bucket!" She wipes her eyes.

"It was all I could think of." I put my hand on her knee and lean toward her, and for a couple of seconds we're happy again, but then both of us remember, and now neither of us is laughing.

Desperation sets in. "Emily, don't go back to the car pool. Please?"

Her eyes fill with tears. "I'm sorry, Ryan. I have to."

"Why?"

She just shakes her head again. "I'm really sorry."

After a minute, I start the car and drive her home. I feel as if that Road Rage Guy had in fact taken out a machete and run it right straight through my heart.

. . .

Today Chrissie's reading a book called The Complete Book of Pregnancy From A to Z.

"Jay and Spencer got it for me," she announces. "They're such worry warts."

"Can I see it?" I take the book and open it. I talk and move on autopilot, as I've been doing ever since Emily stopped letting me take her home. I look and act normal. No one knows that I'm really the walking dead. A zombie, smothered under an avalanche of grief.

"Do you think Mitzi will wait for me?" Chrissie asks. "I'll be able to audition soon, if she doesn't cast the role first."

"I'll talk to her," I say, paging through the book. It is almost five hundred pages long. In careful, alphabetical detail, it explains The Things You May be Worried About in Pregnancy.

"Look at all these things you're supposed to be worried about!" I point to the Table of Contents, which runs for several pages.

Chrissie peers at it. "It doesn't say I'm supposed to be worried. It says I may be worried." She tosses her hair. "Or, I may not!"

"Look at all this stuff." I point to the book. "Morning sickness. Swollen ankles. The pain of childbirth."

"You're a pain," she says, throwing a box of tissues at me.

I catch it. Too depressed to do anything else, I stand up and walk over to the bedside table, putting the box back in its place. I sit down again. "Just take care of yourself, okay?"

She gets a soft look in her eyes. "You're a sweet guy, you know that?"

I give her a mock sneer and put the book up in front of my face.

She reaches over and pulls it down. "Listen. Nothin' bad's

gonna happen to this baby. You know why?"

"Why?"

"Because this baby was put on earth for a reason, Ryan."

When I don't respond she says, "Think about it. I'd finally gotten a good job in Los Angeles. It was my first week workin' at the tennis club." She waves a hair clip at me, nodding in a knowing way.

"So it's nine o'clock, and just as I'm closin' up the Pro Shop, this beautiful boy walks in. And he persuades me to stay open so he can buy some racket strings."

I'll bet he did. I can see Michael flashing the old grin at Chrissie and making her feel like she was the hottest woman on the planet, because at that exact moment in time, he really thought that way himself.

"So then, he says, 'You gonna lock the place up?' And I do, except now he's convinced me to stay inside the shop, and then, well, we have *a moment,*" she says, her eyes widening.

"And I knew, right then, that there was something special about it. And after that, I knew I was pregnant." She gives me a wide, open smile. "And I was happy. I knew this baby was given to me for a reason."

Her smile fades. "And then he died. But he had left a baby behind. It was all meant to be."

"What do you mean, meant to be?"

"I mean," Chrissie says, after a pause, "that Michael was destined to die young, and I was destined to have his baby. And this baby is destined to do something important in the world. Like maybe …. run a bank." Chrissie nods at me as if to say "See?" and sips her water.

I feel a weight lift itself off my shoulders, floating in the air above me, as I consider her words. "You think Michael was destined to die young?"

"Absolutely."

It feels incredible, to let myself off the hook, to believe that Michael was supposed to die now, and that what happened had nothing to do with me and was just part of some larger plan. For a minute, I feel great again. But it's too easy. It's too convenient a way for me to sluff off the responsibility for what I've done. As I put

my books into a pile and start to gather up my papers, I feel the
weight of guilt and blame slowly settle back onto my shoulders.

Chapter Forty-Two

Jonathan and Calvin are standing on the golf course in day-glow golf shirts, plaid pants, and white shoes. To say they are giving me suspicious looks would be an understatement. Calvin keeps glancing around. He *knows* people at this golf club.

Sweat trickles down my back as my stars look to me, waiting for direction.

It has turned out that my "Physics Nerds Go Golfing" script sucks a big one. Lines that I thought were killingly funny when I wrote them now lie dead on the page. Not only that, my two actors cannot act.

A cold wave of terror runs over me. What made me think I could do this?

I force myself to sound cool and confident. "Let's improvise!"

"We have to make up our own lines, too? This is stupid!" Calvin frowns and looks over his shoulder for twentieth time, afraid of being spotted in orange and brown polyester.

"What am I supposed to say?" Jonathan tugs at the sleeve of his shiny shirt.

Now I'm the one who's improvising. "Jonathan, you're the new golfer who needs help with your swing. Calvin, you're the conceited golf pro." I move my camera into position and motion them to start. I suddenly remember when Jonathan and I did a skit in the sixth grade. "Do your cowboy voice."

I pray to the karma gods. *Please let this work.*

Jonathan, looking doubtful, takes on a fake deep bass voice, and improvises. "Howdy, pardner! How 'bout you showin' me a thing or two about that thar swing o' yers?" Jonathan's golfing cowboy, in his turquoise golf clothes, is unusual, to say the least, and bizarrely entertaining. Or maybe it's just bizarre.

I give Calvin the go-ahead. He has suddenly gotten the idea and is ready to wing it.

"My good man, your swing is in dire need of improvement," he croaks, in his best version of a golfing English butler.

While I hold my breath, they wander along in their newly invented characters, taking swings and cracking jokes that stink so bad I am sure we will clear the golf course. They get into it and really start working it.

Jonathan swaggers and says, "I reckon I larned me a lot about golf today!"

"Jolly good, old chap!" Calvin replies. "You're a real swinger now!" He gives a horrible, leering wink, one that would make little girls run screaming for their mothers. Then he and Jonathan collapse into laughter, overwhelmed by their own wit and star quality.

Standing there on the green, we look at some of the footage in the camera. It's unbelievably hokey and bad. Every joke's a groaner. It's odd, but strangely compelling.

I'm starting to breathe again. *Yes.* "I can work with this," I announce. "It's a wrap!" I go home seeing myself accepting the Oscar for Best Director, which Dad had won twice by the time he was forty.

Later that evening, my palms are sweating, and I'm considering an identity change. Anything to avoid facing my partners, who are counting on me. I'm taking a hard look at the footage of their improvised scenes.

I've got a half hour of Jonathan and Calvin talking funny and taking golf swings in bad clothes, but basically nothing that ties things together or makes sense as a story.

What was I thinking? I can't make a film with this. I've screwed up again.

What else is new?

• • •

Since I'm always at Chrissie's or studying or trying to make Emily happy, this is my first time at the tennis club in a month. I'm able to pick up a practice match with a good tournament player who beats me without breaking a sweat.

As the match ends, I look up and see Ben Swanson watching me. I raise my hand, and he nods, but he doesn't come over and speak to me. He's probably not interested in coaching me again. I don't blame him after what he just saw. Plus, I had a bad attitude the last time around. Why would he want me back?

I go home, lock myself in my room, and fall onto the bed. I can't even play tennis anymore. The one thing I was always good at.

I find myself thinking about Michael and the envelopes of white powder in my drawer. I take out a baggy of powder and study it. Pulling my laptop onto my stomach, I type into a search box. "What is it like to take cocaine?" One answer reads, "You feel really good and have lots of energy. But it's an empty feeling and doesn't last." Maybe that's how Michael experienced it, I think. Maybe that's why he went back to it this summer, because he felt empty inside.

I type more questions. "What's it like the first time you use cocaine?" "Can you take cocaine once and not get addicted?" "Does cocaine use lead to use of other drugs?"

As the owner of some cocaine, it's about time that I educated myself. I know I should just flush the stuff. But I don't. It seems like the key to Michael somehow.

I think of Chase standing at my locker. *Do you have anything of Michael's? He was supposed to get something for me.*

At the time, I didn't know what Chase was looking for, but now, of course, I do.

Chapter Forty-Three

My cell rings, and it's Spencer. I'm at home, because spring break has just started.

"Jay and I got a house-sitting job!" He's spitting out words machine gun-style. "In Malibu. This mansion on the beach. For a week."

He tells me they're going to take Chrissie with them. "It'll give her a change of pace."

Finally. Something good. I have a week off from both schoolwork *and* Chrissie duties.

I text Emily immediately with an invitation to the guest house. She answers back. *Can't. My nana's here. From Miami*

The woman who gave birth to Mr. Wintraub. If anything could put a damper on my life, that would be it.

ditch her

not that easy

I fume. I bet Emily could get away if she really wanted to. I go to the club and pound tennis balls all morning, come home, shower, and text Emily. No answer. I text her five times. Still no answer.

Screw it. I'll just go over there. I park in front of her house and run up the front walk. My nerves are tingling, because I've never just dropped in at the Wintraubs' house before. You don't do that to Mr. Wintraub. But it's a work day, so I figure that particular parental unit is out of the picture.

He opens the door.

"Ryan." It's all he says. His eyes glisten. His look says *fresh meat*.

"Oh! Hi. Is Emily there?" I shift around, shoving my hands in my pockets.

"Yes. But she said to tell you she's not available."

My mouth opens. *She said to tell you.*

He shuts the door.

I drive home, his words ringing in my head. *She said to tell you.* Is that true?

I text her twenty more times. No answer.

I can't believe this. But when I add it up with everything else that's happened, it makes sense. She's squeezing me out of the picture, little by little.

I've lost Michael, and now I'm losing Emily, two people that I've loved. It seems almost careless. It's one thing to lose a pair of socks or an umbrella, but I keep losing people. They're not as easy to replace.

I wish that road rage guy *had* slashed me into pieces with a machete. I wish I were dead, like Michael, so I could just lie quietly in the ground and get eaten by snails and beetles.

I hole up in my bedroom. Rosario is in Mexico visiting her relatives. Her niece Yolanda is here, treating my sisters with trips to Disneyland and Universal Studios. My parents have been gone even more than usual, due to a run of movie premieres, fund raisers, and other crucial events.

Without Emily or the daily routine of school and Chrissie, I stay up until two and three every morning, watching old films from my dad's DVD library. I create my own little Alfred Hitchcock film festival, watching a string of the psychological thrillers. Then, I put together and watch a series on The Films of Death Row.

By Day Four of the break, I still feel like an aircraft carrier is parked on my chest at night, making it hard to breathe. I've gotten thin over the last few months, and even I can see how bad I look— like a cadaver, white, with almost sunken cheeks and dark purple smudges below the eyes.

I get up and head for the library again. As I pass by the wet bar, something catches my eye. Through the glass door of the liquor cabinet, I see a label on a bottle. In an instant, I'm at Emily's party again, with Michael's arm clamped around my neck as I breathe in his whisky smell.

Jeez, Michael, get off me.

Stay here, man. Please.

I don't even stop to think. I grab the bottle and head back for my room. I lock the door, scrounge through the egg carton-sized freezer of my mini-fridge, and come up with a mini-tray of ice cubes. Jack Daniels on ice, taken straight out of my Pacific Prep travel mug. Just what I need.

I lie on the bed, getting hammered. I figure, if you don't like the state of your consciousness, then try an altered state.

I've never called Chase before, but I do it now.

"I've found something. In Michael's locker."

A pause. "Oh, yeah? What was it?" Chase's voice scales up in excitement.

"Is there some place private where we can meet?" I ask.

"My house."

"The stuff I found—is it all yours?"

"Half of it. The other half – well, I guess it's yours now." He pauses, then throws down a challenge. "Do you want to bring it by? Try a sample or two?"

"I'll be there in an hour."

• • •

"Mom, there's this guy at school named Chase. He's new this year. We're gonna hang out tonight at his house."

No fool, I've chosen Mom as the parent to receive this information.

"I'll be back tomorrow, okay? Maybe even the next day."

She just nods and says "Have fun, honey," so now I'm covered for up to forty-eight hours.

Chase lives in one of those mausoleum houses made of marble. I walk up a wide set of front steps to reach the front door, which is a polished black with a heavy brass knocker.

He opens the door barefoot wearing a stained sweat-shirt, the hair on the back of his head mashed into a weird cowlick. As he leads me past the stone lions and glittery chandeliers in his entry way and through other rooms, I catch sight of mirrors and dark wood and shiny fabrics with tassels and fringe.

In spite of all the designer furniture and lamps and stuff, the house is strangely free of human inhabitants. We pass through room after room, all empty and quiet. Between my two sisters, their friends, Rosario, all the work buddies Dad brings home, my parents' personal assistants, and our fleet of maids who continuously patrol for crumbs and dust particles, I'm used to having people around.

"Is anyone here?" I ask.

He shakes his head. "Just Dora. She's the housekeeper. She puts in ear plugs and goes to bed by eight."

"Where are your parents?"

"Fiji."

Chase locks the door to his bedroom, just in case one of the nonexistent people in the house might want to pay us a visit. Feeling like I've just landed on an alien planet, I watch him lay down lines of white powder on a mirror. Hunched over the white lines, he looks up with a big grin on his face.

"I can't believe you got hold of this," he says "I paid Michael, and then he was going to buy for both of us. But then he, well, he wasn't around anymore."

Chase has split up the wax bags from Michael's locker into two equal piles. He has put one pile away in a drawer and left the other out for me. "Your half," he says. I notice that the current evening's entertainment is coming from my half.

"Do I need to get a bill from my wallet?" I ask, thinking of how I'll get this stuff up off the mirror.

"Naw, I got straws," he says. Chase has his head down and has vacuumed up a line. He pushes the mirror over to me.

How did I get here? I've lost the people I loved, and am now hanging with a guy I can't stand, preparing to do something I've never wanted to do.

"Close one nostril with your finger," he says. "Breathe in through the straw with your other nostril."

Should I leave? My eyes flick over to the closed bedroom door. *You know where the exit is, Ryan.*

Seeing me hesitate, Chase pushes the mirror closer to me. "Don't be such a pussy."

I shoot him a scowl. "Just *chill*, okay?"

I could walk out of here right now, but if I stay, it's not because I give a flying fart about what Chase thinks of me. It's more as if a force has been pushing me toward the hidden box of white powder.

I need to understand why Michael did this, to become Michael, to become somebody else for a while. I need to leave the old Ryan behind.

I pick up a straw.

My nose and sinuses burn as I breathe in. I do one line, as Chase instructs.

"Now what?"

"We wait. Fifteen minutes maybe." Chase moves over to a wall of expensive sound equipment and slides in a CD. "A little Nirvana, to set the mood."

I'm really nervous now, not knowing what's going to happen. I'm starting to feel warm and heavy. "I've never done cocaine before."

Chase does a double take, although it's kind of in slow motion as the drug starts to kick in. He has a really weird look on his face.

"You dumb dick. This isn't blow," he says. "It's heroin."

• • •

The word *heroin* hits my conscious mind at the same time that the drug hits my bloodstream. It feels sort of like when you hold down the gas and brake pedals of a car at the same time: the car's generating all this internal energy, but it's not going anywhere.

I lie on Chase's bed, thinking *I'm in big trouble,* but I don't do anything about it. I'm on heroin, but it's fine. Everything's fine. The heavy feeling's pleasant, and it occurs to me that Chase isn't such a bad guy after all. All my feelings of fear and loss and grief evaporate. I feel so comfortable, so good in my own skin. Slowly, I begin to realize that I am powerful. Powerful enough to have anything I want. I am awesome. I am a beast. I can do anything.

Chase and I lie around in his room, laughing occasionally and talking. I am warm and have such a sense of peace. Chase feels like my best friend, like I've known him all my life.

But then I feel my stomach ball itself into a knot. I sit up, knowing something's wrong. Chase doesn't even lift his head. "Bathroom's that way." He points.

I run for it, or rather, I stagger and stumble for it. I reach the toilet just in time. I'm kneeling with my head in the toilet bowl. I'm there for, I don't know, a couple of minutes? A couple of hours? I hurl my guts out. Then, I lie on the floor, my cheek pressed against the cool granite.

My left calf itches, and I scratch absentmindedly, thinking *Heroin's not such a big deal.* But the itching spreads down my left leg and to my right. No amount of scratching will help. I am way too unsteady to stand. My whole body itches. I still want to throw up, but I want to scratch more. I tear at my skin with my fingernails, scratching and scratching. The itching's like nothing I've ever experienced. The high's almost gone, and now my whole body's hot, sweating like a pig. The palms of my hands itch. Then all of a sudden, I'm freezing, my teeth chattering.

I crawl on my hands and knees from the bathroom and somehow get to Chase's bed. He's on the floor. "You wanna do another line?" he mumbles.

"No, you go ahead," I hear myself say. I fall into a dark, deep well of sleep.

Chapter Forty-Four

I'm sleeping, but this rude person's interrupting me, waking me up. Lights turn off and on, doors creak open. A door accidentally slams. I'm in a bed, but I'm not sure where. I hear a distorted, bloated voice that turns into Chase's after a minute. Then, a second voice, a girl's. The girl and Chase are outside his bedroom, their voices getting louder as they get near.

I stir and try to lift my head off the pillow. I would call out, but my throat's so dry I can't make any noise.

"Where is he?" the girl is demanding. Then she's in the room and runs over to me, and I have died and gone to heaven because it's Emily who's there beside me, holding me and kissing my face and saying "Ryan, are you okay?"

"We have to call a doctor," she says to Chase.

"Negative. We call a doctor, we go to jail."

"But…"

"He'll be okay. He just needs time."

I slide off into sleep again.

• • •

I wake up to find myself in a strange bed spooning with Emily, both of us fully clothed. She's lying behind me, her face against my shoulders, one arm around my waist. At my first movement, she springs up to a sitting position beside me. I'm nauseated and my head's pounding. Slowly, I roll over onto my back.

I want to ask where we are, but I'm not up for the challenge.

"Chase gave us a guest bedroom," Emily says. She picks up a

damp cloth and smooths it on my forehead.

I try to sit up, then sink back into the pillows as my head pulsates. Emily tells me what happened. It's nine o'clock on Sunday evening, and I've been at Chase's for twenty-four hours. When Chase realized around three this morning that I was not coming down from my one line of smack according to any normal schedule, he checked my pulse and breathing and decided I was going to live and should just sleep it off. It was his own drug-addled way of caring, staying close by me for most of a day, checking my vital signs, but not calling 911, which would have resulted in inconvenient felony charges.

But by four this afternoon, Chase needed reinforcements. He had plans to go out tonight. So he called Emily with what he seemed to think was a reasonable request, that she come and spend the night taking care of me.

He must have told her I was dying, because she recruited Chloe to pick her up and cover for her. Emily's parents think she's sleeping over at Chloe's.

I finally get a question out. "Where's Chase now?"

"Gone." Emily's voice is matter-of-fact. "He'll be back really late. He didn't want to leave you alone, so he called me."

I'm gonna puke again. Luckily this guest bedroom has its own bathroom. I make it just in time. I push the door closed with my foot, not wanting to share the experience with Emily, but she follows me in and strokes my head and helps me over to the sink afterward, where I wash my face. She produces a toothbrush, has me brush my teeth, and helps me back to bed. Her hands are so gentle that I could do this forever, just stay here in this strange room letting Emily touch the small of my back and smooth my hair off my face.

Does she think I'm as big an idiot as I do? Sick as I am, I still manage to throw little glances at her, trying to read her expression. But I can't.

"Do you need to call your folks?" she asks.

I try to remember. When I was younger, I often stayed at Michael's two or three nights in a row, so Mom's used to it. I should probably check in with her, though, and confirm I'll be gone another night. But that means making a phone call and speaking normally. Right now, even the thought of it tires me out.

"Could you manage to leave her a message?" Emily asks.

I nod.

"I'll call her on my cell, just to see if she's answering or not. If she answers, I'll hang up. She won't recognize my phone number. If she doesn't answer, then you call right away and leave her an update."

It turns out Mom's not picking up, so I call her and croak out a brief message that I'll be home tomorrow.

"There," Emily says. "Now you're all set." She tucks the covers around me and sits down on a chair by the bed. We look at each other, both feeling how bizarre it is to be alone, the two of us, in a strange, empty house belonging to someone we barely know or like, who's not around anyway. And we're going to spend the night here to boot.

It figures, that the one time I get to sleep overnight with Emily, she's mad at me and I'm strung out on heroin. I yawn and my eyelids fall, no matter how hard I try to keep them up. With all the energy I have, I reach my hand out to her, and she takes it. Her eyes brim over.

"I was so scared. Why did you do this? You could have died."

"It was stupid," I say. "I wanted to know what it was like for Michael, I guess."

"Don't ever do it again."

"I won't," I promise, knowing I'm telling the truth. Whatever Michael saw in getting high is not clear to me. Then I have to rest, after the effort of all that talking.

Emily climbs into bed with me. "I hate not being with you," she says.

"Same here." Silence. "Emily?"

"Hm?"

"That day that I came to your house." I stop talking to rest for a second. "Did you really tell your dad you didn't want to see me?"

"What are you talking about?"

I tell her, as best as I can. With the drugs still in my system, I think I hear a two-second lag between the movement of my lips and the sound of my voice, like on a bad phone connection.

"Ryan, I didn't know! My dad never told me!"

202

"But you didn't return my texts."

"With Dad and Nana around, I was stuck doing all this family stuff. It was, well, it was hard." Her voice trails off.

"I'm really sorry I let you down. I didn't want the baby to die."

"I know."

We are holding each other's hands, and her face is close to mine on the pillow.

"Ryan?"

"Yeah?"

"I feel bad. I've been keeping away from you. I could have returned your texts."

"Why didn't you?"

"It's just that ... I'm not as strong as you are."

I must be hearing her incorrectly. "What do you mean?"

"I couldn't handle the whole Chrissie thing. It was so intense. A pregnancy, childbirth, life or death responsibility." She moves her hand on my arm. "I just wanted to be sixteen and think about my own stuff, you know?"

"Well, that's what I want, too."

"But you're helping her anyway. You're so good and strong and kind. I'm in total awe of you."

I didn't know heroin was a hallucinogen. But if it keeps producing scenes like this, I will take it every day.

"You're so amazing, Ryan. I'm sorry I ran away."

Maybe this really *is* happening. But I'm so tired. I try to keep my eyelids open, but they drop. We curl up together in the bed in Chase's guest room, our arms around each other.

"I don't want to be apart anymore. I've missed you so much," she says.

"Me, too." I drift off into sleep, thinking *I'm just glad she's here.*

• • •

"You're sure you're not addicted?" Emily asks me the next day. She's worried about that, although I'm not.

"That stuff was like bad seafood," I tell her. "One time, and you're off it forever."

I have the shakes for the next few days, if that can be called withdrawal. For me, though, the experience was mainly about being with Emily, about spending a night in bed with her, so wasted that I could hardly even think about sex more than three or four times, and then only theoretically. Feeling her love and strength lifting me up, her hands touching me, feeling safe and taken care of—if I were going to be addicted to anything, it would be Emily, not some powder in a plastic bag.

Although we're back together, Emily decides to stay in her carpool, so I still go straight to Chrissie's every day after school. It sucks that we can't meet at the guest house ever. I know better, though, than to suggest another round of car sex after our run-in with law enforcement.

Emily talks about our upcoming travels. "Boston's going to be incredible," she says one day in the park, as we sit there on the cold grass, shivering a little, my jacket spread around the two of us. "I want to visit as many schools there as I can."

"Yeah, it'll be good." I couldn't care less about Harvard or BU. I just want to sit next to Emily on every bus and airplane we take, especially if we can share a blanket.

"After the England program ends, it'd be so much fun if we could travel together in Europe," she says. "I wonder if there's a way we could do it?"

It *would* be awesome to travel around and see things with Emily, not to mention laying her down on foreign mattresses in six or seven countries, but I keep remembering that history program. I'd just as soon watch glaciers move as study William the Conqueror. I find myself thinking about the tennis club and the thought of maybe training with Ben again. If I really plunged in this summer and took it seriously, I wonder how far I could go.

Chapter Forty-Five

I'm in the Mills library with Jonathan and Calvin. While I stare blindly at our useless footage, the two of them sprawl in our big leather chairs, wearing cargo shorts and Timberland loafers and swigging Gatorade. Relaxed and confident in my leadership, they are jabbering about something incomprehensible.

"...find the vertical components of velocity and acceleration," Jonathan is saying.

They don't know that we're sunk. We have nothing to work with.

"...raising the plane degree shortens the distance," Calvin says.

Something in there cracks them up. They are both practically falling down, they're laughing so hard.

I close my eyes. They won't be laughing for long.

Get it together, Ryan. Failure is not an option.

What would Dad do?

I take a few deep breaths. You guys," I say, forcing myself to sound strong and confident, "let's brainstorm a little. See if we take this thing up to the next level."

"What do you mean? I thought you said our scenes were great," Calvin says.

"They are! That's why it might be cool to wrap a story around them."

I've seen my Dad on the set coaxing new scenes and better work out of tired writers and actors who just want to go home. The way he puts it is, *Don't require. Inspire.*

"You guys are the golf experts. When a swing's bad, what happens?"

"What happens? Well, the ball flies off where it's not supposed to go," Jonathan says.

"And?" I'm looking for something, anything, that might give us a direction to take.

"You could hit a bird," Calvin says.

Hit a bird. I start to smile. "Or a squirrel," I say.

"Or a golf cart."

"Or a little old lady!"

"So let's say Jonathan is a total menace on the golf course. Every time he swings, he hits something." I think for a minute. "So the golf course tells him he can't play there anymore until he improves his swing. And Calvin teaches him how. Jonathan is saved, thanks to his knowledge of physics. That's our story!"

Over the next week, we film the additional scenes we need, edit the footage, and argue about how to present the physics.

"It has to be clear and easy to understand," I tell them. "Think lowest common denominator. Think *me*. If *I* can understand it, we've got something."

The night before it's due, we hold a screening in the forty-seat Mills home theater. Besides the three of us, my dad, sisters, and Ro are there. Emily had wanted to come, but instead has to scramble to finish a history paper due tomorrow. Mom's at a yoga class.

As it runs, I watch with a director's critical eye. Jonathan careens around the golf course, swinging his club. His girlfriend Samantha, dressed as a little old lady golfer, does a comic crumple under the force of a runaway golf ball. A stuffed squirrel that I got from a props supplier goes flying out of a tree. I can hear my sisters laughing. When Jonathan runs for his life, chased all over the golf course by a cart and its angry owner, even my dad laughs.

I make a cameo appearance as a golf course official, palming a police nightstick and using an accent of my own invention to say, "I em effraid ve must revoke yoor golf course prifileges." Calvin demonstrates his perfect swings and explains the physics in his English butler voice. We include plenty of hard science, but it's clear and easy to follow. The film comes to an end, and I flip on the lights.

"It's awesome!" Jonathan says. "You even made Calvin look good!"

"You should look half so good, Takahara," Calvin replies with a smug grin.

"Great job, son," my dad says. "You made it work."

"You mean it?" Without my telling him, Dad knows the filming difficulties I was up against— inexperienced cast and minimal shooting time, not to mention the nonexistence of a script. I have actually directed a film—a cruddy little student film, but still, a film. And it was fun.

"Yeah," he says. "You have a good eye, good instincts. You should develop them."

Yes. Dad liked my film.

I stand there taking in this strange new feeling—I'm proud of myself—and thinking I could get used to this.

Then, guilt slams into me. It makes me sad to think that this good thing only came my way because Michael died.

• • •

"The doctor says I can go off total bed rest!"

"Really? Are you all healed then?" I'm driving Chrissie home from the medical clinic.

"I guess. I feel good. I'm rarin' to go."

"But don't you have to take it easy?"

"Yeah. That's why I'm only going back to the SaveWell part-time."

"You're going back to work? Don't you think you should kick back a little?"

"And do what for money? I already owe you so much I don't even wanna think about it."

"Then don't. I'll help you with money for now. They don't pay you jack at the SaveWell."

"That's why I need that audition, Ryan."

"I'll call Mitzi." She's casting two other films, plus going back and forth to New York for a TV series. "She's swamped, but I think she's had the Roxanne casting on hold since this happened to you."

"It's not too late, then?"

"I don't think so. I'll let you know."

· · ·

Now that I'm free from my afternoon shifts at Chrissie's, Emily has Songbirds rehearsal every day after school. They're gearing up for the National competition in June, and Emily's going to have a solo, which ups her practice time even more. I stay late every day to take her home, but the guest house becomes more and more of a distant memory.

Jonathan, Calvin, and I show our film to the physics class. The audience laughs in all the places I hope they will and claps when it's over. A couple of kids tell us that this is the first time they ever understood anything about physics.

"See, lowest common denominator," I tell my partners as we pack up to leave class. "If I can understand it, anyone can." We are high-fiving each other, happy that it's done and that it went well.

"Ryan," Jonathan says. He's on his laptop checking the surf reports. "Whaddya say? A little board time later on?"

Mr. Simpson approaches. He's a thin guy with a nervous tic of jerking his head to one side every thirty seconds or so. He doesn't quite meet our eyes. "The physics work was excellent," he says. "Not only were your research results interesting, but you've created a good teaching tool."

He continues. "My one concern's the amount of adult help you had on this. Ryan, I know your father's a film maker. This project was supposed to be your own work."

Our three jaws hit the floor at the same time. I feel a surge of heat as rage starts to build. Jonathan and Calvin put a lot of extra physics in this, above and beyond what we learned in class, and he's not accusing them of cheating. But my two loyal friends are already on Simpson like a pair of Rottweilers.

"Ryan's the mastermind of this project!" Calvin exclaims with a sweep of his arm. He has discovered his dramatic side since the shoot. "He did all the film work himself."

"We were *there* when he did it! We barely saw Mr. Mills," Jonathan says.

Mr. Simpson begins to back pedal. His head jerks a couple of times right in a row. "Okay, okay, I'm sorry, Ryan." He shifts his weight back and forth and runs his hand through what's left of his hair. "I just assumed you couldn't have done it, because it looked so professional."

"It didn't look professional," I say. Like glowing coals, I am still emitting heat. "It looked like what it is. Top-quality student work."

Jonathan, Calvin, and I get an A plus on our physics project. I'm still pissed off at Simpson, but a little part of me is thinking, *so he thought my old man did it, huh?* Even if it's only by a high school physics teacher, it's kind of nice having my work mistaken for my father's.

Chapter Forty-Six

Finally, it's the day of my interview at the Teen League. Its offices are in a seedy part of the mid-Wilshire district, on the third floor of this office building. I park my car at a meter, locking it while a couple of street people ask to wash the windows. I give them each a five and leave, praying the car will be there when I come back.

I haven't told my parents I'm here. On the application, I identified my father as D. Mills, Media Consultant, and my mother as N. Mills, Homemaker. I want to get this one on my own.

I walk in through a reception room where kids and their parents sit waiting to meet with Teen League staff. The room's cheerful, with plants, bookshelves, and an aquarium full of fish. I like the energy of the place.

The receptionist, Linda, takes me past a row of carrels, where kids sit working the phones. A girl in a t-shirt and giant overalls, cut off into shorts, is saying, "Did he hit you or hurt you in any way?"

She listens, sitting very still, as if concentrating on every word. "Good, but still, be sure to document everything that happens," she tells her listener. "Write down dates and exactly what he says and does. Hide the notes where your dad can't find them."

My throat gets tight and painful as I listen. Did Michael ever make any calls to a place like this? Did anyone he called ever try to help him?

After a moment, the girl's off the phone, and Linda introduces us. Her name's Amanda Lewis, and she's a junior at UCLA. She's at the Teen League on a work-study project and is overseeing the high school volunteers.

Amanda shakes my hand. She has these surprising green eyes

and a cute laugh. "I'm sorry we're so disorganized this morning," she says. "Bridgette Connolly, our Staff Director, was supposed to be back from the Children's Court, but she's been delayed. Do you mind terribly waiting? It could be a half hour or more."

"No worries," I tell her. By now, there's just one boy left in the waiting room, maybe twelve years old, along with a woman who's sitting tense and straight-backed in her chair. The kid wears jeans with three inches of boxers showing above them, and a sweat-shirt with the hood pulled up around his face.

"...not like last time!" she says to him.

"You don' be tellin' me what to do!" He scowls and looks at the floor.

I sit down, drumming my hands on my knees a few times. I look around. I go over to the bookshelf, but find only little kids' books. I sit back down. By now, the woman is writing something, while the boy stares straight ahead, frowning.

I dig around in my pockets and unearth some old store receipts. Seeing a trash can nearby, I wad up the receipts, take aim, and shoot. My paper wad bounces off the rim of the can. The boy's watching me from the corners of his eyes.

"*Oh!*" I cry. "Near miss!" I walk over, pick the wad up off the floor, and sit back down. I aim and shoot, a high arcing shot. It's in.

Now the boy walks over, takes my paper wad out, walks away, then whirls and does a jump shot. The wad goes in.

"Two points!" I tell him. "But I can take you."

"No way," he says. "I can wipe the floor with you."

The woman is giving him dark looks, and for a minute it seems like she's going to say something. But then she settles back into her chair.

"Four out of five," I say.

We begin shooting, taking turns. We are tied, four to four.

"Nine out of ten," I say. We keep shooting. On my last shot, I miss. I groan. The boy easily makes his shot and does a victory dance.

"Awesome," I tell him. "But watch out. Next time, you're toast."

"You wish." He's grinning broadly. "I'm gonna take a leak," he tells the woman and walks out. She sits up in alarm.

"Would you please follow him?" she asks me. "Make sure he comes back?"

"Follow him to the bathroom?" I'm puzzled.

"Please?" she repeats. "Make sure he comes back?"

I follow the boy down the hall and duck into the men's room behind him. He's standing at a urinal with his back to me. This is incredibly strange. I feel like a pervert.

The boy looks over his shoulder. "You gotta problem, man?"

He and I are the only spots of color in this bathroom, with its all-white floors, walls, sinks, and stall dividers.

"Your mom asked me to come in here with you."

"My social worker," he says.

"So how come your social worker wants me to keep you here?"

"I dunno." He zips his pants. I step backward to block his path, feeling the hard-edged door handle behind me jab itself into my side.

"You going back?" I ask. "To the Teen League?"

He stops and looks me over, as if he's trying to figure out how hard a punch I pack. "What's it to you?" he says.

"She asked me to bring you back. I can't force you to come. But I can ask you nicely."

"And I can say no."

But I see his shoulders relax as he says it. He reaches up, pulling the hood off his head.

"You don't like the Teen League?" I ask him. "Because I'm here on a job interview. If this place sucks, you gotta tell me, man."

"This is only my second time here." He runs a hand over his hair, which is in a buzz cut.

"How did the first go?"

He shrugs.

"What's your name?"

"Roberto."

"I'm Ryan. Help me out, okay? I can't afford to lose this job." I add, "And I can still whip your ass at B-ball."

"Cannot."

"Can, too."

We walk back down the hallway together, and I ease him through the door of the Teen League. The social worker's standing there with Amanda Lewis and some other lady I haven't seen before. The new lady puts out her hand. She has lots of dark wavy hair and these floaty clothes and big gold earrings that make me think of a gypsy.

"I'm Bridgette Connolly, Staff Director. I'm sorry you had to wait so long, Ryan."

"It was no problem," I tell her. "Roberto and I played B-ball."

"And I kicked your ass!" He gives me this cocky grin.

I point a finger at him. "Only temporarily, my friend. Next time, you go down."

"In your dreams."

"Gotta go. See ya."

I go into the interview and field questions from Bridgette and Amanda. We're in Bridgette's office, which is full of sun and hanging ferns. She has a large corkboard on the wall with snapshots of teenagers.

Her eyes follow my glance. "Those are all kids that have come here for help."

"I'm really interested in this program," I say. "My best friend had substance abuse problems, and I think it's what killed him."

Then, my mouth says something that surprises my brain. "I'm looking for a subject for a school project and was hoping to find it at the Teen League."

"Oh?" Bridgette Connolly is looking at me with interest. She has unusual cinnamon colored eyes that add to her gypsy look.

"I want to make a film as part of my project. A documentary. About some of the kids here. Maybe about someone like Roberto." As soon as I say it, I know it's a fantastic idea. I will do this. I will make a film for Michael, and it will be amazing.

"Well," says Bridgette. "You certainly knew how to handle Roberto. The last time he was here, he wouldn't talk to anyone at all, and then he ran out of the office and disappeared for forty-eight hours. The police had to bring him home."

"Oh." It's all I can think of to say.

"I think you'd do great here," Bridgette says. "Now that you've seen and heard more, are you still interested in volunteering with us?" She moves a paperweight around on her desk as she talks.

"Very," I say. "I'd be available next year, when I'm a senior."

"You'd be required to go through our six-week training program."

"Great," I say. "Sign me up!"

"It's during the summer." She gives me the dates. It's right in the middle of the England trip.

My brain goes into a slide, like a person walking on ice. It's skidding around, trying to regain its grip on the ground, while my mouth continues to speak, saying God only knows what. The interview ends. I shake hands with Bridgette and Amanda and head out to the elevator.

What did I say to them? It comes back to me.

"This summer?" I had said. "Sounds great. I'm very interested."

Chapter Forty-Seven

After a day at school, I drop my heavy backpack on the floor and fall on the sofa in our den. My face is buried in a pillow, and my legs are hanging off the end of the couch. It's a hot day, and I am probably sweating all over Mom's French-Chinese-silk-whatever upholstery.

I have a math test tomorrow and a Spanish quiz. I groan to myself. It's almost five o'clock already, since Emily's rehearsal ran late today.

Someone walks in and sits down, without speaking.

I peer over the top of the sofa cushion. "Hi, Mom."

She perches on the arm of a big chair, as if she's not sure she should stay. She's wearing designer sweat pants and a sweat shirt that I'm sure were never intended to be sweated on for even a moment. She has what seems at first to be this really bizarre necklace, but then I realize it's her glasses hanging on a chain.

"How was school?" she asks.

"I got an A minus on my English paper. And a B plus on my history quiz." I have an A minus average for the semester, and I'm hoping that's good enough for the Honors Project.

"Really? Good for you." She searches for something else to say, then stands up to leave. I remember what Emily told me about how cool and distant I was with Mom and Dad. I decide to make an effort.

"So how's everything going with you?" I ask her.

She stretches. "Fine. I have to go get ready. Your Dad and I are going to an art opening and dinner."

In my belly, this angry red spot of heat begins to burn. *They always go out to dinner.* And then, when they want to know how I am, they ask Emily.

"Are you going just the two of you?"

"Yes, why?"

"Then, don't go," I tell her. "Have dinner with me, Ro and the girls. Be with us."

Mom gives me a surprised smile. "I'd have to talk to your Dad and see how important this thing is."

"We're more important." A stubborn tone creeps into my voice.

"Yes. You are. Let me talk to your dad. I'll see what I can do."

• • •

When Mom and Dad walk into the kitchen, the girls jump up in surprise. Molly runs over and grabs Mom's hand, while Maddy throws her arms around Dad.

"Mommy! Daddy! What are you doing here?"

"Ryan invited us," my father jokes.

Ha ha. Very funny, Dad. It practically takes an engraved invitation to get him to stay home with his kids.

"So. Nice of you to join us!" I sound as fake and elaborately polite as I can manage.

"Any time, kid," Dad answers, brushing my crack off as a joke. He's Mr. Smooth, all right.

We all protest when Ro leaves the kitchen, begging her to stay, but she insists. "I have my television show," she says, leaving with a dinner plate. "Ryan, you know how to serve the meal."

And so the Mills family sits down to a normal dinner together, the way families are supposed to. Nervous tingles are going down my spine, and I get this adrenalin rush as I hand my dad his plate. He looks small and far away, tinged in a red light.

We sit at the table in the bay window. Since it's spring now, the garden's filled with flowers. I tell Mom and Dad about school and my interest in the Teen League.

"I keep thinking that a program like that could've helped Michael, you know?"

"Yeah, poor kid," Dad says. He gives a heavy sigh. He's not the type to get all worked up about things on the outside, but I know Michael's death hit him hard.

"How's Miss Cruella?" I ask Molly.

"Better," she says. "She's not as mean as I thought."

"Why's that?" I ask.

"She gave me all A's on my report card."

I raise my water glass to Molly, who clinks it with her milk.

"Ryan, I need help with my serve," Maddy says.

"You just need to put more top spin on your second serve. I can give you some pointers."

Dad is looking at me with a funny expression.

"What?" I ask him. He shakes his head.

"Nothing, just thinking."

"Mom? Dad? Will you have dinner with us more often?" Maddy asks.

They look embarrassed. "Of course, kitten," my mom says.

"Yeah," I say, "We could actually act like a real family, for once." There's a hard edge to my voice that makes everyone get quiet for a second.

My mom's looking down at her plate, cutting her food in tiny pieces. She spears some chicken and puts it in her mouth without raising her eyes from the plate.

I can feel it happening. My mouth's disengaging itself from my brain. Emily had said I was distant toward my parents. I say the first thing I think of.

"Have I seemed withdrawn the last few years?" I ask. I can hear Emily's voice. *Tell them how you feel.*

"Well, that's a big question," Dad says, taking a hard look at me. "I dunno. Has he?" He turns to my mom.

"It's hard to tell with teenagers, particularly boys," says Mom. "All my friends say their sons never talk to them about anything."

"Oh, I'd talk to you if I weren't so fucking pissed off."

All movement in the kitchen stops.

I've even startled myself. I don't usually swear. And I'd only meant to say "Pass the butter." On the other hand, I've been building up to this confrontation for a long time.

"Language, Ryan!" Dad snaps.

Mom glances back and forth between Maddy and Molly. "*Ryan.*

Not in front of the girls."

"They can hear this," I tell her. "It's about them, too."

"We're staying," Maddy announces.

"Why didn't you guys come home after Michael overdosed?" All my anguish of the last three years pours out with the question.

They look like they don't have a clue what I'm talking about. "We did," Mom says. "Michael was fine. It was Nat and Yancy's decision."

"A week later," I say. "You left us twisting in the wind for a week, while you played in the South of France!"

"It was Michael's issue, not ours," my mom says.

"It was our issue, too!"

Molly's lower lip is trembling. "Yeah! It was our issue, too!"

"Don't you remember, Mom? Molly and Maddy had nightmares for months after that! They saw Michael lying in the driveway. They thought he was *dead!*" Now Molly's crying openly, and Maddy's starting to sniffle. A second later, the dams burst. Both girls are spewing tears.

"I hope you're happy, Ryan!" Mom gets them up from the table and propels the sobbing girls out of the room. "Now what am I going to do with these two?"

"Ring for Rosario. She'll show you the ropes."

Silence. I sit there with my dad, pissed off and making no apologies. Dad has no expression on his face at all. I know he's not happy with me right now. *Tough,* I think. I'm not happy with *him.* Mom and Dad have done me wrong, and I'm calling them out on it, big-time.

"Why don't we continue this in my study?" he suggests. The study's the only room in the house, besides Rosario's quarters, that has escaped Mom's fleet of designers. The leather sofa's worn and comfortable. I've spent thousands of hours on it, listening in on Dad's meetings, talking to him about scripts, casting, locations, editing.

Dad intercoms up to the master bedroom. "Nadine?" Mom's there, sounding tearful. "This may take a while. Why don't you get some sleep, okay? Ryan'll come talk to you tomorrow." He rings off and sits in his old Lazy-Boy, another cherished survivor of the designer wars. I am sitting low in the sofa, legs splayed out in front of me, arms crossed on my chest. I am looking at Dad through narrowed eyes.

Dad's voice could slice a diamond in half. "Tomorrow, I expect you to apologize to your mother and sisters."

From the set of his jaw, I know he means business. I stare at the edge of the rug. "Okay."

"I mean it."

"*Okay*. I will. "

"And Ryan? Don't *ever* speak to your mother that way again."

I feel his anger now, slicing through me like a thin, steel blade. I nod, unable to look at him. "I won't. I swear."

One good thing about Dad is, when something's over, it's over. My promise is good enough for him. He moves on.

"So let's hear it," he says abruptly. "What's on your mind?"

I let him have it. The whole overdose story, how scary it was, the aftermath for me and the twins. Mom and Dad's frequent absences from home. Their lack of involvement. I hold back nothing. I am shaking with rage. I didn't even know I had this kind of anger in me.

When I'm done, Dad says, "So I guess it wasn't a dinner invitation. It was more like an ambush?" Behind the irritated words, I hear something else, though—embarrassment or regret.

"Probably, but you deserved it," I tell him. "Besides, what kid has to invite his parents to dinner in his own home? Parents are *supposed* to be home having dinner with their kids, at least once in a while."

"All right. Point taken," he says. He goes over to his bar and pours himself a Cognac. "Want one?"

"Yeah."

He started doing this when I was twelve, serving me no more than a splash of liquor – it was the ceremony that mattered, not the drink. Today he measures me out a shot glass full, pouring it into a brandy snifter and handing it to me.

We sit there, being manly together. I know what he's doing. My dad's a master negotiator. Right now, he's slowing things down, cooling me off, before we go at it again. I can feel it working, particularly after a few sips of the Cognac.

"Did you know your mother and I almost divorced?"

"*Really?* When?"

"Four years ago."

"Why?" I ask.

"That's between me and your mom. Let's just say, we both made mistakes." After a minute, he continues. "We went to counseling for a year, right before that trip to Cannes. That week after Michael's overdose, we weren't with Nat and Yancy."

I think back to my conversation with Yancy. She had said Mom and Dad weren't there and she would pass them a message. "Where were you?"

"Paris. We renewed our marriage vows and had a second honeymoon. It was important for us."

"We're important, too."

"You three are the most important," he agrees. "I'm just telling you what happened." Dad swirls the Cognac in his glass.

"To be honest, I don't think Nat and Yancy even told us that Michael had OD'd until we met up with them for the flight home." Dad stares off into space, trying to remember. "Right or wrong, we thought of it as the Westons' problem."

"How can you say that, with Molly and Maddy crying every night and waking up with nightmares?" I can't believe he didn't notice that.

He goes to a shelf, pulls out one of his old calendars, and leafs through it. "Right after Cannes I was filming in Morocco for four months. So, I was gone during the time you're talking about." He and I look at each other from across the room. "I realize," he says, "that didn't do you much good. I wasn't there for you."

"Mom was here. She should have helped us."

Dad suddenly looks tired. He walks back toward his Lazy-Boy. "Ryan, your mom loves you kids, and she tries. But she doesn't have a clue how to deal with you." He stands there by the books on his shelves, tracing a hand across a couple of them.

"She's really kind of fragile, okay? Could you just back off for once, give her a little bit of a break?"

I nod. I'm staring at my shoe. I study the ins and outs of my shoelace. "Okay. I can try, too."

"It hasn't been easy," Dad says, "with my schedule and the problems Nadine and I have had. I've focused on work and the

220

marriage, and Ro's handled the three of you. We've kept all the balls in the air, but barely. And you kids haven't gotten much from me and your mom."

He stands up. "Let's go outside for a minute, get some air." He opens the French doors on one wall of his office that lead out to our garden with the reflecting pool and fountains. We step out and walk down in that direction.

The fountains are all lit with white light. There's a little wind, which sends spray from the fountains against my face. I've always loved the sound of the running water and usually keep my bedroom window open so I can hear it at night.

We stand there for a moment, then I ask, "Why do you guys have to go out so much?"

"It's important for my work. And it helps Nadine to get out, too." Dad hesitates, then says, "And frankly, you weren't such good company for a while there. We were having a lot of problems with you, acting like a belligerent smart ass. We thought it was hormones, but now I realize it was this thing with Michael."

We walk along the reflecting pool and look across the lawn to the swimming pools, tennis court, and small basketball court. We have a long lap pool, a deep pool with a slide and diving board, and a separate shallow pool for little kids. I remember many outstanding summer afternoons with a pack of boys over to shoot hoops, play tennis, and have diving contests.

"Yeah, well, if you'll have dinner with us sometimes, I'll stop being a smart ass," I tell him.

Dad gives me a dry look. "How about you stop being a smart ass, regardless," he says. Then he goes on. "It takes hard work, you know, to have all this." He sweeps an arm toward the pools and the rest of it.

"I'd rather have you than some tennis court."

"I'll work it out so we're home more. Maybe not as much as you'd like, but more anyway. The truth is, I'd like to see you kids, too."

For a while, we talk about other things: about school, the upcoming summer, the work on *Mystery Moon*. I update Dad on Chrissie's condition.

"She's okay to audition now."

"Good! I'll have Mitzi set it up."

Dad and I have walked back through the French doors into his study. "In a way, it's too bad you're spending the summer in England," he says.

"Why?"

"If you were here I'd ask you to work with me on the set. On *Mystery Moon.*"

"Really? You mean, as an assistant?"

He nods. "You've got talent, Ryan. You did a great job on that film."

He sits down at his desk again, while I go over to this big free-standing globe he has. Dad thinks I've got talent. He's never said anything like that before.

The globe's one of those things that, using modern technology, has been carefully aged to look like it's a two hundred year old precious relic. Ever since I was little, I've tried to see how fast I could get it to spin. I put a finger on it and start it twirling.

I did a great job. I give the globe an extra whirl.

"How are you feeling these days? With Michael gone?" Dad asks.

"I really miss him. But, it's weird how so much has happened to me since he died. Even *because* he died. I feel like more has happened to me since September than in the whole rest of my life."

"It's a damn shame about Michael," Dad says. "But I've been really proud of you this year. You've grown up a lot."

"You think so?"

"Sure. Working hard, good grades, beautiful girlfriend." He pauses. "Getting laid."

I jump, almost knocking over the globe, my face on fire. There's no point in denying it.

"How'd you find out?"

"The gardeners mentioned all the guests we were having for a while there. As a matter of fact, it was all because of Alberto's little boy."

"Hector?" I ask, incredulous. It was my buddy, Hector, who finked me out?

"Yeah, it was funny. Apparently, Hector discovered a baseball cap on the doorknob of the guest house, got all excited, and went back to pinch a couple of them." Dad doesn't comment that there haven't been any caps to pinch for a while, and I don't bring it up.

"But they were always still there... afterward!"

"Yeah, Alberto kept making Hector put them back. That's when he mentioned the guests to me."

Betrayed by a four-year old. I don't know what to say. I throw Dad a cautious look.

"Are you being safe with her? This is important."

"Yes." When he looks at me closely, I say "Really, Dad. It's okay. I promise."

"Be good to that girl. Treat her right."

"*Dad*. I do."

"I believe you. You're a good boy. A good person."

I suddenly feel tears at the back of my eyes. I turn toward the globe again and twirl it, getting it spinning crazily. No crying allowed. It wouldn't be manly.

Chapter Forty-Eight

"Mom?" It's the morning after the Dinner from Hell. I am standing in the doorway of her office, where she sits at this super-rare, valuable antique desk she found and then loaded up with the latest, most up-to-date computer equipment.

I take a close look at her. She's so thin and frail, I could blow her over with a single puff of breath. She's really pretty, actually, once you get past the fingernails and jewelry and designer clothes. She has this wounded look in her eyes.

"I'm sorry about last night. I was a total dick."

"Language, Ryan." She looks at me over the top of her glasses.

"I was a total jerk."

"That's better," she says. And then she laughs. My mother has made an actual joke. I'm so surprised that I laugh, too. I try to think of something more to say to her, something real. The problem is, I realize, I don't know my mother at all.

"I talked to Dad for a long time last night," I tell her. "I got a lot of stuff out of my system."

"So I heard. I guess I haven't been such a good mother, have I?" Slowly, with great care, she picks up several paper clips, dropping them one by one into a heavy crystal bowl on her desk.

"Mom..."

"No, I understand. It never came naturally to me, you know." She speaks slowly, as if from some sad, dark place deep inside of her. "But I do love you kids. I didn't mean to let you down." She stares, sad and dry-eyed, at the top of her desk.

I can't believe what an asshole I was, that I hurt my mother this way. I'm beside her in two strides, patting her on the shoulder. "You didn't let us down," I tell her. "We love you, too."

The first part of that isn't true. She did let us down. But I let Michael down, too. I guess if I want him and the karma gods to forgive me for my mistakes, I ought to forgive Mom for hers.

And the second part of what I said is true. I do love my mother, and so do my sisters.

Mom smiles at me. "Thank you for being so good with the girls. We could really see that at dinner last night."

"I assume you mean before I went postal."

"Yes, that's what I mean." And now she laughs again, and so do I.

"I'm really sorry for the times we've disappointed you," she says. "Next time, don't wait three years to tell us. No need to suffer in silence."

"Okay." Mom and I have a long way to go, but this was a first step anyway.

• • •

Now it's the girls' turn. I knock on the door of Maddy's room, where the two of them are sprawled in bean bag chairs, pretending to do their homework. Maddy's room is all pink carousel horses, and Molly's is all yellow birds and butterflies. I give the girls another year before they rebel with lava lamps and posters of boy bands.

"I'm sorry, you guys," I say.

"For what?" asks Maddy. She's been growing out her hair and has started wearing it in long blond braids.

"For being an idiot."

"You're not an idiot," Molly replies. "You're a dufus."

"You're a dork," says Maddy.

I grab a foam basketball and aim it at a small hoop on the wall. I put it there for Maddy, but I'm the one who usually uses it. I shoot the ball while I talk, but it hits the rim and bounces away, while I scramble after it.

"Watch it, you guys. We're from the same gene pool, you know," I tell them.

"What does that mean?" Molly wants to know. She's just gotten glasses, and I'm not used to the way they look on her.

"It means we come from the same parents, so anything I am, you guys are the same."

"Oh, well in that case, you're *beautiful!*" shouts Maddy.

"You're smart!" That's Molly.

I shoot again and this time score two points on the hoop.

"I knew you'd see it my way." Then, I ask them, "Are you guys mad at me for yelling at Mom and Dad last night?"

"We were kind of freaked out. But then Daddy told us you were just venting." Molly is always pleased to learn a new vocabulary word. "He said you're all better now."

"He's right. I *am* better. And you know I think Mom and Dad are pretty cool, right?"

"But not as cool as us, right?" Maddy gets up and takes the ball from me.

"No, you guys are way cooler."

Maddy shoots the basketball from across the room and sinks it. It's a perfect shot.

Chapter Forty-Nine

Chrissie's a month from her due date when Mitzi finally schedules her audition for late on a Friday afternoon. Luckily, Emily's in rehearsal, so I can escape to get Chrissie without telling her what I'm doing. Since Emily doesn't know Chrissie went to the party, I can't tell her about the audition.

Unfortunately, that's not the only secret I'm keeping. Nat's going to be there tonight, and I don't plan to tell Chrissie he's Michael's father. No point in getting her worked up.

We are at Dad's pre-production offices, sitting in an audition room. A couple of hard chairs sit in front of a white wall. That's where the actors do their thing. The rest of us pile onto one of the sofas on the other side of the small room, facing the two chairs. Mitzi has just five actresses waiting, with Chrissie on last.

Jared's there ready to read. In *Mystery Moon*, he plays a private eye in a romance with Elaine, a rich young widow played by his co-star Melinda Radnor. Roxanne's a waitress at a coffee shop he frequents. He and Roxanne flirt and talk only three times, but the experience affects him deeply, destroying his relationship with Elaine and changing his life forever.

"So for it to be believable," Dad tells me, "Roxanne's gotta burn up the screen. She needs to have major chemistry with Jared and make a big impact on the audience in just three scenes."

Mitzi brings in the actresses one by one. Trisha Hamilton, who's gotten great reviews in a new TV drama, is really good, and Nat talks to her for a while. She's a redhead with long legs and a sexy whisky voice. But I know Mitzi's biding her time. She's met with Chrissie a couple of times and has coached her.

"The last up is Chrissie Valentino. You met her at the party," she reminds Dad and Nat. "She's Ryan's friend from the tennis club."

When Chrissie enters, Dad and Nat both draw back a little to study her. She's so massive it's almost impossible to believe she'll ever be thin again. She's wearing her SaveWell uniform, the buttons pulling and gapping across her belly.

"It'll be fine," Mitzi tells Dad. "She'd be down to the right weight long before the shoot. It'd be a condition of the contract that she had to get in shape in time."

Walking in, Chrissie looks tired and worried, but when she sees Jared, it's as if she switches on this inner light. She's suddenly this beautiful, exciting red-hot mama.

"Hey, gorgeous, you been waitin' for me?" Chrissie says it in a way that jolts every man in the room upright in his seat, holding his breath to see what happens next.

"There she is!" Jared bounds to his feet, looking at Chrissie as if he's Adam and she's Eve, and he's seeing a woman in a fig leaf for the very first time.

Without a break, Chrissie and Jared move into their scenes, which they've memorized, while Mitzi sits back, looking pleased with herself. Nat looks at Dad, and Dad looks at me, and I breathe this huge sigh of relief, because from the first line, it's obvious and we all know it.

Chrissie was born to be Roxanne.

• • •

Afterward, I run up to Chrissie, hugging her and yelling about how incredible she was. "You got it! You got the job, Chrissie!"

She looks dazed. "This is way better than my commercial for Tidy Litter."

Dad invites us all back to the house for dinner, where Chrissie takes up two places at the table. Totally up from the success of the audition, she's sparkling, talking to Dad and Mitzi, her fingernails flashing bright pink whenever she moves her hands. Jared's gone home, but Nat is sitting across from me. He's so much quieter since Michael died and has gained a lot of weight. His hair's gray everywhere now, instead of just at the temples.

Rosario brings in trays of her awesome Mexican food. I jump up to help her. "Thanks, Ro," I tell her. I hand Nat a platter of quesadillas, feeling guilty. *He has no idea his grandchild is sitting at the table with him.*

"You'll need an agent," Dad says to Chrissie. "I'll introduce you to some people over at Hollywood Artists."

"Hey, Chrissie," I say, "Movies pay better than the SaveWell!"

"Thank the Lord," she says. Then, "Ryan, now I can return the money to you for all those bills you paid!" Dad quietly chokes on his chimichanga.

Everyone's looking at me. I examine my plate, noting the exact coordinates of my cheese quesadilla in contrast to the position of the refried beans. Choosing my words carefully, I say "Dad, I told you before. I've been helping Chrissie out, because she's a friend. But it's not my baby."

Chrissie leaps into the conversation. "Oh, no," she assures my dad. "This baby's father passed away very suddenly. In a vehicle accident."

Nat sits back in his chair, going pale. As he looks up, his eyes meet mine. In that instant, I see the light go on for Nat.

"Chrissie," he says. "My son died this September in a car accident. His name was Michael."

"*Oh!*" Her mouth pops open. For an instant, her eyes shoot over to me, with a look of total panic. I try to signal her back with my own—*it's okay*—but the truth is I don't really know if it's going to be okay for her.

I'd be relieved that her secret is out if I didn't have to worry she was going to disappear again. This time for real.

Meanwhile, Chrissie and Nat are staring at each other. But Chrissie never loses her cool for long. Her head goes up. "My relationship with Michael was brief," she tells him, "but profound."

Nat's voice is choked. "How brief?"

"Once. In the Pro Shop." She sets each word out so carefully, it's like she's afraid they'll break. Looking as if he's on autopilot, Nat moves over to where Chrissie's sitting, and Mitzi gives him her chair. Chrissie's very still and Nat's chalk-colored, but the two manage to smile at each other anyway.

"Michael had a beautiful spirit," Chrissie says after a minute. "This boy does, too."

"It's a boy?" Nat asks. His voice is shaking with emotion.

Chrissie nods. "I'm namin' him Michael."

I can hardly look at Nat. So many expressions are crossing his face at the same time: joy, grief, shock, regret. "It's a gift," he says. "From heaven."

"Yes. It is." Chrissie gives him a warm, beautiful smile, then jumps a little and takes Nat's hand and puts it on her belly. "Your grandson's waving to you right now. Feel that?"

An expression of wonder comes over his face. "Excuse me." Nat reaches for his cell phone and punches a number. "Yancy?" he says. "You gotta get over here. Now."

Chapter Fifty

As Yancy hurries in, you can almost see the emotion in the room. Nat looks dazed, as if he'd like to be overjoyed but he's afraid to be. Mitzi and Mom are in tears. Only my dad is expressionless, as if he's thinking hard. I'm glad that I don't have to keep this secret from my parents any longer.

"So you've been helping her for… what… months?" Nat sounds incredulous. He and Chrissie are transfixed by her belly. She keeps moving his hand around on it, yelling out "There's another one!" and "Oh boy, that was a big one!" Yancy sees the two of them and stops short, her eyes narrowing.

I nod in answer to Nat's question. "I was doing it for Michael. I'm sorry we didn't tell you sooner. She's due in a month." The adults in the room are looking at us, astonished.

Yancy walks up to Chrissie, unsmiling, and extends her hand. "I'm Yancy Weston, Michael's mother." Nat takes his hand off Chrissie's belly, giving Yancy a confused look.

Chrissie pulls herself to her feet. "How do you do?" she says, shaking hands with Yancy. There's an awkward pause.

"So, you knew my son?" Yancy's tone is neutral.

"Yes, ma'm."

"And this is his baby?"

"Yes, ma'm." Chrissie's smiling, but I suddenly realize I've never seen her this pale. And, although her mouth's smiling, her eyes aren't.

"Time for dessert!" Mom calls out as Rosario comes in with platters in each hand. Mom bustles around handing out slices of cake that no one seems to want.

Dad has pulled Nat and Yancy aside, and now they come for me. The four of us go into the kitchen.

"Ryan," Dad asks. "Are you a hundred percent sure this is Michael's baby?"

"I asked her that," I say. "She swore it was. And I know for sure Michael slept with her, because he told me himself. The night he died."

They look as if they're wondering just how many more secrets I've got hidden away.

"Did she approach you about this, ask you for money?" Dad asks.

"No way," I tell them. "I looked her up when I found out she was pregnant. She's never asked me for a dime. I paid some bills while she was on bed rest, but I had to twist her arm first."

"But there's no absolute proof he's the father?" Nat asks. I shake my head.

"We need it," Yancy snaps. "We need to know for sure." So a few minutes later, I pull Chrissie aside, pluck up my courage and ask her. She says "Of course I will take a paternity test." Being a great actress, she sounds cheerful and confident as she says it. But I know better.

Is she going to disappear again now? Then I think: Roxanne. Would Chrissie bolt from a major film role?

I don't have the answer. I stand there, making conversation, while my intestines tie themselves into a series of pretzels.

· · ·

After dinner, I give Emily a quick good night call, then take Chrissie home. By now, my car could drive itself to Chrissie's house. It makes this powerful hum as I gun it up the 405, passing the few cars on the road with us. The whole way up, I'm thinking *what's Chrissie going to do now?*

As we reach the top of the ridge, the lights of the San Fernando Valley spread out before us like the jewelry spilled across my mother's dressing table before a big event.

Chrissie leans her head back against the headrest, closing her eyes.

"You okay?" I ask her.

"I'm just tired."

"What are you thinking? I mean, are you worried about Nat and Yancy?"

"I'm so tired right now I can't think anythin'," she says.

I help her up the stairs and to her apartment door. As she opens it and enters her place, I find myself hanging in the doorway, not wanting to leave. "Are you really okay?"

She nods. "I gotta go to the bathroom." She disappears, while I flop down on some pillows on the floor. I hope Chrissie will be fine now. Nat and Yancy won't cause any trouble. They'll get to know her, and they'll help her with the baby.

Her career, for sure, is off to a good start in Mitzi's hands. Mitzi's like a giant searchlight, always on the move. She's one of the best new-talent spotters in Hollywood, and right now the beam of her searchlight has stopped on Chrissie. I lie on the carpet and give a double thumbs up to Lucille Ball, looking down at me from her poster on the wall.

Chrissie, I'm noticing, has been gone a long time.

"Ryan?"

A warning shiver streaks up my spine. My head snaps around.

"Ryan, are you there?"

I'm on my feet in an instant and heading for the bathroom. When I touch the door, it swings open, and Chrissie is standing there, ghostly pale, one hand gripping the sink for balance. She has changed into a dress that hangs down past her knees, and her legs and feet are bare.

She has a leaky faucet; I hear the steady *drip, drip* of water. But I can see the faucet, and it's not leaking. The *drip, drip* continues.

"Ryan, help me." Chrissie stands as if she doesn't dare to move.

Then I see it. It's not water. A drop of red hits the vinyl floor between Chrissie's feet and splashes up onto her ankle. A second drop and a third. The drops keep coming, joining the pool of blood on the floor at Chrissie's feet.

Somehow, I wrap her up in a big towel, find her purse, lock her front door, and half-carry her down the two flights of stairs on the outside of her building. *Don't let her fall, get to the car.*

"Your beautiful car seats!" she wails, as I set her down on the soft, buttery leather.

"Forget it," I say. I gun my car toward the hospital, pulling in at the Emergency Room and stopping with a jerk that snaps both of us forward.

An orderly takes her off in a wheelchair, while I park, then sprint back to the ER. It's a different hospital, but the same smells, the same plastic tubing, the same needles in bruised arms. It's the same exhaustion, the same fear, the same indifferent faces at the admitting desk.

I shake my head a little, thinking *Dude! Pull it together!* I find Chrissie lying on a gurney while a man in blue hospital scrubs puts a needle in her arm. They're giving her blood. They're not wasting any time, wheeling her up to a machine and laying a sheet over her waist and legs. From what they're saying, I gather she's getting an ultrasound.

Working fast, they pull up her shirt, exposing her belly, and put some kind of gel on it. They move a detector device around on the belly, while gray and white shadows swirl across a screen. Everything in their faces and movement says urgency, fear, danger.

Chrissie stares straight up at the ceiling, holding my hand for strength, like a little girl. I'm focused on the screen, looking for something, anything that will tell me the baby's okay. From within the gray mass, a small foot emerges and disappears, and then a nose. I send an urgent mental message to the little guy. *Help's on the way! Hang in there!*

Two blue-dressed hospital people are leaning into the picture before them. At the same moment, they both point at a wrinkle of dark grayness in the swirling light gray picture. Wobbly tracings are coming from yet another machine they've attached to Chrissie, and some change there suddenly pushes both doctors into action.

I hear the words "hemorrhage" and "fetal distress," as one runs from the room calling out orders. Blue-dressed people swarm in, grabbing Chrissie's gurney and pushing it out of the room and down the hall.

"What's wrong?" Chrissie asks the doctor, a thin guy with cold eyes and long pale hands. "Is it serious?"

The placenta has broken away from the uterus a second time. She is bleeding internally. The baby's heartbeat is abnormally slow.

They are practically running down the hall while I keep pace alongside. Chrissie needs an emergency C-section to save her life and the baby's.

"You have to stay out here." They disappear through a set of swinging doors, leaving me alone in the hallway.

I feel like I've been kicked in the stomach. I thought we had solved this problem. The doctor said it was cured.

I somehow get out to the waiting room and try to ask a nurse how long Chrissie will be in there. "No way to tell," she says to me. "Sit down and make yourself comfortable."

Comfortable? My brain keeps saying *not again*. I pull out my cell and call home. Nat and Yancy are still there. I deliver the news. The grandchild they learned about less than two hours ago is in danger and may die.

"We're coming," the four of them tell me.

I sit there alone for what feels like a long time. After a while, I realize I have my arms wrapped around myself, and I'm rocking back and forth. I am dry-eyed, more frightened than I've ever been in my life.

The exterior door to the ER flies open, and my parents burst through. They have Nat and Yancy between them. Nat looks the way I feel, terrified. Yancy's mouth is set in a grim line.

Sinking heavily into a chair, Nat says what I've been feeling. "I don't think I can do this again."

Chapter Fifty-One

Mom has her arm around Yancy. They sit down with Nat, across from me, while Dad sits next to me, facing them.

"I don't even know why we're here," Yancy says to Nat in a low voice.

"I do," he says. They sit side-by-side, staring straight ahead, not touching.

We wait. Several hours pass. I doze in my chair, but dream of things self-destructing, exploding, coming apart. Cars crushed against road dividers, mountain tops erupting in smoke and flame, bodies eaten by disease, and worst of all, blood dripping, dripping, dripping as little Michael curls himself into a tiny ball and slowly disappears.

A couple of times I jerk awake and sit there staring at the stained ceiling tiles. What am I doing here? I suddenly want Emily so badly that every part of me hurts. As I doze off again, I feel my body slump sideways in the hard waiting room chair.

Finally, around three in the morning, a doctor comes out. It's that same cold-eyed guy we talked to earlier. I try not to look at the blood on his blue surgical scrubs.

"The patients are out of surgery. They're alive, but in critical condition," he says.

"But will they be all right?" I ask.

"Too soon to say. The mother has lost a lot of blood. The infant was deprived of oxygen for a short time. We will have to wait and see how they do." His eyes go past us, as if he's looking for someone else, ready to move on to the next case.

"Can we visit them?"

"Not yet." For the first time, he seems to see us, how tired and scared we are. "It'll be hours. This would be a good time to go home and get some sleep."

The others decide to take his advice.

"I'm staying here," I announce. My voice cracks from exhaustion.

"You don't even know if this is Michael's baby," Yancy says in a flat voice.

I turn away from her. *"Yes, I do."*

"Ryan." Mom puts her arm around me. I almost draw back, but then stand there and let her do it. "Don't you want to go home, too? Get some sleep?" Her make-up's all smeared, and she looks a little shy about standing so close to me, but her eyes are saying *I love you. I want you to be okay.*

I put my hand on hers and squeeze it. "I want to stay. But thanks, Mom."

She squeezes back. "Alright then. We'll call you."

They leave, and I sit there alone, thinking I can't freaking believe what's happening. After everything we've gone through, Chrissie might still die, or the baby might. With Michael, I could see why it happened, but what did Chrissie or the baby ever do to deserve this? I want to sink my fists into something or someone, knock down a building, be like one of those gunslingers on the old cowboy shows who throws a bad guy over the bar in the saloon, smashing the mirror and about a million glasses.

As morning comes with no news, I call my folks and the Westons. Nat's already on his way back here. He wants to be at the hospital in case we're allowed in to visit. My cell rings, and it's Emily.

"Hi," I say, getting up and walking out of the ER and into the driveway outside. I don't want her to hear the sounds of the hospital speaker system.

"I'm so excited! Are you all ready?" she asks.

"For what?"

"For the trip, silly!"

A vague memory surfaces. The junior class trip. To New York and Boston. The trip is this coming Saturday—we leave in the evening on a red-eye flight.

"What day is it?" I ask Emily.

"Saturday. You know we're leaving tonight, don't you?"

"Tonight?" I can't go pack for a trip right now. I can't fly to the East Coast tonight, not with Chrissie and the baby the way they are.

I always let Emily down. I try not to, but I can't seem to help it.

Nat approaches me from the parking lot, walking slowly, like an old person.

"I'll call you back in a minute." I hang up, then say, "Nat, I have to leave for a while. Will you stay here and call me if anything changes?" I want to tell Emily in person.

"No problem," Nat says.

"Where's Yancy?"

"She's staying away for now. She doesn't want to get involved until we confirm it's Michael's baby."

"But you're sure it is?"

"I'm sure I want it to be."

I call Emily back. "I have to talk to you." An ambulance rolls around the corner and pulls into the driveway, its siren making a series of chirps as it turns off.

Her voice falters. "Where *are* you?"

"I'll tell you when I see you." I look at my watch. "I'll pick you up in an hour."

• • •

When I pull up at her house, Emily walks out to my car. I take a quick look around the front seat. Everything looks normal—no blood stains despite Chrissie's fears. Too late, I remember that I haven't adjusted the passenger seat for Emily, the way I usually do after Chrissie's been in my car. Emily practically falls backward as she gets in.

"Wow! Who's been sitting here?" she asks. Then she looks at me. "What's wrong? You look so tired."

I drive around the corner and park under a tree. I feel like I'm standing on top of a hundred-story building with a parachute that might or might not open, staring down at the cars moving far below, not knowing whether I'm going to walk away from this or splatter.

I look at her, memorizing her eyes, the dark hair that falls past her shoulders, her lips, which are a shiny cherry color today. "Emily, I can't go to Boston tonight." Since I can't handle the look of shock on her face, I start to babble.

"Chrissie started bleeding in her bathroom around eleven o'clock last night, and I rushed her to the hospital. I'm really sorry. I wanna go on the trip, but she and the baby are both in critical condition." I watch a leaf drift down onto the hood of my car.

She sits there stiff and unmoving. "You were at Chrissie's place at eleven o'clock last night?"

"Oh. Yeah. But that's just because I had to take her home from the audition." I lick my lips. *The parachute has failed to open.*

"What audition?"

I free-fall.

"Mitzi wanted to audition her for a role in *Mystery Moon.*"

"How did Mitzi meet her?"

"At Dad's party. When you couldn't come, I invited Chrissie. To help her get an acting job." *I'm falling faster and faster.*

Her face holds hurt and disbelief. "You took *Chrissie?* And didn't tell me?"

I nod, feeling sick. "It was just to help her get work."

She leans away from me as much as she can in the small front seat of my sports car. I want to take her hand, but I don't dare.

Her eyes are starting to tear up, and her hands are starting to shake. "Well, I guess I'll need another ride to the airport then." Rosario had offered to drop us both off at LAX.

"Wait a minute! We need to talk about all this!"

"No! I just want to be alone. And I need to arrange a ride to the airport."

Her flat, stunned expression is scaring me. "I'll take you!" I say.

"No! Can I use your cell to call my mom? I left mine in the house."

Wordless, I hand it to her. Everything was fine. We had survived a crisis. And now this happens.

Her face crumples. Too late, I realize why. There, on the screen of my cell phone is the photo of Chrissie, smiling for the camera in my Pacific Prep athletic shirt. It comes down to her knees, with her bare legs sticking out below it.

"She wears *your* t-shirts?"

I splatter. "No, I just gave her that one, because she didn't have any pajamas!"

Emily opens the car door. Her lips trembling, she hands me my cell and puts one foot out. "I need to go now."

"But Emily!"

"Don't say anything! Just don't!"

Fear swamps me. I'm going to lose Emily, the only girl I've ever loved. I picture her—her eyes when she looks at me, her soft hair, her beautiful body. Is it over? My eyes fill with tears.

"Don't go without letting me explain!"

"*Now* you want to explain? It's a little late for that, don't you think?"

"Please, Emily?"

She shakes her head. "I can't be near you right now." She takes off, leaving me alone, the door still open on the passenger side.

My cell rings in my hand. Automatically, I answer it. It's Nat.

"The baby's off the critical list."

"That's great." I hear my voice as if it's coming from the bottom of a well. "What about Chrissie?"

"They tell me she's awake and talking."

"Okay. I'll be there soon."

Nat's voice is gravely. He clears his throat. "We can't see them right now, Ryan. I'm going home for a while, and you should, too. Get some rest."

"Okay." I sign off. I start to drive off, then realize the passenger door is still open. I get out and close it. I sit back down in my car, staring straight ahead. I should be glad they're okay, but I just feel dead. Until the anger rolls in, that is, filling me with red heat.

All along, I've just tried to do the right thing. It seems like that should count for something. I need to catch a break here.

I don't want to go home, so I pick up my cell and text Jonathan.

can I come over? I need to talk to u

sure

Chapter Fifty-Two

Entering Jonathan's house, I follow his family's custom of taking shoes off, Japanese-style. In our socks, we pad down a hallway to his bedroom. It has a narrow bed, a couple of big bean bag chairs, and an entire wall full of surfing posters. A microscope sits on a small TV table.

"You mind if I do my sets?" he asks. "I'm on a schedule here." He's going on the East Coast trip, too. He has a duffel bag lying open on the bed, but it's still empty except for a phone charger and a can of shaving cream.

"No worries." I sink down onto a bean bag chair, while he drops to the floor and begins his push-ups.

"I'm not going, Jonathan." I tell him what happened last night and this morning, ending with, "So it's all screwed up with me and Emily now."

He stops to rest for a couple of seconds, sweat beading his upper lip. "Be honest. This isn't *your* baby, is it?"

"*No!* Jeez, Jonathan!" I can't even believe he said that.

"It's just that you feel so responsible for it." He begins another round of push-ups, his arm muscles bulging.

"How many of those do you do?"

"Fifty, but I'm working my way up to a hundred."

"Anyway, I'm only helping with the baby because of all my bad karma. I had to do *something* to work it off."

"What are you talking about?"

Anguish sweeps over me, and my eyes burn. Chrissie and the baby almost died and maybe still could. Emily may never speak to me again.

I don't say anything for a long moment, until Jonathan finally stops his push-ups and lies there staring at me.

Then, I tell him. How selfish I was that night at the Breakers Club. How I persuaded Michael to drive his own car. How I wouldn't listen to him and left him alone in the stairwell.

"After that, my karma was shot, you know? So I had to make it up. To myself and to Michael." My chest's being crushed in a vise, and I blink furiously, looking down so Jonathan can't see my face.

He gets up and sits on the bed. "Dude, your karma's fine."

"No way! How could it be?"

Jonathan's shaking his head. "You were trying to *help* him! But no one could have. He was freaking *crazy* that night!"

"I *didn't* help him. I left him. I did something bad and screwed up my karma."

"*Intentions*, man. Karma's all about intentions." He moves over to a bar mounted inside his bathroom door frame and begins doing pull-ups. "You meant well. That's like ninety per cent of the battle."

"*It is?*"

"Yeah. You're allowed to make mistakes." He is pulling himself up and down in smooth controlled movements. "You just ... have to have"—he puffs—" the right motivation and ... do your best."

A wisp of something calm and mellow drifts through me. "So I'm not gonna get reincarnated as an invertebrate?"

"Dubious," he says. He drops from the bar and walks around, shaking out his arms and hands.

I struggle to sit up in the bean bag. "Why didn't you tell me that?"

"When?"

"When I asked you about bad karma that time?"

Jonathan lies down for ab crunches. "I didn't know you were asking about *yourself*! Besides, would you have done anything differently?" He cocks his head at me from his position on the floor.

"What do you mean?"

"Let's say you *hadn't* felt guilty." He stops talking for a minute, breathing hard. "Would you have blown off Michael's kid? Would you have just said *whatever* and let him disappear?"

I think about it, surprising myself with my answer. "No." I

would have done the same thing.

"See, a lotta guys ... wouldn't a done what you did." He continues to crunch steadily up and down, although he's really puffing now. "But that's just ... who you are, Ryan."

"What do you mean – just who I am?"

"I don't know the exact word for you in Japanese," he says, in between breaths, "but the English word for you ... is *mensch.*"

"That's *Yiddish*, Jonathan." Yiddish, meaning "a person of integrity and honor."

He stands up and wipes his face again. "Whatever... but that's what you are, Ryan. You're a *mensch.*"

• • •

I reach the hospital, arriving outside what I call the Capsule. It's the special glassed-in area, where Chrissie's baby is staying with other newborns. Nat's already there, making his daily visit. He and I stand in the hallway, peering through the window at a bundle of blankets in the third crib from the left. Both Chrissie and the baby are going home tomorrow.

Since mothers are allowed inside the Capsule, Chrissie's there with the baby, leaning over and talking to him. She has what looks like a blue shower cap over her hair. I see her lips moving, but can't hear her.

"Yancy's going to call any minute," Nat says. "She's getting the results of the paternity test."

Yancy has given the hospital a hairbrush of Michael's for a DNA sample. She and my folks, the Skeptics, decided to stay out of all this until the test results came in. Meanwhile, Nat and I, the Believers, have been at the hospital every day, helping Chrissie out. Nat even went with me to her place yesterday to pick up her laptop and some books for her.

Nat clutches his shirt pocket, which is vibrating. "This is Yancy."

I stand there, waiting. Sure enough, a minute later, Nat is beaming and giving me a thumbs up. He's a grandpa.

"Congratulations." I shake his hand. Even though I hadn't worried about it or anything, I'm glad we have it now. Proof for all

243

the non-believers.

"Listen, tomorrow, do you mind if Yancy and I pick up Chrissie and the baby at the hospital?"

"No," I say, as I think of Chrissie and all her fears. I study Nat, trying to read his mind.

"Can you keep a secret?" he asks.

I nod, praying I'm going to like what he has to say.

"We're going to offer her and little Michael our guest house. To live in." Nat's face is taken up in the kind of smile I haven't seen on him since before Michael died. "We'll be gone a lot this summer, but still, she'll be safe and comfortable there with him."

"That's a great idea!"

"Yeah. We couldn't let our grandson stay where she's living now!" Nat claps me on the back, beaming. "Thank you for helping her so much. She's a good girl. Who knew that our Roxanne would turn out to be a daughter-in-law! Well, sort of!" he adds, when he catches my expression.

Then, like the sun popping behind a cloud, his face changes and he is fighting back tears. "Sorry." He pulls out a tissue and blows his nose. "It's just …."

"I know."

I wish Michael were here, too.

• • •

Emily's coming back from the East Coast trip tomorrow. I only spoke to her once while she was gone. *I need to think,* she told me.

So do I. In my hand is a letter, which came today from the Teen League. *Dear Ryan,* it says. *We are delighted to offer you a place in our summer High School Counselor Training Program and a position as a volunteer counselor thereafter.*

It's as if the Teen League was custom-made just for me. I like everything about it: working with kids, helping them stay away from drugs, the chance to make a film – my own film that says the things I want to say. It's perfect for a Senior Honors Project, which I'd *better* qualify for. Failure is not on my radar screen.

I drive to the tennis club, where I have a three o'clock practice match with one of Ben's students. He's fourteen, and he's good. I pretty much wipe the court with him, but in a constructive sort of way. Ben's watching and stops us occasionally to throw instructions to the kid, Jonas.

Afterwards, Ben calls me over to him. "You're looking better and better," he says. "If you got into regular strength and cardiac training, along with the right practice drills, you'd be—well, you could be *really* good."

"You talking about me going back into training?"

"It's all a matter of how committed you are."

"I think I'm ready for it," I say. "But I also have to keep my grades up."

"Good for you. That's important."

"Can I let you know in a couple of days?" I think I know the answer I'll give, but then again, maybe I don't. I just need to sit with it for a while.

"Sure."

I go home and throw myself on my bed. It feels like everything about my future and who I am hangs on what I do this summer.

I see two possible Ryans next fall. The Ryan-who-stayed-in-LA is a scorching hot tennis player—an actual contender at tournaments. He's great with kids and has really helped a couple from the Teen League. He's making this amazing documentary that he wrote himself.

The Ryan-who-went-to-England is a loser who followed his girlfriend there because he had nothing of his own to do.

My arms close around my pillow.

It's pretty clear which Ryan I like better.

On the other hand, Ryan-in-England is also a guy who keeps his word to his girlfriend, a guy who doesn't let people down. Ryan-in-LA doesn't worry so much about stuff like that.

Ryan-in-England will have great sex with his girlfriend all summer. Ryan-in-LA will live on his fantasies.

It's not until I realize that no choice is going to make me happy that I finally decide what I'm going to do.

Then I change my mind.

Chapter Fifty-Three

"How was your trip?"

"Incredible." Emily's voice sounds thin and remote over the phone. "I just knew, Ryan, the minute I got to Boston. That's where I'm going to school."

"Well, that's great."

"We need to talk," she says.

I would want to see her, but this heavy feeling weighs me down, like I'm trying to peer through thick fog or walk through knee-deep water. A vise closes around my chest and squeezes the air out of me. Is it over, between her and me? I don't know how I'll live. Emily is like air, a necessity.

Later that day, I bring her to the guest house. Ever hopeful, I glance toward the bedroom door, but Emily is already sitting on the sofa in the living room, twisting her hands together and clearing her throat. I sit down beside her. I still can't quite believe what I've decided to do.

"Emily, I'm really sorry I didn't tell you about some of those things with Chrissie. But you have to know that there's nothing between her and me. She's a friend. That's it." I stare at the edge of the rug, following its zigzag pattern with my eyes.

"I know," she says.

I look up quickly. "You're not mad at me anymore?"

She shakes her head. "You should have told me about the party and the audition. But I know you, Ryan. I know you wouldn't cheat."

I'm glad she's forgiven me, but it makes it even harder to go on. "I've been thinking a lot since you left."

"Me too," she says.

My smooth prepared speech deserts me, and the words come out of my mouth in a single blurt. "I'm not going to England."

She takes in a sharp breath and stares at me.

I'm explaining it to myself at the same time that I explain it to her. "Being with you would be awesome. But … I don't *like* history! I wanna get back into tennis. And work at the Teen League and make a film for my Senior Honors Project."

She looks down at her hands.

"And you'll do your own thing this summer, too," I say. "It'll be great for you. And then we'll have all of senior year together."

Emily just keeps staring down at her hands for a long moment, while I inspect what I can see of her face, trying to read her expression. Then she looks up.

Her eyes glow. I'd expected her to be mad or disappointed, but instead she looks … proud.

"You're so smart, Ryan. You're doing the right thing."

It never occurred to me that Emily would also like the Ryan-in-LA better than the Ryan-in-England.

"Really? You think so?" She's okay with it!

"Yes. We're only sixteen," she says. "We *should* try new things, branch out."

"Exactly."

"Like in your case, doing the Teen League."

Something in her tone makes me ask, "And what about in *your* case?"

She looks down again. "Well, *since* you're staying here, and I'll be in England, maybe we should consider…. you know … seeing other people this summer."

I feel a muscle start working in my jaw and hear a rushing sound in my ears. "You really have been thinking."

"Ryan, we're too young to tie ourselves down! And if we're going to be apart this summer…."

I feel a strange prickly pain behind my nose and eyes, like something in between tears and a beginning migraine. She's been thinking about this for a while. I know what it's about.

Derek won. He got Emily away from me.

"We both have so many things we want to do and try," she says.

"So you're gonna go out with Masters?" I have to know.

She shakes her head. "He's not nearly as much fun as you."

Confused, I jump up and pace the living room. "What is it then? You just want a break from us over the summer? Check out some English guys?"

Her eyes are welling up, and she's shaking her head. "This is too hard, Ryan."

"What's too hard?" I'm getting a sinking feeling in the pit of my stomach.

"Us, together, next year. It's too hard to be together, getting closer and closer, while the whole time, all I'll be doing is applying to colleges so I can leave!"

A hard band coils itself around my chest and begins to squeeze. "But, leaving for college—that's more than a year from now!"

"I'm not like you, Ryan. You're so strong. You can handle anything. I can't be with you *and* be planning to leave you, both at the same time."

"You want to break up *now* because you might move to Boston next year?"

When Emily doesn't answer, it bursts out of me: "Don't you love me anymore? Am I not enough for you?"

"You *are!* It's just …" She wraps her arms around herself. "Our love scares me. It's so intense. I wasn't expecting anything like this now, in high school. I want to go places, do things!"

"Then go places and do things with me!"

"You don't understand, Ryan."

A strange, painful energy is running through me, making me want to climb a wall or run down the street really fast or maybe throw something out a window. "I can't talk about this anymore right now. I'm taking you home."

"I really love you, Ryan. You have to believe that."

"You want to leave me and date other people. That kind of love I don't need."

• • •

As Emily steps onto the curb outside her house, I floor the gas, my tires screeching as I pull away. I know where I'm going. I drive through the Palisades, following Sunset Boulevard's snake-like, curving path toward the ocean.

Even in my misery, I see the colors as I drive, the colors of Los Angeles in springtime. It looks like we've had a city-wide paint ball war. The fences and walls are thick with purple and red flowers and these pinky-blue things, too, the size of cabbages. And other flowers are all over the place in huge splashes of peach, yellow, red and orange.

Why Emily would want to leave here to live with snow and cold and concrete walls is beyond me. What's her problem anyway? Some people wouldn't know a good thing if it went up their ass.

I hit the gas pedal and roar along to the beach, leaving Sunset and heading south on Pacific Coast Highway. I feel this brief, savage joy in accelerating to twenty miles per hour above the speed limit, but then scenes flash before my eyes: Michael's black Mustang crumpled into scrap metal, him lying there while the paramedics try to save him, his coffin being lowered into the ground. I slow down enough to screech the car into a beach parking lot, and tear at the parking brake. Somehow I rip a gash in my thumb, but barely notice it.

I run down the sand to the water. And who does she think she's going to date in England anyway? Some skinny, pale, pimply faced English dude? I don't *think* so. What would someone like that know about loving a woman? I'll bet the average dick over there's the size of a number two pencil.

There are stones on the beach, which I start picking up and launching into the water. They are too small to make a really satisfying splash, but I throw them anyway. I look for a really big one, something to make a tidal wave as it hits.

I see nothing. I start to run along the water's edge, digging deep in the sand with each step. I still can't believe what she's throwing away.

Nobody knows Emily like I do. For sure, nobody knows her body like I do. Man, is she gonna be sorry when she comes back here this fall, sees me, and realizes what she's given up. Within a week, she's going to be begging for a sweet-n-slow, heart-pounding, do-it-to-me, don't-stop Ryan-style lay ... and it'll be too late. I'll have moved on.

I've been running in deep sand for maybe twenty minutes. My

lungs are on fire. My heart's about to burst. I walk out into the water until it's past my knees, rolling up my pant legs a little. The pants still get soaked, but I don't care.

I stand there for a long time, letting the waves push and pull at my legs. If she thinks I'm gonna sit around this summer waiting for her, she's in for a shock.

My heartbeat slows, and my breathing returns to normal.

Who am I kidding?

Of course I'll be waiting for her.

The thing is, Emily and I still love each other. I think of the card I gave her, the one with the Grand Canyon on it. That card pretty much said it all. My love for Emily is like the Grand Canyon, enormous, wondrous. It's epic love. But epic love can't work at sixteen. Or can it?

The sun drops lower and lower in the sky until it's just a slice of fire on the horizon. I wade out of the water and walk slowly back to the car.

Chapter Fifty-Four

"Don't be a stranger!" Molly says. It must be her latest new expression.

She stands over me as I lie in bed, a pillow covering my face. It's been two days since Emily and I broke up, and we haven't spoken to each other since. I've dragged myself to classes and down the stairs to dinner— but only because Ro made me. The rest of the time, I've been in bed.

"Get up," Maddy says. She's standing next to Molly.

That's what Emily had said to Chase at her birthday party. I moan, remembering how amazing she was that night.

"He'll be okay," Molly says. She pats the pillow.

"No. He's doomed." Maddy's voice is dark.

I groan to myself as I hear them leave.

I know I have to get up though. I'm supposed to go to Chrissie's. Besides being with Emily, meeting the baby is probably the only thing I actually want to do right now.

As I stumble toward Nat and Yancy's guest house, I hear Chrissie before I see her. She's singing "She'll Be Coming 'Round the Mountain," and seems to be making up her own verses for the little guy. "Michael's comin' 'round the mountain, here he comes…"

It's been a week since he was born, but because of Emily, and because of the baby's time in the Capsule, I am only now meeting him. You would never know Chrissie gave birth seven days ago. She's half her former size. I find her outside the Westons' guest house with a pair of gardening shears, clipping roses. She's wearing a wide brimmed hat and has her hair in braids.

Baby Michael sleeps in a sling at Chrissie's waist. With a strange feeling of unreality, I peer into it. Here he is, finally, the baby I fought for.

He's a squishy, red little guy. He yawns in his sleep and waves a walnut-sized fist in the air. I put out a finger and touch his hand.

His skin is so soft.

"You wanna take him?" Before I can protest, Chrissie has him out of the sling and is handing him to me. I somehow get him up on my shoulder. He's so tiny, but he's solid too, moving restlessly and digging his feet into my chest. His face is turned toward my neck, and I can hear him making funny little sounds.

I hold my friend Michael's child, thinking *you'll never know your daddy*. But maybe I can tell him a few things. I'll keep the good stories alive for him.

"You wanna hear his full name?" Chrissie asks. "Michael Ryan Fellars."

"Really?" Starting to feel my throat close up, I quickly say, "How 'bout we call him Mikey?"

"Mikey! He'll get the crap beat out of him."

I have to admit, she's got a point. "Before he's old enough to get beat up, we'll switch over to Michael."

Chrissie leads me inside, fills a vase with a giant bunch of roses, and puts it on a table. Unpacked suitcases and boxes fill much of the space, but she has hung crystals and wind chimes and put fresh flowers everywhere. There are two small bedrooms, a bathroom, and a tiny kitchen.

"How's this going so far?" I ask. I still have Mikey on my shoulder, one hand on his back and the other hand cupped under his diaper. He's wiggly, so I keep a good grip on him.

"Perfect!" she announces. "I told them I wouldn't live here unless I could pay them rent. So I don't feel like I owe them anything. They're gone a lot. Nat's such a sweetheart. He's been great. And Yancy's okay, too, once you get to know her." She's beaming.

"Where's the baby crib?" I ask. "I heard Yancy wanted to make a nursery."

"Ssshh," Chrissie says. "I put the crib in my bedroom." We walk into the small room, filled entirely by a bed and baby crib. The crib's full of stuffed animals and toys.

"Where does he sleep?"

"In my bed with me, of course. Do you know that in other cultures, they wonder why Americans make their babies sleep alone in cages?" Chrissie looks outraged. "That's probably why we're all killin' each other right and left in this country."

"Won't Yancy find out and get mad?"

Chrissie winks at me. "Her Highness doesn't come out here much. Mikey and I make appearances at the main house, so she can see him."

"And Nat?"

"Oh, he comes to visit. I been making him wheat grass juice with my new machine."

"Wheat grass juice?" I twist up my face.

"You, too, mister," she says, pointing at me. "I might even put it in Mikey's bottle. When he's older. Make him grow up strong!"

"Chrissie, you are a force."

"You should meet my momma," she replies. "Speakin' o' which, you *will* meet my momma!"

Darnell Fellars is arriving in six weeks. She's leaving her job at the Mayfairs and moving to California to help Chrissie with the baby after she goes back to work.

"She'll live in the guest house with me, in my second bedroom!"

"Whoa!" I look down. Mikey's diaper is expanding underneath my hand, like a balloon filling with water. "What do I do?" I stick him out at arm's length, where he dangles in my hands, his feet kicking the air.

"Whoops!" Chrissie says. "I'll take him." She lays Mikey on a blanket on the sofa and starts to take off his diaper. "Yancy wanted to use some fancy agency to find a trained nanny. She said my baby needed 'stimulation.' No, thank you, ma'am!" Chrissie practically snorts as she says it.

"What does she think of your mom coming?" I look out the window, having decided I don't need to see what's inside the diaper.

"Nat knows. He'll tell Yancy when the time is right."

"There!" She picks Mikey up. "All done!"

Her new agent has a few auditions lined up for her. With help from her family and from Nat and Yancy, Chrissie's taking the summer off, shooting her Roxanne scenes in September, and going back to the tennis club after that.

"Unless I'm a star by then!"

She walks me to my car. "Ryan, would you do something for me?"

"Sure," I say, not even asking first what it is. This baby forms a bond between me and Chrissie that's like family. It's just there and will never go away.

"Would you be Mikey's godfather? My friend Raylene's going to be godmother. But the only guy I've ever met who's good enough to be my child's godfather is you."

I feel that stinging behind my eyes that I get in mushy situations. "Really? Thanks. Sure, I'd like that." I'm not sure what I'm supposed to do as a godfather, but I guess I'll figure it out.

I hug her good-bye. "I'll see you tomorrow." She's bringing Mikey over to our house to meet my family.

"Thank you for everything," Chrissie says in my ear. "As my Momma would say, you are the sunshine in my garden."

Chapter Fifty-Five

I try to focus my eyes on the paper in front of me. I'm on the last problem of my last exam of the year—physics. The problem's about the universal wave equation, something really important to my daily life and personal happiness.

Not.

I scribble down everything I can think of and turn my paper in, hoping all the work I did this year will make up for my total failure to study for exams after Emily and I broke up. It really bites to think I might lose out on the Senior Honors Program because I choked at the last minute.

Calvin is already off to the golf course, having finished five minutes early. Jonathan and I walk out of the classroom together.

"Emily leaves for England on Wednesday," I say.

"What's happening with you two?"

"We're taking— a break."

"You mean, for the summer?"

"Longer than that." It hurts too much to say more.

Jonathan has to be suffering, too. His girl Samantha blew him off for a guy on the soccer team. "Samantha's gonna be sorry," I tell him. "She'll see she made a big mistake."

"Nah, it's cool," Jonathan says. "It was bound to happen eventually."

"Really?"

"Yeah. Me and her, we had fun, but we weren't that tight, you know? Not like you and Emily."

His words hit me as if he'd punched me right in the gut.

He's already changing the subject. "You thought about where

you're applying next year?"

"I think USC and UCLA. They both have great tennis teams." *And*, continues a tiny voice in the back of my head, one that I've just barely started listening to, *they have great film schools, too.*

"What about you?" I ask Jonathan.

"I want Cal Tech."

"Awesome."

We make plans to go to Surfrider Beach together, while in my head I keep hearing the words over and over again that Jonathan said.

We weren't that tight. Not like you and Emily.

• • •

Emily's last evening in LA, I pull up in front of her house and get out to stand by my car. I've already told her I'm just stopping by for a few minutes. "To say good-bye. I'm not even coming in."

All day, I've been thinking about her and me.

She walks out to meet me. Neither of us speaks. I put my arms around her and crush her in a hug, my face buried in her hair. We stand that way for a long time.

She starts to pull away, but I tighten my arms around her waist.

"Listen. Date other guys in England, if you want to. But then… come back to me, Emily." Every ounce of love I have for her is in my voice.

She's looking up at me, reminding me of that first night we danced together on the beach.

"Ryan…"

"Come back to me." I feel as if I've just taken out my heart and handed it to her. "Promise you'll think about it."

She puts her head against my shoulder.

"We have something good. Think about it!" I kiss her cheek.

"I'll write to you." She walks away.

I drive home and sprawl on my bed, channel surfing the TV. I miss Emily so bad right now that I can't even stand up. I click from channel to channel, not bothering to stop to see what's on. Just random clicking, an exercise for the thumbs.

After a while, I go to my ski clothes drawer and pull out the envelope of photos belonging to Michael. There it is: the one of us at Soldier Rock. I put it up on my cork board where I can see it all the time. As I'm returning the other photos to the envelope, I feel something small and hard down in the bottom. I pull it out. It's a red, plastic lobster on a key chain.

It's Michael's crawdad from the Lobster Barrel restaurant. I have to smile. So he had kept his, too.

• • •

Grass covers Michael's grave now. It's quiet and peaceful under the trees here. Much more quiet and peaceful than Michael ever was in his lifetime, I think, with a pang. But maybe he likes it. Maybe Michael was looking for a little peace and quiet all along.

I can feel his presence here, in the shade, looking out at the city. *Hey Michael. Sorry I didn't come sooner. But you know I've been thinking about you.*

I have news for him. A letter came from Miss Anderson saying I made the Senior Honors Program. Good thing, since I had already arranged to do a project for it through the Teen League.

My folks are totally psyched about it and took all of us out to celebrate at dinner—me and my sisters, Ro, the Westons, Chrissie, and the baby. Mikey spent the whole meal getting passed around from one lap to the next.

Your kid's awesome, Michael. I'm gonna tell him all about you.

I look at my watch. I've got to get going pretty soon, but I have something to do for Michael first.

I fish in my pants pocket and pull out the small red plastic crawdad. It's the one from the envelope. Mine's in my desk drawer at home, and I'm going to make sure right now that Michael has his.

I place it on the grave, but find myself frowning. The crawdad will be gone within a day. I look around for a big stone or something to put on it. There's nothing like that in sight.

Thinking I can bury it, I find a stick and start digging. It's tough going through grass and roots with a crummy stick. I stop for a minute to rest.

"Hey! What are you doing?" It's a maintenance guy in a golf cart. Brushing dirt off my hands, I walk over to him.

"I'm trying to bury this crawdad," I say, showing it to the man. I notice that his name tag says "Bruno." He studies the red plastic thing in my hand.

"Wait a minute! Weren't they giving those away over at the Lobster Barrel?"

"Yeah, but think of it as a crawdad." I tell him about Camp Evergreen and crawdad fishing.

"He was my best friend," I finish by saying. "He was only sixteen when he died."

Bruno gets a strange look in his eyes. "My son's sixteen," he says.

He looks around for authority figures. "If you tell anyone I did this, I'll say you lied." He pulls a shovel out of the back of the golf cart and takes one scoop of earth from the top of Michael's grave, making a little depression. I drop the crawdad into the hole. Bruno pours the earth, still in the shovel, back into the hole, burying the crawdad. He tamps the earth down good and hard.

"The grass will grow back over within a week," he tells me. "He'll keep your friend company."

I stand there a few more minutes, looking at the big grave holding Michael with its mini-grave holding the crawdad. The familiar pain in my chest hits me again. I think I'll always have it, but by now I know how to ride it out. I stand there, waiting, until it passes.

Rest in peace, buddy. I'll be back.

My flashy sports car is gone, traded in for a dark gray hybrid. I find my new car in the parking lot and get in. My cell, which I'd left in the car, is beeping: I have a text message.

It's from Emily. It says *I'm thinking about it. A lot.*

Humming to myself, I drive out the cemetery gates. Ahead of me, a row of impossibly tall, skinny palm trees guards the horizon, making a crazy zig zag silhouette. I wonder suddenly how those things stand up, when they're so tall and thin. It's a physics question, for sure. I'll ask Jonathan when I meet him an hour from now at Surfrider Beach.

Finding the westbound freeway entrance, I rev my car up to proper cruising speed and hit the fast lane. The sun roof and windows are open. I put on the radio and start to sing along, emptying my mind of anything but the music and the hot wind whipping through my hair.

I'm headed for the ocean.

THE END